I0524832

Mercy Springs

Mercy Springs

Jennifer Osufsen

LITTLE TYRANT press

MERCY SPRINGS by Jennifer Osufsen

Little Tyrant Press
Aurora, Minnesota 55705
www.littletyrantpress.com

This book or any of its parts may not be reproduced, stored, or transmitted in any form by any means – electronic, mechanical, photocopy, recording, etc. – without the express written permission of the author and/or publisher, except as provided by United States of America copyright law.

Copyright © 2014 by Jennifer Osufsen
All rights reserved
ISBN-13: 978-0692236086
ISBN-10: 0692236082
10 9 8 7 6 5 4 3 2 1

All characters, places, and events are either products of the author's imagination or are used fictitiously. Any resemblance to actual persons, living or dead, businesses or locales is entirely coincidental.

Visit **www.jenniferosufsen.com** for more information about the author and her upcoming projects.

For Jesse, for always believing in me. You are my heart.

Acknowledgements

This story was the work of many hands, and without them, my lifelong dream of writing a novel would never have happened.

First and foremost, to my husband, Jesse, who pushed and encouraged, and made me trudge upstairs to write while he watched all the kids and made supper for six weeks. Teamwork makes the dream work, babe.

To my good friend Mack Hayes, who was and continues to be rooting for me from the sidelines for nearly twenty years. To friend and author Jayna Morrow, for slogging through the first draft with her virtual red pen. To Nancy Harp, who works for baked goods, and for reading a novel she normally wouldn't suffer, and not leaving too many red marks on the pages. To Paula Chapman, librarian extraordinaire and one of the kindest souls I know, for reading and offering sincere encouragement. And to Dawn Breen, my first and most faithful reader; a truly wonderful friend, a great cheerleader, and I am so blessed to know and claim her.

And with each breath, I am thankful for my God, my Father,
who is the infinite wellspring of mercy and grace.

"Let us therefore come boldly to the throne of grace, that we may obtain mercy, and find grace to help in time of need."

Hebrews 4:16 (AKJV)

PROLOGUE

Ferret Landing
Missouri District, Unified Socialist America

He pulled back from the embrace.

"I guess this is goodbye, sis."

Calloused hands rested on her shoulders, squeezed. Her brother's eyes were red rimmed, his face drawn, tired. Sandalwood from his aftershave mingled with the sharp, acrid smell of rotten fish from the dock. Drawing him into a hug once more, she inhaled his scent, committing it to memory.

Cora forced a smile, despite the tears. She hated crying. Her lips and eyes puffed and swelled, red and blotchy, like a jellyfish victim.

"I'll write, John. Call as often as I can, too, once I get the cable set up." She laughed to lighten the mood, sniffled as a tear escaped, trickling down her cheek. "You'll never know I'm gone."

"Are you sure there isn't another way, Coraline?"

Cora closed her eyes, weary. She blinked away the hesitation, swept a glance around what would be the last earth her feet would touch in Missouri. Ferret Landing was a small port, primarily local trade, but a few dozen people milled around, waiting to board the steamship that would transport them southward. Some smiled, others hugged tearful goodbyes, but a handful bore a twinkle of anticipation in their eyes, ready to conquer the world and start life anew.

"Wilkes won't stop until he locks me behind bars, wads my license in his vindictive fist and lights it on fire." She forestalled him with a hand. "You know it's true. No, John, I see no other way. Texas will be my new home. You agreed the town photos in the ad looked nice, idyllic even. I'll be fine. You fret too much."

"But to flee to another country? Cora, it seems excessive." Her brother exhaled, disappointment painted on his face.

"Remember the burning cross, the attack on our parents' home? Or have you forgotten?" Gordon Wilkes was on a witch hunt. She had no choice but to leave America, escape Wilkes and his misguided grudge. She longed for an alternative to seeking asylum in a foreign country.

She tucked a stray red curl back into her kerchief. "Don't worry, big brother. I've got a new place to live, to set up shop, to make a life. I know you want to be able to control all … this!" She threw her hands up in the air, frustrated. "I don't like it any more than you do, but I know there's a plan. I know God is in control."

John hissed, looking around, shoulders tensed. Though dozens of waiting passengers loitered nearby, none seemed to be paying attention. John rolled his shoulders and neck. "Coraline, you need to watch your mouth. It's the reason we're standing at this dock in the first place. Why must you cling to this misguided belief?"

The corners of her mouth curled up, but sadness clouded her face. Her big brother, so solid, dependable, trustworthy. And lost. She would keep praying for him, no matter where she lived, and for as long as it took.

"I will not deny Him, John. It may be the root of my troubles, but I'll live by my faith."

For a moment he stood there, silent. "I know. I know, I do. Maybe one day I'll understand."

2

She stood up on tip-toe, and grabbed his head with both hands, looked into his eyes. "One day." She kissed the end of his nose, hugged him tight, and stepped back.

The shrill call of the boarding whistle pierced the air. People rushed by, jostling one another, suitcases nudging and satchels bumping. Uniformed attendants tugged a wagon full of small livestock cages, the handled cubes stacked one atop the other. Rabbits huddled in furry shivering mounds, and chickens bounced around the wired sides of their temporary homes, frantically flapping wings. Cora envied the simplicity of their lives.

John stooped, picked up her rucksack. "You've got your ticket?"

"Right here, hot shot." She pulled it out of her back pocket and waved it in front of his face. The tears had evaporated, thank goodness. In their place Cora felt the warmth of determination, a resolution to start fresh and not dwell on the past. She shouldered her pack, adjusted it, and punched his arm.

"Ow! You know, you're a little stronger now than you were at age six, little sister." John rubbed his arm, a frown tugging his mouth. "Keep packing punches like that and I *won't* worry about you."

"Yes, you will. But it's what I love about you, big bubba."

Though her heart begged her to stay, to find another way, Cora turned to go. When she was a few steps away, she cocked her head and yelled over her shoulder. "Go home to Sally, John, and kiss my nephews. Keep them safe."

One last kiss blown into the wind. She waved, and marched to the landing, boots smacking and squishing in the muck of river mud masticated by hundreds of feet. She joined the line of folks already queued up to present tickets to the bored travel administration official at the base of the ramp. The beep of his handheld scanner was lost in the din of crying toddlers, squealing children playing tag around their mothers' legs, businessmen discussing their trades. A ray of sun shone down, breaking through the cloudbank. The southern wind gusted, giving a momentary reprieve from the mingling smells of unwashed bodies, the dockside fish market, and the swampy-silt odor of the riverbank. The breeze chilled the sweat trickling on her chest, down her back. Though only May, the sun packed a punch.

Cora waited. If patience was a virtue, she considered herself a righteous woman. Besides, she loved people-watching. The interactions, the subtleties, body language. A coy grin and an eye-flutter, a shuffle of the feet, a boisterous laugh turning heads. Slugging ahead in line at a snail's pace, it seemed as though she had all the time in the world to get on the boat and sail away. Well, not sail precisely, but paddle. Whatever the propulsion, the steamship was taking her to a new life.

She couldn't help it. She looked back. John lingered where she left him, stoic in his jeans, blue flannel shirt and worn leather boots. He had his arms locked in front of his chest, shoulders and back ramrod straight as was his habit, but he waved when she caught his eye.

One day, John, she thought. She prayed daily, asking God to soften John's heart. She longed to see the light of true joy shining from her brother's face. When John hugged his wife, Sally, or tussled with the twins, Hunter and Heath, Cora caught a glimpse of happiness, the lines of his face relaxing in a crooked smile. Or on the nights when they played games as a family, and the dice rolled true, John laughed and clapped their father on the back. John's joy centered on family. Cora prayed one day he'd know true happiness in his soul, the joy gained in knowing God.

"Ma'am?" She jumped in surprise. "Ticket and identification, please?"

So engrossed in her thoughts, she didn't realize she had inched her way to the front of the line. The bored official spoke politely as he covered a yawn. "I need to scan your ticket, ma'am."

"Yes, sorry. Got a little distracted." Cora placed the ticket under the red laser light, and her thumb on the fingerprint scanpad.

"No problem at all." The attendant compared her face to the image which appeared on the handheld. "Your cargo has been scanned and is stowed below, and your trunk has been placed in your cabin for your convenience. Have a nice trip, Miss Thomas. Watch your step on the ramp."

The wooden incline was slick with the muddy footprints of travelers already aboard. Once again she was thankful for leather boots and rubber hiking soles, despite them being clotted with river muck. The young girl in front of her in the pretty blue calico dress wasn't so lucky, and Cora reached a hand out to steady the barefoot toddler as she slid back a foot. "Careful there, little one."

The harried mother glanced back and hurriedly mouthed, *Thank you*, before scooping up the girl and toting her the rest of the way up the loading ramp. At the top, Cora looked back, careful to step away from the rest of the boarding passengers. The final whistle blew, much louder this close to the steam stack, and a few passengers' hands flew up to cover their ears. The last of the travelers boarded, and the ground crew began hauling on the pulley cranks to withdraw the ramp to the shore.

Families on the riverbank waved goodbye, calling out to their loved ones. Others wiped at eyes and blew noses into cotton handkerchiefs. Near the rear of the throng John stood, arms locked in front of him. He didn't wave, and Cora didn't expect him to.

John simply nodded once, and executed a crisp about-face. You can take a man out of the military, but you can't take the military out of the man.

She watched his retreat, into the tree line where their horses stood tethered on a picket with a dozen or more others. Her brother untied the lead from her horse first, then his, and swung up into his saddle as easily as breathing. She would miss Winnie, but she simply couldn't afford the fee for shipping the quarter horse on the livestock barge. No doubt her nephews would soon spoil the animal with too many sugar cubes and apples. Cora imagined those boys racing and jumping Winnie in the pasture as their dad checked the fence line.

The deck beneath her feet rumbled as the giant paddle shuddered to life, backing the steamboat away from Ferret's Landing. Farewells faded out of hearing as the riverliner inched into the mighty Mississippi, the steam-powered paddlewheel hauling the medium-sized craft into the swiftly moving coffee-brown currents below.

At the edge of the forest, John turned the animals and walked them to the horse lane, a twelve-foot wide swath of packed dirt running parallel to the paved road a hundred yards away. The last Cora saw of John was the black tail of his big bay horse swishing at flies.

Cora stayed at the bow rail until the *Adeline* reversed its engines, the trembling of the common deck dwindling as the massive paddle eased to a stop, but increasing once again as the engines propelled the wallowing craft downriver. Around the bend they cruised, murky waves rippling from the bow of the steamer to the willow-lined shore.

A cormorant dove near the middle of the river. After mere seconds, it broke through the surface in a splash, fish in its beak and its powerful black wings beating the air as it lumbered to the far bank. Near the rock where the fisher bird landed to enjoy its meal, a snapping turtle wallowed into the water. The reptile's shell spanned two feet across! She stood amazed, enchanted.

Then, for the second time today, Cora was caught off guard.

"Would ya look at that!" The man at her shoulder jabbed a finger toward the eastern shore near the jut of land the boat had rounded only moments before. Passengers gathered near the railing, pointing and whispering to one another at the gang of men astride lathered horses skidding to a stop at the edge of the river. All but one stayed in their saddles. A lone rider dismounted, hastily flinging the reins to the man next to him.

The gray-haired man stomped into the river, took high jumping steps until the water lapped at his thighs. Unmindful his soaked jeans, or the steamboat's wake rippling over him, he stood, glaring at the *Adeline*, raking his eyes over the passengers until he found the one he sought.

Hastily, Cora stepped behind the traveler next to her, but not in time. She recognized the man in the river and his steely stare, watched as he raised his finger and pointed at her. The crowd parted like the Red Sea at Moses' command, and she stood alone in a ring of strangers. Surrounded, but alone. Vulnerable. But for the moment, safe.

Gordon Wilkes arched back his head and bellowed at the sky, the guttural cry scattering a flock of jays from the nearby trees. He raised his hand with a finger outstretched, swiped it across his throat with a slash. The sun glinted off the golden badge on his chest, even as the *Adeline* churned down the Mississippi, sweeping Cora towards her new life and away from his vengeance.

1

The punch of the pneumatic framing nailer sang in her ears. Two months of patience and planning was paying off. Finally! Three framed walls lay on the browning San Augustine grass, their pine skeletons absolutely beautiful to Cora's eyes. She shaded her eyes with a hand and surveyed the east side of her little slice of heaven. The clinic addition to her home was coming together, one pine stud at a time.

"Hand me a hammer, will ya, girl?"

Cora flicked it off the loop of her belt with a practiced hand, and passed it to Dabney. He reached back without looking and snagged it. "Daggum nailer's been double-tapping," he complained.

"I'll go get the oil. It's still in the wagon?"

"Hmph." Dab's lips gripped the errant nailed he pulled from the two-by-four stud.

Taking the grunt as a yes, Cora strode over to the big oak where the buggy was parked in the shade. Dab's wooden toolbox sat at the rear edge near the tail gate, as did his jug of water. She grabbed both, the oil and the water, walked it back over to the construction site.

She passed him the oil can. "It's happening, Dab." Cora danced a jig in place, happily shook her backside, and had Dabney chuckling at the sight.

"It's happening all right. Just wish the sun would let up. September should be cooler, if you ask me."

She snorted. "Oh, come on. You are honestly not whining about the sun, are you? How else would you power that antique you call a compressor?"

"Hmph. Thanks for the water. You're a sweet girl."

"Why do you still use that old thing?" She nodded at the air compressor. "I've seen modern, less bulky ones at the hardware store in town."

The older man swiped at sweat beads trailing down his face, shrugged a shoulder. "It belonged to my granddad. When I was in high school shop class, we had an electric-to-solar conversion class, and the compressor was my project. I keep it because it still works. Same reason we still ride horses. After the Collapse, well, we just learned to make do with simpler things. Horses don't require battery cells, just love and feeding. Every little thing helps, you know. Sometimes, the basics are best. Technology has its place, but not everywhere. And you can't rely on it. Just ask all the old timers that went through the Collapse and Reformation."

"Dab, that has to be the longest speech I've ever heard from you."

"Hmph."

The Crockett reputation was well-known throughout town. Dabney had six sons and one daughter, all grown and on their own, two of the boys married with children. But every one of them worked for Crockett Seven Construction in one capacity or another, from running crews to marketing to accounting. Dab groaned about retiring one day, but dedication to his family and work ethic were the reasons he busted his hump out in the heat on construction projects like Cora's new office. In many ways, Dabney was breathing life into Cora's dream by building this moderate-sized room where she could bring healing to the community.

"You going to be home tonight? Mae's hands are bothering her again something fierce, and she ran out of the goop a few days ago."

"Tell her to swing by. I'll be here. How's your back?"

"Hmph. Part of the reason she ran out of the goop. I had to use it after building Timpson's barn last weekend."

Sixty-nine years of hardscrabble life demanded their due from Dabney; but like he always said, *"Hard work is its own reward."* Crockett Seven Construction branched out to cover Angelina County, and more than forty years in the building trade exacted a toll on his body. His knees popped and cracked as he stood. Leaning back, hands on hips, he stretched his spine. He glanced down at his right hand gripping the hammer, so he passed it to Cora. "Much obliged. You're handy to have around."

Cora's face brightened. "Thank *you*. You're making my dream become a reality."

"Hmph."

"Is that all you ever say?"

"Hmph." He chuckled, rolled his shoulders. "What do you say we get these walls up on the foundation?"

No sooner than the words were out of his mouth, however, than pounding hooves pummeled the dirt driveway, announcing urgent arrivals. Cora and Dab exchanged a rapid glance, ran to the front of the house. Red clay dust preceded the riders, but not by much, as they barreled through the ruddy cloud. Two lathered horses pawed the ground. A rugged older man flew from the saddle of the smaller animal.

"Doc! He's hurt bad!"

Shock faded as habit grabbed the reins. Cora snapped into action.

"Dabney, thank God you're here." The aging stranger panted,

wiped the sweat away from his face. "We'll need your help getting him off the horse."

Strapped facedown across the saddle of an enormous horse lay one of the largest men she had ever seen. Blood soaked through a hastily applied bandage on his upper forearm. The wadded fabric was dingy and stained, bound by a once-white paisley bandanna. A slow crimson stream oozed from the wound to drip off the end of his fingers. She immediately untied the restraints holding him on the horse. Other hands joined her, and soon they had the patient lying on the ground. Gravity helped, since he all but fell from the saddle.

Dabney asked the question before she could. "What the heck happened to him, Burt?"

Cora listened intently as she assessed the arm. Satisfied the man wasn't in danger of bleeding to death, she loosened the dirty and blood-stained bandanna to peek at the wound. Deep, but not too deep. It wasn't a clean slice, and Burt confirmed her suspicions.

"We was up to Tom Bradley's place. He had some trees fall in the big thunderstorm a couple weeks ago, and he asked us to cut and stack 'em." The burly man jutted his chin at the unconscious man across the horse. "Ben here's been helping me out some since he got back into town. Knows what he's doing, Ben does, just a bit of bad luck out there today. The chainsaw skipped on him, kinda flailed back. He lost control of it, and somehow it got turned around and chewed his arm. Nasty."

Nasty, indeed. But while it was traumatic, she didn't understand why the man was unconscious. She voiced the thought aloud for Burt.

"Did he hit his head?"

"You could say that." Cora raised an eyebrow. She knew hedging when she saw it. "Now don't go thinking bad about the man, but well … he took one look at his arm, saw the blood, and passed plum out. Whacked his head good on the splitting log on the way down."

Ice the head first, then treat the arm while he was unconscious, and after he wakes up do the concussion evaluation. He had a goose egg on the left side of his forehead. The external swelling was a good sign. Poor guy. "Let's get him into the front room, lay him out on the table. His legs may have to hang off a bit."

Ben was a giant, or as close as they come these days. Easily six foot seven, six-eight, broad through the shoulders, and *good grief* the man had to weigh close to two seventy-five. The three huffed and dragged Ben up the two stairs to the porch, then sweated him through the front door and into the dining room. All three were breathing deeply once they got him in the house, and Cora realized the futility of trying to heave him onto the table.

"Stretch him out on the floor. I'll get my kit and an ice pack."

She wasn't gone thirty seconds, one of the benefits of having a small house. When she returned she found Dabney and Burt restraining a writhing Ben, Burt kneeling on the enormous man's shoulders while Dabney immobilized the knees. Black kit bag and ice pack smacked the floor as Cora dropped to help the men stabilize her patient, taking ahold of his hands and holding them to his sides.

Burt leaned over her patient's face. "Calm the heck down, Ben. Doc's gonna take good care of you!"

The thrashing continued as Cora, Dab and Burt wrestled him. She adopted her no-nonsense tone and commanded, "Be STILL!"

Ben ignored her. Cora suspected panic and pain were colliding in the man's mind. He continued to writhe on the floor, arching his hips and bucking as if he was the victim of torture. No amount of wrestling tamed him, so Cora did what came to mind. She ripped the

12

hasty bandage off his arm and held the blood-soaked cloth in front of Ben's face.

Ben took one look at the gory bandanna, and passed clean out.

2

"Girl, I like your quick thinking." Dab patted her on the shoulder. "Didn't know you had it in you. Kind of cruel in a funny way, though."

"Not sure he'll ever live this one down," Burt added around a laugh.

Both men wiped at their brows, clearly exhausted from hauling her enormous patient into the house and battling to keep him there, but they kept the complaints to themselves.

"Well, gentlemen, let's take a look at this forearm. Wait. Y'all aren't going to pass out, too, now are you?" Cora grinned to let them know she was joking around, and both men chuckled. "Burt, hold the ice pack on the goose egg."

He nodded and placed the pack on Ben's forehead. "Trust me, Red," Burt said to Cora, "we've seen our share of blood and guts. Both of us were in the Second War of Secession. Different companies, but a bloody mess all the same."

"Yeah, for a little while. 'Course, you were there a year before me."

Burt bobbed his head, waving his arm to Cora to tell her to get busy. She was already plucking vials, muslin strips, and suture gel out of her kit and placing them on a clean, quilted cotton pad. A chainsaw wound was most often a jagged mess, the chain biting and chewing the skin and leaving a deep trench behind. This wasn't her first encounter with the beast tool, and she doubted it would be her last, especially in this part of eastern Texas, where pine trees towered and oak trees hovered above. Suture gel was an all-natural option to antiquated silk stitches, a combination of natural polymers like those found in slugs and mollusks. Though Cora knew the sticky, binding gel was completely sterile, thinking of the slug slime as a medical application both fascinated her and gave her the shudders.

She laid another quilted pad beneath Ben's arm, and opened the large glass container of grain alcohol. It was the next best thing to a flash disinfector, which she hadn't acquired yet for her practice. Beside her, the men were deep in recollection, talking about a second lieutenant from Bravo Company who couldn't find his butt with both hands, and who had the distinction of leading his company in a circle three times before running headlong into Socialist Forces. Burt guffawed at the memory and slapped Dabney on the shoulder. "You ain't heard the half of it, lad. We had this sergeant major with a big hankering for cigars, and one night this mangy mutt of a puppy …"

Cora tuned them out, concentrating instead on the jagged laceration on Ben's arm. Nasty was right. Nearly four inches long, the gaping wound was almost dead-center on the top of the forearm, a shredded trench half an inch wide. The skin on either side was gnawed, but not as bad as a case she'd treated in the Missouri District. Bits of bark, leaf and sawdust littered his arm, the clotted blood acting like a viscous magnet. She grabbed the sterile water first and began irrigating, washing away the loose pieces, the pad below the arm turning pink with the blood-soaked water. Next, she used a cotton-topped swab to wash and probe the area, dislodging more debris until the gash and surrounding forearm was clean.

When she looked up, she saw the men watching her, their nostalgia put aside. Cora directed Dabney, "Take hold of his shoulders, and do not let go."

To Burt she instructed, "You take his knees. Sit on them if you have to. I don't know if he'll stay out through this part. It could get ugly."

Inhaling swiftly, she uncapped the jar of grain alcohol and slowly poured it on the wound, careful not to slosh it. The stuff was hard to come by, and she despised waste. Her patient groaned, turning his head from side to side, his jaws clenched, but so far, unconscious. Cora sighed in relief, and nodded to the men to release him.

With a clean applicator she applied the suture gel, deftly arranging the chewed ridges of skin before coating them with the healing adhesive. Minutes passed. The old men's conversation was a buzz in the background as she focused on the wound in front of her. She exhaled and sat back on her heels, rolled her shoulders. A few minutes drying time, and then she would apply a compress to aid the healing and fight infection.

She stood up and strode into the kitchen, opened the white-painted cupboards, then grabbed the jar of honey, opened the drawer beside the sink and snagged a spoon.

"Kind of a strange time for a snack, eh, Doc?"

Cora lightly punched Dabney in the arm, and said, "Quiet, old man. Didn't your grandmother ever put honey on a cut or burn when you were a kid?"

"Can't say she did. But it was a long time ago, as you were so nice to point out."

She snorted a laugh and bathed the spoon with alcohol, then poured some of the golden liquid onto the utensil. From there, she drizzled it onto the wound, lightly covering the bloody gash and the surrounding skin. Cora laid the spoon aside and picked up the coated muslin strips. Each time she went around the arm with the strips, she applied a measured amount of pressure. Enough to bind and compress, but not interfere with circulation. He'd scar, but most men wore them as honor badges anyway. On the last time around with the bandaging, Ben mumbled, shaking his head side to side, but staying blessedly still.

"Mighty fine work, little lady."

Her cheeks pinked at the praise, and she smiled her thanks to Dabney. He was such a sweet old man.

"It's the beginning, I'm afraid. The bandage is going to have to be changed a few times over the next couple of days, and different poultices put on it. The honey's the first step. We'll pray he doesn't get an infection, hmmm?"

Cora stood up, knuckled her back and stretched a bit. Burt remained at Ben's head, applying the ice pack to the goose egg. Her immense patient was coming around slowly, and as Dabney gathered the soiled soaker pads, she took a good look at Ben.

Even lying on the floor as he was, she could tell the man was a slab of solid muscle. Whatever job he had in real life, it was physical. He was broad and thick, a bull of a man, his tousled hair the gritty brown of beach sand. Firm jawline, and a full lower lip, with a smattering of freckles across his nose and onto his cheeks. He reminded her of a mischievous school boy, in a way, and she could imagine him putting a little grass snake in the lunch pail of an unwary victim. As she smiled at the thought, Ben opened his eyes.

Brilliant green emeralds shone at her, and she gasped. Never had she seen eyes as green, as verdant. Entranced, she leaned over, hands on knees and stared, lost in a rare beauty.

"Who are you? Where am I?"

The daydream snapped closed.

"I'm Cora, and you're in my home. Well, my home which is also a clinic. Burt brought you to me after your accident. Do you remember anything?"

Ben's eyes glazed a little, closed briefly, and opened wide.

"The chainsaw," he breathed. He tried to sit up, but Cora firmly, yet gently, put a hand on his chest and held him down.

"Please, don't try to sit up yet. You lost a lot of blood and whacked your head."

At the mention of blood, the color drained from his face, leaving a white sheet in place of the healthy tan of working outdoors.

"Whoa! Take it easy, big guy! Relax. Breathe." His rapid breaths began to slow. "The arm is all cleaned up. But I'll warn you it's ugly, and it's going to take a few weeks to heal. Now, as soon as you feel like it, I'm going to have Dabney and Burt, here, help you sit up so I can assess your head injury. Sound like a plan?"

He nodded, winced, reached up with his good hand to touch the bump. Gingerly at first, but gaining confidence, cautious touches becoming more assertive probes until Burt had no choice but to remove the ice pack. Satisfied, Ben turned his head, eyes resting on Cora's face again. Unsettled, she looked away and busied herself with replacing vials in the leather bag that served as her kit. She snapped the top shut. "You ready to sit up?"

Ben halted mid-nod with another wince of pain. "Yep. Let's do this."

She clicked on the solar-powered flashlight, and shined the beam first into his right eye, followed by the left. Both pupils contracted, but not equally.

"Your right pupil isn't reacting as well as the left. Do you remember what day it is?"

"Thursday?"

"Good. How about the president?"

With a questioning look he answered, "Nicolas Titus."

18

"Um-hmm, okay, what year is it?"

"Is this necessary?"

Cora nodded. "Yes. I need to know how fuzzy your brain is. So, the year?"

"2094."

Satisfied, she replaced the flashlight on the window charging strip and returned to sit cross-legged beside Ben.

"You have a mild concussion. Looks like you have a thick skull. As far as the arm is concerned, it's pretty ugly. Not going to lie. I've applied a suture gel and a honey poultice to it, wrapped it in sterile strips, and you'll need to …"

"Wait. Honey is sticky. Changing the dressing will rip off scabbing, open the wound, right?"

She shook her head no, saying, "These strips are soaked in coconut oil first, so it makes a barrier of sorts between the honey and the cloth. The suture gel allows the antibacterial properties of the honey to penetrate without adhering to the wound itself. This is the first poultice of many to come. Do you have anyone that can help you?"

"Only if you count my 80-year old grandmother. Most days she does good to get out of the bed and into her rocker since the stroke."

"Well." Cora took a deep breath, uncertain of the offer, but willing to help a patient. "You're welcome to stay here. I have the second bedroom set up as a kind of hospital room, though it's not quite as sterile as the fancy ones in the cities. Actually, I'd prefer it if you stay overnight, because of the concussion. I can keep an eye on you, check in on you while you're sleeping, and teach you a little about changing the dressing on your arm. What do you say, Ben?"

He grinned, and she saw an impish boy in her mind. "Why, Doc, I'm flattered you want me to spend the night, but I don't even know your last name."

Laughing, she said, "Thomas. Coraline Thomas, at your service."

He extended his right arm, took her hand in a firm handshake. "Benjamin Tucker."

His green eyes sparkled and he held her hand a breath longer than customary. Whoa, boy! This ought to be interesting. As if he could read her thoughts, Ben smiled again, this time his whole face alight. "Everyone calls me Ben, by the way."

"And I suppose when you were a kid you were called Big Ben?"

"How'd you know?"

Chuckling, she shook her head, a few stray red curls sweeping her shoulders as one tickled her nose. She blew it up and away from her face, then tucked it behind her ear.

Dang those green eyes!

3

The sun kissed the tops of the yellow pines as she walked the two older gentlemen out to their horses. Dab and Burt returned to their earlier conversation as they moseyed down the dirt drive. Two weeks had come and gone since the last rain, and the earth was parched, dusty. She shaded her eyes, surveyed the sky. Not a single wisp of cloud dotted the broad, blue expanse. Rain would return, but not today. Burt slung himself up onto the horse, the practiced action belying his age. With a wave over his shoulder and a shouted, "See around, Doc!" he was trotting down the lane, headed back to Cotton Springs and his supper at Dixie's Café. Cora ambled along next to Dabney.

"Mae still coming out tonight, do you think? I can get an ointment together pretty quick. Say, an hour?"

He rubbed his bristly jawline. "Yes'm, I think she'll want to come on out. Should she bring anything? Looks like you'll be home with your patient tonight. Although," he paused, looking over her shoulder and gestured with a jut of his chin, "I don't think he's exceptionally patient."

Cora glanced back and saw Ben standing on the front porch. Looked more like he was trying to hold up the porch column, but she was pretty sure it was the other way around. America or Texas, men were the most stubborn creatures, no matter the country. She rolled her eyes, gave Dabney a tight hug. "Tell Mae it'll be ready in about an hour. No need for her to bring anything. And don't," she said with her hand out in a halt motion, "send any payment for the goop. Your help today took care of it, and then some. I owe you a lot more."

"I put Ben's horse in the pasture."

"Thanks. For everything. Get out of here and go kiss your lady. She misses you when you work so much."

"You're a good girl, Red. Those fellas in Missouri don't know what they're missing. I'll be back tomorrow to help raise those walls."

Once his horse and buggy were down the lane, she stalked back over to the little house, her sternest look in place. She wagged her finger at Ben. "Back in the house, mister."

"No."

Wait. "What?! You need to be resting, not holding up my porch. Go on, scat. Get back in there."

"How about I sit out here, and you can watch me rest in the fresh air? Supposed to be good for recovery, right?"

Mules like fresh air, too. "The only place to sit is the swing or the steps, and I do *not* want to try to pick you up off the ground myself if you pass out and fall down the stairs. If you haven't noticed, you weigh about three hundred pounds."

"Ouch. That hurts. Two-eighty and not a pound more. Swing suits me fine." He shuffled the six feet over to the bright white swing. "You gonna stand there swishing your tail or come on over here and supervise?"

Hard to be mad at the man, smirk plastered on his face, the chiseled lines softened somewhat by the mirth in his eyes. Fine lines winged his emerald eyes. Cora held the swaying chained seat steady as he lowered himself down. She squeezed into the tight remaining space next to him. Good grief, but he was a big man.

It was her favorite part of the day, when the midday heat subsided and yellow fire blazed through the trunks and needles, casting gangly shadows on the ground. Sunset was fairly late, the skies lit well into the evening. Most nights she roamed the woods, meandering deer trails and listening to the squirrels chatter and squeak. There was a creek that trickled across the corner of her five-acre property. One of these days she'd build a little footbridge over it. Charming, that was the word. This country had charmed the socks off her.

"How's the arm?"

"Hurts like a beast," Ben admitted. "Bearable since I swallowed one of your poppy pills."

"You did *what*?! I had those in my kit! In an unlabeled vial!"

Of all things, the man blushed. Well, if that didn't beat all. A blushing giant with a concussion and a chainsaw wound was sitting on her front porch swing. Strange days.

"You don't seem a bit ashamed, either."

Ben shrugged. "I'm what you would call the curious sort."

"Nosy. And how, pray tell, did you know it was opium?"

"Top secret, Doc."

"You, sir," she said, lightly poking him on the good arm, "are an infuriating man."

Ben smiled, sat there pleased like a cat in the cream, while the golden sun bathed his face in late summer glow. "Oh, fine. As you are well aware, they appear different at times because different hands make them. Hands like yours. I like your freckles, by the way." He laughed when she glanced down at her hands and frowned, but he continued explaining. "Most apothecaries tend to shape them roughly the same. It's the smell."

Intrigued, Cora's eyebrows rose. "So you can identify opium by smell?"

"Yep. Got a sniffer like a bloodhound. Just one of the many aspects of my career."

"Which is…?"

"I'm a tracker. A bounty hunter at times, but not always."

"I thought you were a logger."

He went on to explain he returned to Cotton Springs after receiving a letter from his grandmother, Annie, telling him she was recovering from a stroke. She didn't want to be a bother, but she could use some help, at least for a few weeks until she could find someone to help her out with meals, cleaning and outdoor chores. Ben was in the Panhandle at the time, finishing up an escaped prisoner pursuit. The day after he received the letter, he packed his saddlebags, rode to the nearest track station and bought a standby solar-rail ticket for himself and his horse.

"From the station in Lufkin, I rode on down and I've been here for a couple weeks. Nan's doing better, but I think you already knew. Eh, Doc?"

The pieces fell into place. Cora had been summoned to Annie Hayes' house four weeks ago mid-morning, a call on the emergency line. Annie's best friend, Millie, had arrived for their daily coffee and gossip session to find Annie on the floor, dragging herself towards the door. Because Doc McMullen was five miles out of town at a farm setting a broken arm, the call was directed to Cora. It was her first crisis response in the new town.

"I checked on Miss Annie last week. I was so happy to see her on the mend. She has a strong constitution, an even stronger faith. She told me she was getting help around the house from her grandson. I guess I pictured her grandson as someone … smaller?"

"Nan's a feisty little lady." His eyes were beginning to droop, and hand came up to cover a yawn. "Even a stroke can't keep her down for long."

Cora stood up, careful not to disturb the swing too much, and faced Ben with hands on hips. Time to get this big guy inside before he fell asleep.

"Up. Now. I'll help, but I need you to move. Those meds are kicking in," she said, leaning over to put an arm around and under his arm, bracing herself for leverage. "Ain't no way I could drag you to bed."

"Aw, Doc, you say the sweetest things," he teased. But he didn't argue. Nice progress.

They grunted and shuffled at a snail's pace, through the living room and down the short hall to the bedroom across from her own. The room was simply furnished, with a full sized bed and a nightstand. Cora had refinished both pieces of furniture in the first few days after moving in. An intricate quilt in bright colors covered the mattress, a gift from the city council. Log cabin, the piecing was called. The crimson and turquoise were lively, and she believed joyful colors helped stimulate the body. She had kept the solid-wood bedframe white, except sanded and freshened with two new coats of paint. The nightstand, however, got a bright layer of turquoise, two shades lighter than the hue in the quilt.

Maybe he would appreciate the décor another day, she thought, as he settled onto the mattress. Cora winced as the frame squealed in protest, and prayed it would hold. She helped him lay back on the pillow as his eyes closed in sleep.

She couldn't help but laugh at the sight of his boot-clad feet hanging off the end of the bed. Once the boots were off and neatly placed on the floor in the closet, Cora busied herself placing a pillow under his arm, checking for fever, taking his pulse. She ducked out to get her stethoscope and cuff. Satisfied with his blood pressure, heart rate and lung sounds, she draped the stethoscope around her neck and charted the results on a clipboard she kept in the nightstand drawer. She pushed a shock of sandy hair away from his forehead and noted the swelling was going down. All good signs.

Awake, Ben Tucker's face was a study in stern determination. At rest, the hard exterior softened and gave a glimpse into what she thought was the gentle inside.

Cora was fascinated.

She was also behind schedule, since Mae would be coming for her arthritis ointment any time now.

***

Cora was humming and mixing when Mae rapped on the screen door.

"Anyone home?" Mae called as she came in.

"In the kitchen. Almost done."

"No hurry, Doc."

"Pull up a chair and sit a while. Talk to me. I need some information."

"Hmph. About a particular patient, I suppose?"

Cora laughed. "Am I so transparent?"

"Ha! No, honey, not at all. The man's got all the single ladies fanning themselves. You'd think he was a porterhouse steak with all the drooling going on around here." She slapped the table at her joke, and Cora smiled, her eyes sparkling.

"Do I look like I'm drooling to you?" She wiped her hands on a plaid towel and slung it over her shoulder. She grabbed the jar cap and screwed it on, not too tight. Cora passed the glass container to

Mae. "Ben seems like a huge contradiction. Big burly guy, a bounty hunter no less, riding home at breakneck speed to be with his grandmother? Not a lot of men with the personality of a tracker would drop everything to come home to an eighty-year old infirm woman."

Mae nodded, a finger aside her nose. "Exactly. Ben *is* different. You fit in here so well I forget you weren't raised here. Take it as a compliment, by the way." She placed her gnarled hand on top of Cora's. "Annie raised Ben and his sister. He'd do anything for his grandmother."

"Where are his parents?"

Sighing, she shook her head. "Dead. Killed when Ben was six and his sister was four." She lowered her voice and leaned in a little. "Murdered."

At Cora's sharp intake of breath, Mae added, "I know. Horrible. The whole town buzzed for weeks, people locked doors during the day, looked sideways at everyone, especially strangers. They eventually nabbed the killer, but it didn't bring their parents back."

She thought of the man lying in bed down the hall, so peaceful in sleep, obstinate awake, and saw him in a different light. Ben intrigued her, for sure. She didn't know what to do with these sudden and unwelcome feelings. Stop it, Cora. He was a patient. Nothing more.

She remembered those brilliant eyes, and knew there was a connection, however small. But for now, the most important thing was to get him well, make sure infection didn't set in, and insure his head injury healed without lasting damage.

Mae eyed her across the table, a sweet sadness in her smile. "Watch yourself, girl. He's kind, generous even. Funny and smart, loyal. But he's lost. So very lost."

"What do you mean, Mae?"

"He's an angry man, deep down. Annie's talked to me about it some, how she's tried to break his shell. But the truth of the matter is no one ever gets through. I once told him I'd pray for him. He was out at the cemetery, standing by his folks' graves. I think he must have been about eighteen at the time. I was walking one morning, and it struck me how sad and lonely he looked, his head bowed low and his hands laced in front of him. I had to walk over, you know?"

Cora nodded, and Mae continued. "So we stood there side-by-side a few minutes, and when he looked over at me, there was flint and fire in his eyes. Not what I expected to see at all. Set my heart galloping for sure, but I patted him on the back and told him I'd pray for him. He looked straight at me and said, 'Don't bother, Miss Mae. God doesn't exist. If he did, my parents wouldn't have been killed. Or if he does exist, I want nothing to do with a God who allows good people like my parents to be killed for no reason.' And he turned on his heel and stomped off."

Cora was silent. A deep sadness filled her heart.

"This was over fifteen years ago. He was gone the next day, enlisted in the army. Annie got some letters, some calls. He came home on leave when his grandfather passed, but didn't stay long. These last couple of weeks have been the longest he's been back home. I think Annie's afraid if she sneezes wrong it'll send him back out north, tracking and racking up bounties.

"He's a troubled man, Cora. Can't tell from the way he acts, all swagger and charm. Inside, though, he's still an eighteen-year old, angry at the world and God. Guard your heart," Mae said. "Guard it well."

4

Ben awoke to the smell of jasmine, moonlight filtering through lacy white curtains, the faint voice of a woman singing, and a thousand hammers pounding his skull. His left arm blazed, and as he stared up at the white beadboard ceiling, he had a hard time getting his bearings. Where the heck was he?

He tried to sit up and got halfway there before collapsing. He hadn't hurt this bad since his horse threw him two years ago, when he had bounced and skidded down a rock-riddled slope in the hill country and landed on a cactus. Blinking flecks of light sparkled around the room, and the hammers pummeled joyfully. He touched his forehead, and his fingers brushed against the edges of a fair-sized bump, the bruise raw and sore to the touch. Something greasy oiled his fingertips. His first instinct was to smell. Garlic?

As his breathing leveled, he tried to recall how he got into what was obviously a woman's bedroom, and why he was lying on the bed, fully clothed and covered with a crocheted afghan. Rolling his head over to peer down his left side, he saw his arm was bandaged thickly, with a spot or two of red seeping through.

Hold it together, man, he pleaded. Deep breaths, deep cleansing breaths.

He remembered. He had been helping Burt Clausson chop logs over at the Bradley's place. His chainsaw bit into a hidden knot and skipped back. He lost control for a split second, and the weight combined with the momentum of the power tool whipped it back and into his forearm. There was yelling, a lot of yelling, he remembered. He recalled the whites of Burt's eyes as he looked down and over, and following Burt's eyes he found ... his arm. Bloody. So much blood.

Next thing he knew he was staring up at brazen red curls and big, blue eyes, flat on his back on a hard floor, with Burt and Dabney Crockett, of all people, watching him carefully. Ben remembered thinking the men looked exhausted and wary, as if he were a cornered rabid dog. Then, a porch swing, the red-headed lady, and now he found himself in a bed. He wondered if it was hers.

He turned his head as the singing drifted closer. It wasn't a song he recognized. Then again, he never paid much attention to any bands when they played. He appreciated a good tune, one he could whistle or hum, but hardly paid heed to lyrics. Some days on the trail, when the rain was falling in sheets and darkness was descending, humming a playful melody kept him sane, focused.

"Good, you're awake." The woman actually bustled. "Saves me from waking you."

"You're the doctor?"

She had a beautiful smile, sweet and mysterious. "Sort of. People around here call me Doc, but I'm a Level One physician, certified apothecary and midwife. Not a full M.D."

"What?! Midwife! Now hold on a second, Doc ..."

She laughed. Laughed!

"Why is it men only hear the 'midwife' part? I'm a Level One physician, board certified in emergency and trauma medicine, primary care, apothecary, pharmacology, and yes, midwifery. Would you like to see my license?"

Might not be a bad idea, Benjamin. Instead, he grunted.

"All you men and your grunting." She shook her head him, looking amused. "You'll be happy to know I've treated your laceration and you're not feverish, which is a good sign. I'm assuming your head hurts?"

"Understatement of the year," he said under his breath.

"Hmm, yes, I'd imagine it does. You hit it on the splitting log. After you passed out. From the sight of blood."

He narrowed his eyes. "Are you laughing at me?"

"Maybe."

"Only happens with my own blood," he mumbled.

"Don't worry, your secret is safe with me." She exaggerated a wink. "Once upon a time there was such a thing as patient confidentiality. Though it's not standard practice, I still abide by it whenever possible. Are you ready to sit up?"

What the heck, he gingerly nodded. With her assistance, he sat up in bed, his back resting against the pristine headboard, with a pillow supporting his back. He felt as weak as a day old kitten. This wouldn't do.

"Got anything to eat?" She raised an eyebrow. "What?"

"Didn't think you'd be ready to eat. Kind of figured your stomach would be heaving from the headache. Concussions often cause nausea."

"I have a concussion?"

"Yes," she nodded, "a mild one."

Doc slid open the nightstand drawer and withdrew a slim tablet. She whipped her stethoscope from around her neck, warmed the chest piece against her shirt one-handed and laid the tablet on the bed beside him. After poking, prodding and squeezing, she extracted the hidden stylus, scribbled notes on it.

"What?"

"Hmmm?"

"You're staring."

"I know." Dang, the doc was a pretty little thing. Wild red hair, pulled back on top of her head, a few curls escaping around her face. She tucked an errant lock behind her ear. He pointed at her and she jumped. "I remember that. You, the hair-tuck thing."

Again with the eyebrow raise, huh? "Well, yes, I've been told I tend to do that. Old habits, and all. Can you blame me? It's got a mind of its own," she answered, pointing to her head.

"I like it. You should wear it down. Hey, do you have a name or should I call you Doc, Doc?"

Ben liked the way she tilted her head to the side. "You don't remember?"

"Well, now I get the feeling I should," he shrugged, "but I don't."

She laughed, a tinkling little sound with sultry undertones. "Cora Thomas. And you are Benjamin Tucker, a tracker and bounty hunter, and your grandmother is Annie Hayes. You're home helping her while she recovers from the stroke."

It was his turn to raise an eyebrow.

"You can also identify the smell of opium and find it hidden in my medical bag. Oh, and you snore."

"Do not!"

"Do so. Now, let me go see about some broth, hardhead." Bossy little thing. He must have been gabbing like a cheerful drunk earlier. Too bad he didn't remember a thing.

Doctors tended to be strong-willed, no-nonsense bullies, ordering people around, telling them what to do and how to do it, at least in his experience. Rare to find one as sassy as this, though. And attractive too. A dusting of freckles on her sun-tanned face, thin but not skinny. Her curves were in all the good places.

She returned with a bowl of broth and a spoon, balanced on top

32

of a white wooden bed tray, and placed it over his lap. A napkin lay neatly beside the bowl. Cora left the room, but quickly returned, glass full of water in one hand and a white pill in the other.

"What is it?"

"You tell me, Mr. Bloodhound."

"What if I don't want to take it?"

"Hmm. I guess I can't *make* you swallow it. You're much bigger than I am. But you may want to reconsider since I'll be changing the dressing soon."

Ben hadn't forgotten about the arm. The place where the chainsaw bit him throbbed and burned, a smoldering slash pulsing with every heartbeat. But he had learned long ago to tune out pain, to ignore discomfort that interfered with duty or his bounty. There was a saying passed down from the old country, from his great-grandfather's time: *Pain is weakness leaving the body.* Ben had a lot of weakness on the retreat.

He grunted, but took the pill, washed it down with the full glass of water. And he'd drink the broth like an obedient patient, butter her up a bit. Work some of his infamous charm on her.

He chuckled when she patted him on the head and said, "Good boy."

"Where you going, Doc?"

"I'm going to let you eat the broth while I update your chart. Holler if you need anything. I'll be right across the hall."

A few minutes later the unmistakable sound of an alto saxophone drifted through the house, a sultry jazz tune floating lazily in the air. Girl's got good taste. He slurped the broth slowly. He hated to admit it, but the feisty doc was right. His stomach protested and his head still throbbed, despite his efforts to discipline his physical response to the hurt. Ben found himself humming, the fingers on his right hand tapping along with the beat.

Something else occurred to him. Quite urgently, in fact.

"Uh, hey, Doc? Cora? Um, well, I kind of need to …"

Cora peeked around the doorframe, an eyebrow raised in question. "What's up?"

With his good hand he motioned in the direction of his lap, the building pressure in his bladder making him restless. "It's been a while since I, well, hmmm. I need to pee!" he blurted. "Dagnabbit, woman, don't make me beg!" Were her jaws clenched a little too tightly? "Are you laughing at me again?"

"Not at all," she lied, the corners of her eyes turning up a bit in repressed hilarity. "Let me move the bed tray for you."

She reached under the bed and brought out a glazed ceramic container, a roughly bottle-shaped vessel with a handle.

"What the heck is that?"

"Do you need some help with your pants? Remember, I'm a professional."

He growled, waved her away. "Shoo. I got this. But this is the first and only time I'm peeing in a jar for anyone."

***

Cora couldn't help it. She eased the door closed and hurried back to her office, quietly shut the door, grabbed a pillow from the bed and broke out in a belly laugh. He looked so adorable sitting on her quilt-covered bed, lace curtains in the background, cheeks tomato red, asking to use the bathroom! It had to be the sheer size of the man making the whole thing hilarious.

She wiped the tears streaming from her eyes, replaced the pillow, and attempted to compose herself. Attempt being the key word.

34

The man had her in stitches. Mae's warning echoed in her mind, a whisper in the dark. *Guard your heart.* And she would, because deep down she knew she could never have a relationship with a man who didn't first have a relationship with God.

But it sure felt good to laugh a little.

5

He woke for the second time in her guest bedroom, early morning sun filtering through frilly curtains, with the smell of coffee heavy in the air. His stomach grumbled noisily, and thank all the stars in the midnight sky, the blacksmiths in his head were taking a short break. Ben wasn't pain-free, far from it, but it was manageable. He sat up without any dizziness, albeit sluggishly. The small amount of movement necessary to sit up jarred his forearm, aching shivers running both directions to his fingertips and up to his shoulders. Still, better. The salve Cora applied at last night's dressing change was working.

Reaching over with his right arm, he snagged the quilt and threw it back, momentarily surprised to find himself in only his underwear. He vaguely remembered his face burning as she helped peel him out of his jeans, humiliated at his weakness. Ben couldn't recall the last time he had blushed as much as he had within the last twenty-four hours. Time to man up and stop acting like a schoolboy.

Sitting on the edge of the bed, he gathered his courage, grabbed the post of the headboard and his jeans, and stood up, the hardwood floor cool on his bare feet. So far, so good. He cradled his left arm to his stomach, disdainfully staring at the handheld bed pan perched neatly on the nightstand. There wasn't a chance in Hades he would touch it again. He took a deep breath and a step, then another, gaining confidence with every foot. Boards creaked under his weight as he shuffled across the hall and into the tiny bathroom. Ben quietly shut the door behind him, exhaled in relief. He made the mistake of looking in the mirror above the sink.

"Oohhh," he moaned aloud.

He looked rough. Above his right eyebrow a bump protruded, the skin scraped and abraded, shiny with one of Doc's magic ointments. The bruising was glorious, all red, purple and blue. Dark circles pulled at his eyes, red veins making tracks across his eyeballs. A stubbly beard cast a shadow on his jawline, and his hair stood out in wacky tufts and clumps.

He miraculously snagged on the dusty jeans, and with the business at hand finished, set out to find Cora. The humming led him right to her. She was standing at the sink, elbow deep in bubbles, shaking her backside and tapping a toe to the beat.

"Song stuck in your head?" He laughed as she jumped three feet in the air, soapy water sloshing out of the sink and splatting onto the floor. She juggled the slippery plate in her hands, pinned him with a steely stare.

"Do you always go around scaring nice ladies?"

"Only the ones holding the coffee hostage." Her features eased into a lazy grin as she placed the dish in the drainer and bent down to mop up the floor with a red plaid towel. She raised her chin towards the countertop and said, "Mugs are in the right-hand cabinet. Help yourself. Cream is in the fridge, sugar bowl beside the coffeemaker."

"Cream and sugar. Bah. Sissy stuff."

"Of course. Don't know what I was thinking. Would you like some rocks to chew this morning, or will eggs and toast do?"

He pointed at her. "You're laughing at me again."

"Guilty as charged."

Later, they sat at the table, his left arm propped on a pillow at her suggestion, his right arm shoveling cheese laden eggs into his mouth. The toast was long gone and only a swallow of orange juice remained in his glass. Cora didn't shovel, but she wasn't a debutante when it came to eating. He admired a woman with a healthy appetite.

"What did you put in the crud on my arm, by the way?" he asked around a mouthful of bacon. "Smells like a spice cabinet."

"It's a combination of coconut oil, cayenne and cloves. They're natural anesthetics, and the oil diffuses the other two so it's easier on the raw wound. I also added garlic and honey, both antibiotics. The coconut oil is, too."

"Where'd you learn all this stuff?"

"I studied at the American University in St. Louis."

"Missouri? As in the Missouri District in Socialist America?"

She nodded. "That's the one."

"Hmm."

"Hmm?"

"Didn't figure you for a socialist," he admitted, catching her eye across the table.

She was quiet for a few moments, her food momentarily forgotten. She pushed the scrambled eggs around the plate and continued, "I suppose I'm not. I was born in America. You don't get to decide where you're born. But let's say I don't agree with the propaganda and restrictions imposed on the citizens."

She was hiding something. He knew the look of evasion, knew it well. You couldn't track deserters from the army over the entire Republic of Texas, and not know hedging when you saw it. He tried another tactic.

"So why apothecary instead of traditional physician?"

Cora took a bite of eggs and toast together, swallowed.

"Because I felt if the human body was sick or injured, that something in nature could heal it, since both were created by the same God. Apothecary allows me more freedom to treat the person and underlying condition, not only the symptoms. Think of it as whole-body medicine."

Animated, she gestured with her fork, circles in the air. "Look at it this way. Action, reaction, you know. All the choices we make, the foods we eat, genetics, everything combines in the human body. And there's all of nature existing in harmony with itself, with humans, animals. Deep down, at a cellular level, everything is connected. Like a symphony. Harmony and melody combine to form the whole.

"When I was in the medical school portion of my training, I had this crazy idea. Maybe there is a cure in nature which corresponds with a physical ailment in the human body. There has to be something pure, not manufactured, which would heal the human body. So I explored plants, flora and fauna, the symbiosis of plants and animals. And the more I studied the more I saw the pattern, a beautiful intelligent design seen throughout creation. It sealed the deal for me, for apothecary. Pharmacology is one of the basic tenets of apothecary, producing healing medicines from the fruit of the earth. Midwifery came as a natural progression. For me, helping a child come into the world is one of the most beautiful things on this earth."

"Hold up. You believe everything was created, designed? Scientists have laughed at the theory for centuries. Come on, now, Cora. You're a smart lady. There is no design, no glorious connection between everything. It just ... is. Fortunate for us it all worked out the way it did, but it was incredible chance. Coincidence."

She was shaking her head, both hands on the table and fire in her eyes. "No. Existence happened because God created it. Breathed it. Spoke it. No cosmic accident happened to produce life as we know it. Something doesn't come from nothing. It's the law of the conservation of mass, right?"

Ben sat flabbergasted, stunned. How could such a passionate and intelligent woman suffer from the delusions of religion? Never in a million years did he expect this.

He leaned in, his voice deepened, stern. "There is no God, Cora. Wake up."

"Oh, Ben, you're wrong." Tears welling up in her eyes. Why was she looking at him with pity on her face? She was deluded, brainwashed.

Pushing back his chair he stood, heedless of the stars dotting the room in flickering pulses, ignoring the burn in his arm. "I had no idea you were one of *them*." Scorn dripped from his voice. "You are, right? A so-called Christian?"

Cora raised her chin, her jaw clenched. "Yes, Ben Tucker, I am. So what?"

"Don't you dare look at me like you're sorry for me, like I'm the one out of his mind. You do good work, Doc. And thanks for the help, for getting me back on my feet. But it's been nice knowing you, Cora."

The sun blinded him as his feet hit the front porch, the screen door slamming in his wake. He barely heard her yelling behind him, "Wait, please wait, Ben! Your arm, your head! You need a doctor."

A ruddy dust cloud rose around his knees as he spun and pointed at her, saying, "Doc McMullen will do fine. Just … stay away, Cora. I can't handle this right now. Ever."

Ben was down at the end of her driveway before he stooped over, his wounded arm cradled to his stomach, his good arm resting on his knee. What just happened? How could he have been so wrong about a person?

He didn't know why it hurt so much.

6

Cora was crouched on her hands and knees in a corner, covered in plaster dust when the rider appeared at her door, out of breath and red-faced from the rushed journey to fetch her.

As she quickly washed up and changed out of her grungy work clothes into her clean cotton scrubs, she thought about how thankful she was she had been on the last wall of sanding. Tomorrow she'd finish the trim work, both base and ceiling, and sweep up as much plaster dust as possible. The fine, chalky powder had the uncanny ability to settle everywhere and on everything, whether it was in the construction zone or not. Like confectioner's sugar, the dust coated the large, heavy duty paper sheeting which protected the newly laid oak planks, the unfinished wood lying in wait until the stain and protective sealant could be applied. Her work boots left perfectly shaped footprints in the dust and trailed it down the hallway, away from the new clinic addition.

No, she wouldn't be sad to see an end to the plaster work.

She pulled her unruly hair back into a hasty bun. No matter how many times a day she pulled it back, a few curls would escape, refusing to be tamed. She blamed her Irish genetics for the red, and for the stubborn. She left the bathroom and peeked down at the end of the hall, caught a glimpse of the newly built room. The thought of treating patients in a medically equipped room made her belly quiver with excitement.

The summons to deliver the baby was overdue. Nelda Hall's first child didn't seem anxious to make its appearance into this world. At her last visit, Nellie had been miserable, and Cora couldn't blame her. At forty weeks, she still hadn't begun to dilate. The poor woman had sobbed for half an hour before Cora could calm her down and let her know it was perfectly normal for first babies to take their sweet time. She had encouraged Nellie and her husband Norman to take walks around the homestead, allowing gravity to work in her favor. Looks like baby was finally ready to be born.

"I don't believe we've met," Cora said, extending her hand to the grimy rider. "Cora Thomas."

"I'm Norman's cousin, Fenton. I work around the farm, helping out since Nellie's ... uh ..." He held his arms way out in a circle in front of him. "Anyway, Norman sent me to fetch you since Nellie's screaming something awful and she's been having contractions."

"It's about time," they said in unison, looking at each other sideways. Fenton snorted a shook his head, a smile on his face.

The Hall's farm nestled snug in an oak grove two miles east of town, a sixty-acre combination livestock and wheat farm which supplied local beef and grain for the businesses in town. There were a number of similar farms ringing Cotton Springs: homesteads, ranches and farmsteads passed down from one generation to the next.

Cora's mind wandered as they rode. Rusty galloped after Fenton's bay mare, but her thoughts flew to Missouri. Comparing the two countries happened naturally, as Cora flew through the countryside.

Ironically, many suburban cities and towns in America operated in the same way small towns in Texas did, with local suppliers meeting needs of citizens. The main difference between the two countries rested in the policies governing the supply and demand of provisions. The farmers surrounding Cotton Springs relied on the townsfolk for support, supplies, medical treatment, schools, and a variety of other services. In turn, the town depended on the local produce and crops, freshly butchered meat and dairy yields the farms produced. It only made good sense to work together. Communal responsibility remained the driving force of the relationship between the farmers and the townsfolk.

In the U.S.A., however, the similarities stopped at the surface. Sure, there were farms around towns, and towns circling the cities. But where Texas farmers sold and traded goods, American farmers surrendered the majority of their crops or livestock to the government. Bureaucracy controlled the collection and distribution of all material wares within the country. For the greater good of the people, or so the president liked to claim. Goods, materials, services, businesses, medical care, education. All were rigidly controlled and monitored by the government.

She had tried to explain it to Dabney one day. If the Second Tuesday Farmer's Market were in America, it would operate something like this. Weights and Measures attendants would be on hand to certify all scales were calibrated correctly. A trade official would be on-hand to insure all produce carried government analyzed and approved prices. Food and Drug Administration monitors would randomly test crops for sale, and cite or fine the smallest carrot or turnip which didn't conform to published standards. Citizens would be allowed to purchase their regulated allotment, so no family had an abundance when some may have none.

In short, the Second Tuesday Farmer's Market wouldn't exist. Cora couldn't remember seeing anything like it in Missouri District, or hearing of such an establishment anywhere else in America. Despite the disappointments and circumstances leading up to her asylum in Texas, Cora couldn't help but be thankful for God's provision in providing a new home in a generous community.

Rather than riding with a dusty farmhand to a home birth like she was today, more than likely she would have been back in her sterile office, providing health care using techniques and methods strictly sanctioned by government standards. True, only a decade had come and gone since medical schools were approved for apothecary studies. Cora was one of the first students to graduate with the new, unique licensing. Many people were leery, not truly understanding what an apothecary provided.

Practicing as a Level One physician meant she could provide primary care services; x-ray, splint and set broken bones, and act as a first responder in emergencies. A midwife was more easily recognized, more readily accepted with the general populace. In Missouri, Cora was one of a handful of certified midwives in the county.

She had been in practice for only a couple of years before the tragedy with Missy Wilkes happened. The day haunted her still, and she hastily put it out of her mind as she and Fenton neared the Hall farm.

Norman came into view as they crested the hill. He paced the front porch, wringing his hands. His gaze landed on Cora. Bypassing the steps, he leapt from the porch to the ground, rushing her. She dismounted and grabbed her saddlebags, and was practically drug into the farmhouse by the fidgety father-to-be.

"She's making awful sounds, Doc. I mean, it's not the first time I've seen a little one born, but usually it's a cow. Oh, good grief, don't tell 'er I said that. She's already cussed me a blue streak for putting her in this position." He shook his head, and looked at Cora with saucer-sized pleading eyes.

She put a hand on his shoulder, gave it a little squeeze. "Don't worry, Norman. Women can be a bit more, um, vocal than a heifer." She smiled, and opened the front door, and was immediately met with a wailing groan.

"She's in the bedroom," he gestured, "down the hall on the right."

"I'll take it from here. I need your help, though. Go get some water boiling, gather as many clean towels as you can find, and meet me back in the bedroom. I'm going to check on Nellie and see how she's doing."

Thirty hours later, a nine pound and eight ounce baby boy entered the world, squalling and beet-red as he hit the air. Sweat-drenched and shaking, Nellie cradled her infant son to her breast and beamed at Norman, who looked poleaxed and joyful in turns. A slow smile spread across his face as he leaned down to gently kiss Nellie's forehead. A cooling breeze fluttered the curtains, carrying the earthy scent of hay and livestock.

"He's absolutely beautiful and completely healthy."

Cora was wired, the last day a blur in the wake of the birth. Nothing made her soar more than delivering a baby. Mother and son were doing great. She packed her saddlebags, and promised to return in two days to check their progress. She was a kite, soaring and dipping in a crisp, azure sky.

The high had worn off about the time her horse passed the mailbox at the end of her drive. Fatigue crashed into her, and she felt herself sway in the saddle. She gripped the pommel for stability, tightened her thighs to keep from falling to the rocky clay below.

Mae Crockett swayed on her white porch swing, a tan wicker basket at her side.

"Mae? I'm happy to see you." She stumbled from the saddle. "But I'll confess, I'd like to see my bed more."

Mae smiled, her dentures bright and straight, and motioned her up to the porch. "I've got something for you. Won't take long, but I think you'll like it. Now take off those boots and come with me."

Mae led her through the house, holding her hand, until they arrived at the door to the new addition. The door was closed, and Cora was curious. Exhausted to the point of delirium, but curious nonetheless. Mae instructed her to close her eyes.

"Keep 'em closed, or I'll kick your butt."

"So bossy! Okay, okay, they're still closed. See? Hands on eyes, too."

She heard the turn of the doorknob, felt Mae's slight push forward, putting her in motion. Cora baby-stepped into the room, hands out in front of her like the blind. Her words echoed back to her off bare walls.

"I don't know what the big deal is anyway. I've been in this room a hundred times already. Remember? I helped build it? It's not exactly a surprise."

"Trust me, you haven't seen this part. Open your eyes!"

Light flooded the room through six gleaming windows. Cora gasped. "How? When? Who?"

Mae clapped her wrinkled hands together. A gleeful and husky laugh bounced around the room. Cora stared in awe at soothing sea foam green walls, trimmed in smooth white. Stained and glossy floors the color of maple syrup gleamed under foot. The glass panes of the window sparkled, not a streak or a fingerprint to be seen. She inhaled the scent of fresh paint. It smelled new, full of hope.

"Seriously, how did this happen? I was only gone a day!"

"Many hands make light work," Mae quoted, a toothy grin shining on her face, her eyes crinkled happily. "I'm so glad you like it."

"Like it? I love it!" Cora crooned, amazed at the feat accomplished in her absence

Jaw-dropping awe at seeing her project, nearly complete, wiped the fatigue from her mind. She was blown away.

"A couple of the ladies from church were real thankful you did the free clinic a couple weeks ago and wanted to do something nice for you. We've been waiting for Nellie Hall to have her baby. Took her long enough." Mae looked baffled when Cora busted out with a loud guffaw.

"Sorry, sorry. Fenton and I said the exact same thing to each other on the way over. And I'm a little slap-happy at the moment. I can't believe you got all this done!"

"Jenny knew the wall color you wanted because you showed her the paint chips, and you already had the floor stain sitting in the corner. Turns out Trish is real handy at mitering corners and she tacked the trim up in no time. After, it was a matter of getting everything on the walls quick-like so we had time to stain the floor. Actually, we should probably step off it," Mae admitted, "but I do like looking at it from this angle."

"It's all so gorgeous, Mae. Truly. You guys are the best! Where are Trish and Jenny? I need to thank them."

"Tomorrow's soon enough, I think. You're dead on your feet." Mae planted a kiss on Cora's cheek. "We're the blessed ones. I thank God every day you moved to this town, girl. You're exactly what we need around here."

They reluctantly backed out of the room, leaving the door open. Cora couldn't help looking over her shoulder as she walked with Mae back to the living room. "I don't think everyone is happy I'm here."

Mae looked at her, eyes squinted in thought, lips pursed. "If you're talking about a mule masquerading as a man, then I'd say not to waste your time worrying."

"Oh, Mae, I handled the whole thing so badly. You told me all about him, advised me to guard my heart. I should have let it go. But he asked why I became an apothecary and I got carried away. I'm pretty passionate about my work and I guess, well, I got carried away is all."

"Don't you go making excuses for the knucklehead."

"I was at the hardware store in town three weeks ago, a couple of days after Ben high-tailed it out of here. I stopped in to buy light bulbs and sandpaper. When I took my basket up to the checkout, Ben walked in the door. I looked up when the bell tinkled, and there he was, filling up the doorway." She shook her head slowly. "He glared at me and spun around, marched right out the door, and down the street he went. I didn't even get a chance to ask how his arm was healing."

Since the horrid encounter at the hardware store, she bumped into Ben Tucker four other times. The first was the worst, but by the time they nearly collided in the bread aisle at The Green Grocer, all the infuriating man did was ignore her. Acted like she wasn't even there, an apparition. Not worth his time. Each time Cora ached to say something, anything, to make it better. But she would not apologize for speaking the truth! Dagnabbit, if the man wanted to act like a mule, so be it!

Mae waved her hand in the air, dismissing him. "His loss, dear. Don't worry about him anymore. You're loved in this town, and everyone – hardheaded animals excluded – is happy you're one of us."

Later, after Mae trotted her horse and buggy down the lane, and the sun had dipped behind the trees, Cora sat with her knees tucked underneath her, gliding slowly in the porch swing. The wind gusted, skittering broad oak leaves and whispering between the pine boughs, giving her swing a careful nudge. There was a bite to the air, and she snugged a crocheted lap blanket around her shoulders. The yarn was soft from many washings. Even though it didn't carry her smell anymore, the blanket always brought her mother to mind. She missed her family, yearned for them. What she wouldn't give to poke fun at her brother or ruffle the twins' hair as they scampered by. Cora longed to stand side by side with her sister-in-law, Sally, rolling out flaky butter crusts for warm apple pie. Wished she could stand by her dad like in the old days, foot propped up on the creosote fence boards watching the horses lazily swat flies with their tails as the sun dipped low in the sky, while a lazy summer wind tickled their bare arms.

Wistfulness and exhaustion sat heavy in her heart, but a warmth surrounded and encased it, walling off the knot of depression inside a cocoon of slow-burning joy. She laid her head down, pillowed by her arm, and watched the breeze rustle through the trees. As she said a prayer of gratefulness, a chubby brown squirrel chittered and scuttled up the oak tree nearest the house. Her eyes slid closed, and the wind rocked her to sleep, a lullaby sung by a late September breeze, nature's symphony interrupted by the small squeak of the chain as the swing cradled her in dreams.

7

The letter arrived on a rainy and dismal Tuesday morning. Cora sat at the table, a porcelain mug of coffee steaming in front of her. A freshly stoked fire took the chill out of the October air, but she wore wooly socks to keep her feet warm.

She noticed the international postage first, the lack of a return address second. Curious, she carefully sliced open the plain white envelope. The missive was written on non-descript paper, a hasty scrawl slashed across the small page.

Witch,

Thought you could hide, huh? I know where you live. Just a matter of time and justice will be served. I'll see you soon.

GW

The note glided to the floor, more graceful than it had a right to be. She rushed to the window, shoved the lace aside carelessly with trembling hands. It was foolish to think he was out there, watching, but her skin crawled with fear as she frantically scanned the tree line, visually searching the area surrounding her home. Cora covered her eyes, felt tears burning behind her closed eyelids.

"Please, God, no," she begged.

She dropped to the floor, weeping. Anguish swept over her in waves as she sobbed. It had taken weeks to get the threatening image of Gordon Wilkes standing hip deep in the Mississippi River out of her mind, a couple of months before she felt comfortable walking or riding a bicycle into town for errands without imagining his menacing face in the crowd on Main Street. She cried for the loss of her patient and best friend, Missy Wilkes, Gordon's wife, who had died in Cora's arms after delivering the son she had waited ten long years to conceive. She wept in frustration, anger, hurt. Her heart was a maelstrom, the tears streaming down her cheeks the evidence of the storm.

Agony consumed her; but slowly, gradually the hurt diminished and was replaced by a slow-burning anger, stoked by the surety she had done no wrong. Women died in childbirth, had since the beginning of time. Even the healthiest lifestyle, the best prenatal care available couldn't one hundred percent prevent heartrending endings. Sadly, life wasn't always a happily-ever-after story.

***

Cora and Missy had been friends since Cora's freshman year of college. Missy was older by eight years, but neither woman cared. They were thrown together in a biology lab, and the friendship grew as quickly as streptococcus in a petri dish.

Missy had married Gordon a year before she met Cora. She told Cora his confidence dazzled her and she liked the way his deputy's uniform fit his trim and well-muscled body. It seemed to Cora that Missy had the perfect life, and most days Missy would have agreed with her.

By the end of their second year at the university, Cora found herself consoling Missy, lending a shoulder when necessary, rubbing her back, holding her close.

Try as they may, Missy and Gordon weren't able to conceive. Both desperately wanted to begin their family, longed to hold a precious baby in their arms. But every month at the same time, Missy met disappointment head-on. She continued to circle the day on the calendar in the hopes that one day soon, the ringed number would be critical in knowing the due date of their baby.

Missy finished her nursing degree in four years. While she was joyful her friend had begun her career, Cora missed seeing her friend around campus. They still met for lunch twice a week, at the little organic café a block away from the college. A sad acceptance had settled over Missy. Despite fertility tests and treatments for both her and Gordon, they remained childless. She claimed she had moved on, acknowledged she wasn't meant to have children. Instead, she was committed intensely, almost obsessively, to her husband, and to her patients. More than anything, Cora prayed for Missy to see a positive pregnancy test.

Yet another year passed. Missy no longer talked about children, and had even focused primarily on hospice nursing and elderly care. Timidly, one sunny day as they sat beneath a pavilion eating lunch in Pearson's Park, Cora took a chance.

"Have you considered prayer?" Cora inquired.

Missy snorted. "Pray to what? God? Buddha? The Great Life Force? Don't you think if there was a God, he would know how much I wanted a child? Give over, Cora. Let's not talk about it."

But Cora pressed on, gently. "Missy, I don't know what you believe."

"I'm a good citizen, Cora," she said, a disgusted chuckle escaping. "Belief in all ways, in all gods, so I'm tolerant of everyone and hateful to none."

Cora hesitated, uncertain. Now or never. "I never told you, but when we were sophomores, I found a bible in the library. I stumbled on it while researching the history of herbal use in medicine for a paper. What I read changed my life, Missy. For the better. I've watched you over the years. You don't smile anymore, honey. Not really. It never reaches your eyes.

"I love you, like a sister," Cora said, pleading. "I know we're supposed to embrace all religion as one true belief, but will you at least read it? The Bible?"

"Why are you so interested in this now, Cora?" Missy demanded. "I've tried for nearly seven years to get pregnant. I don't see how reading an ancient book of mythology will help."

"What could it hurt? These pages radiate hope, Missy. Real hope. Real joy. Promise me you'll read a little?"

Missy acquiesced, and at their next lunch date Cora handed her a wrapped package.

Over the next few weeks Missy asked questions, shyly at first and not without looking over her shoulder to make sure no one was close enough to listen, but growing in boldness in her desire to know more. Cora convinced Missy to join her in an underground Christian Bible study, and Missy seemed to thrive and thirst for knowledge.

One of the happiest days of Cora's life was the day Missy told her she had accepted Jesus as her savior. They cried and laughed together, hugged and sat quietly, celebrating together but cherishing the secret.

"I hate to mislead Gordon," she confided at a meeting. "Do you think I should tell him about it? About God, Christianity?"

Cora urged her to seek the opportunity which God would provide to mention it to Gordon.

And then mysteriously, Missy dropped off the face of the earth. A month, six months, a year passed and Cora heard not a word from her friend. She no longer worked for the rehabilitation home, and when she inquired as to her whereabouts, the employees she questioned were as puzzled as Cora. Letters were returned unopened, emails rejected as recipient unknown, and an automated voice denied service for all her calls. Their modest townhome had been abandoned.

For all intents and purposes, Missy had vanished. Cora knew Gordon had severed their friendship, but she couldn't prove it.

Until one day, eighteen months after the last hug they took for granted, Cora walked home from the government hospital where she was on staff, and found Missy sitting on her front steps. She dropped her backpack and stared, dumbfounded.

"Missy?" she asked. "Where have you been?"

They rushed into the embrace, heedless of the stares of inquisitive passersby. Cora whispered into Missy's long hair, "I've missed you so much."

Missy let the tears flow down her cheeks, but she smiled. Oh, how she shined! "I'm so sorry, Cora. It was Gordon. I couldn't convince him, he wouldn't listen. Cora, he was so mad!"

She had waited until she thought Gordon would be receptive to listening to her newfound faith, she said. He went ballistic, railing at her. The wife of law enforcement officer upheld the law, he yelled, never flouting strictures placed on the citizenry. How did she dare endanger his job by singling out one religion? What she did was illegal, he blustered, and he forbade her from seeing Cora again. Like she was a child!

"He screamed, yelled at me. Forbade me from seeing you again," she admitted. "He frightened me."

"Did Gordon lay a hand on you? Did he?!"

She shook her head, "No, never. I promise." She grabbed Cora's hands in hers. "He made me swear our friendship was over."

"So how is it you are here now? I tried to find you, but it was like you were abducted by aliens!"

Again, Missy beamed, and she placed Cora's hands on her belly. "I'm pregnant, Cora!"

"What?! Why didn't you say so in the first place!" Cora was ecstatic! Laughing and hugging, they danced on the sidewalk, earning more stares and not a few frowns. "How far along?"

"Four months. Four glorious months full of all-day sickness, aches and pains. But who cares! I'm going to have a baby!"

"Come upstairs and tell me all about it!"

Gordon grudgingly acquiesced to Missy's pleas for Cora to serve as her midwife. Ultrasound imaging showed a robust and healthy baby who liked to suck its thumb. Both mother and child sailed through with a picture perfect pregnancy.

Missy's labor was arduous and lengthy, as it typically was with a first baby. Textbook, normal and uncomplicated. Their son entered the world in the wee hours of a Sunday morning, when the moon was high in a cloudless sky. Mother, father and son huddled close together, picture perfect, as the baby nursed at his mother's breast.

As Cora massaged Missy's abdomen to deliver the placenta, Missy complained of a headache. It wasn't unheard of right after delivery, so Cora wasn't alarmed. The placenta was delivered, and the bleeding under control when Missy gasped and raised a hand to her head.

"Something's wrong, Cora! My head. It hurts so bad," she groaned.

Cora knelt by her head, supporting the baby on her chest.

"Pray for me, please, Cora. Something is wrong."

Immediately Cora asked God to guide her hands, give her wisdom. Her training took over. Though outwardly she appeared cool and efficient, instinct screamed danger through the adrenaline shooting to her fingertips. Cora examined her once again, and everything postpartum was normal, no hemorrhaging. Keeping one hand on the little one, she checked Missy's pulse. It was weak, erratic, with galloping and pausing in odd intervals.

"Gordon, you need to take the baby. Here, gently," she coaxed.

With the baby wrapped tight and snug in his father's arms, Cora was able to take Missy's blood pressure, and found it dangerously high. Her friend went limp, collapsing in on herself, breaths shallow.

"Hang in there, Missy. Missy! Wake up, honey. Good girl," Cora urged as Missy's eyes opened a fraction. *"Stay with me. Gordon, hit the emergency line, NOW!"*

Behind her Gordon stopped his pacing, the heavy steps no longer beating a dark staccato, the baby still cradled tight to his chest. "What is going on? Tell me! What is wrong with my wife?!"

"Now, Gordon!"

She heard his footsteps pound into the other room, but all of her attention was on Missy, who had begun gasping and wheezing. Her fingertips and lips changed to a horrid shade of blue. Realization dawned on her. Oh, God, no, not an embolism.

"No, no, no, no. Come on, honey, stay with me!"

Gordon yelled, "Five minutes! They're five minutes out! Oh, God, Missy, don't leave me!"

Cora was doing chest compressions and emergency breathing when the wail of sirens assaulted her ears. Flashing red and blue lights flooded the house, lighting the dark sky outside with a menacing strobe.

Five months after Missy Wilkes came back into her life, Cora cried helplessly as her friend died in her arms. The baby Missy had waited to hold for ten years wailed in his father's arms as his mother's lifeless body was wheeled to the ambulance outside.

Cora saw the hatred boiling in Gordon's eyes as he cradled his mewling son. At the moment, Cora couldn't bring herself to care if the man hated her or not. Her friend was dead. She was numb.

***

She huddled on the dining room floor as memory faded. Cora swiped angry tears from her eyes, her cheeks. She scooted across the hardwood floor and grabbed the letter, reread it. Gordon still harbored a grudge, his animosity evident where the pen tore the paper at the end of his signature.

Cora had worked too hard to establish a new life for herself in Texas, had invested herself in friendships and relationships, just to have a bitter, angry man destroy it all. Wilkes forced her away from her home, but he would not intimidate her anymore. She vowed to fight him and anything he threw at her.

Starting today.

8

Crisp autumn air stung her face as she pedaled into town, her unruly hair streamlined into a ponytail threaded through a ball cap to keep it out of her face while she rode. The bicycle wheels crunched dry leaves and kicked up dust as she rode the scant mile into Cotton Springs. A surfaced bike trail was sandwiched between the paved two-lane highway and the hard-packed earthen horse lane. She needed to feel the wind in her face, have the biting chill cool her hot temper. Her wallet, a jug of water, emergency beacon, and the threatening letter from Gordon Wilkes rested in her backpack. Her calves throbbed as she pumped her legs. She had dressed in a hooded sweatshirt and jeans, but now regretted the heavy top. Sweat rolled down her back.

She flew down Farm-to-Market Road 58, south towards the town seated at the junction of 58 and Farm-to-Market Road 1818. Cora waved to Billy Bates at the feed store and he nodded as he tossed a fifty-pound sack of dog food into a rusty old wagon. Two other wagons were parked at the store, their horses looking bored at the hitching posts. A heavy-duty pickup truck sat off to the side of the lot, nearer the road. Curious. Motor vehicles were a costly expense the majority of people in both Texas and America chose to do without. She idly wondered about the owner of the truck, wondered if he was local or driving through. Not many people passed through Cotton Springs. The town was a destination, rather than a thoroughfare.

Modest houses dotted the side of the road. Most were decked out in harvest-colored decorations with a few pumpkins scattered about; a few dried cornstalks were tied together in clumps around mailboxes here and there. Older men straightened from the raking to wave as she passed, and Cora returned the courtesy. This was part of what she loved about this town, civility and friendship. People here made it a point to smile, give a pat on the back, or tip their hat in hello. This must be what history professors talked about when they discussed the manners of the Deep South, before the Second Civil War, before the Collapse, even. It amazed Cora, behavior so ingrained in a people that it endured for hundreds of years. She was thankful for it.

Cora slowed as she neared downtown. The bank clock flashed 10:40 on its outdoor display screen, switched to show the temperature, a cool sixty-eight degrees. October was a respite month in the south, a soothing balm from the heat of summer, a time when rains soaked the parched ground left in August and September's wake. She imagined her brother, John, would be seeing the first snows soon, in Missouri District. The locals in eastern Texas said she might see a dusting, but most of the white fluff stayed north near the panhandle. One of Cora's elderly patients, Miss Marty, had showed her a brittle old photo taken back in 2014. The pictured showed a two-year old Marty Hamlin bundled up in a pink, puffy winter coat with a scarf wrapped around her neck and shoved under her nose, mittened hands holding a white snowball. A miniature little snowman stood sentinel in the background. Miss Marty's face radiated joy, despite a negligible inch of snow on the ground at her feet. No, it rarely snowed in this part of the Republic, but when it did, it was photo-worthy.

Here, on the outskirts of town, the travel lanes merged into one wide paved road, with stripes painted as they were on the highway. Shod horses clopped along the far right side of each lane. Cyclists and motor vehicles drove slowly through town. Cora pulled off the main road past the bank, and walked her bicycle along the sidewalk to the nearest parking rack. She paid the toll with a swipe of her identification card, and slid the bike into its slot. The locking mechanism clicked shut with a dull thud, and she pocketed the receipt as she looked around The Square.

The Square was a central meeting point in the town of Cotton Springs where the two main roads converged to form the downtown district. Businesses flanked the square on all sides. Patrons staged their horses or personal vehicles in the parking area opposite the grass-carpeted park and walked in to shop. Cora loved the mottled gray and brown cobblestones forming the walkway around The Square, and adored the old gaslights lighting the path at night. Central to The Square was a quaint park, with playground equipment for the children and a few picnic tables scattered about. On Friday nights the city showed old movies projected onto the white brick wall of Wainwright's Pharmacy.

Today, Cora hoped to see Jimmy Wilson, one the deputies with whom she was friends. Jimmy was one of the first people to welcome her, a hesitant asylum-seeker unfamiliar with the country, but granted sanctuary by the Texas government. The lawman had put an arm around her shoulder in welcome, and Cora felt like she had made her first friend before walking out of the sheriff's office. His affable ways and crooked smile often put the people of the town at ease, but he was no pushover. Cora had heard tell from a dozen patients that Deputy Wilson was a pit bull at enforcing the law, and showed no favoritism to those seeking to buy a pet lawman for their back pocket.

She spotted him across The Square, standing under a pecan tree heavy with nuts and speaking with another deputy in front of The Black Bean. He looked up and she waved, crossing through the still-green grass of the park. He smacked the other deputy on the arm and laughed as his colleague left with a wave.

"Coraline! What can I do you for, girl?" Jimmy asked with a smile. He reached around to hug her, squeezing the air from her lungs. She wouldn't have it any other way.

"Got a favor to ask of you, Jimmy." She reached around and pulled off her backpack, withdrew the letter from inside, and handed it to him. "I've got a situation."

"Hmmm," he said, opening the envelope gingerly and extracting the letter. His eyebrows rose as he read the short missive.

"This is the guy, huh?" he asked with one eyebrow raised.

She nodded. "Yep. And you know what? I'm tired of being scared."

"Good for you, honey," he replied with a slow nod. "But it was kind of stupid of him to send this to you. Either stupid, or he has some reason not to fear retribution."

Cora had thought about Wilkes' motivation on the ride into town and she told Jimmy her theory. "I think it's a scare tactic. He knows I was granted asylum in Texas, and he obviously can't touch me. Still, I thought your office should have the letter for evidence, in case we need it."

"Good thinking. Listen, this guy seems a little, well, off his rocker, you know?"

"Yeah, he was furious and a little obsessed. In his case, it appears time has not healed the wounds."

Jimmy nodded slowly again, clearly thinking. He looked down at her, or up and over her shoulder, not meeting her eyes. When he did focus on her again, it was steel she saw in his face, a resolve. "What about your family, Cora?"

"My family? They're still in Missouri District."

"Exactly."

"Surely he wouldn't hurt them! Not physically, I mean. There were those threats and pranks a while back, but nothing violent toward them."

Jimmy rubbed his stubbly jaw in thought, scrunched his face up so little lines framed his chocolate brown eyes.

"Let me do a little digging, Cora. I'll see what I can find out about this Deputy Gordon Wilkes. I've got a guy, well— ," Jimmy said, hedging a little. He cleared his throat. "Anyway, I may have a contact who can obtain solid information."

"Would it be the same someone who covertly inserted an advertisement for Cotton Springs in all the American newspapers targeting young professionals?" Cora asked sweetly, a smirk on her face.

Jimmy's eyes widened and he cleared his throat. "I have no idea what you're talking about."

"You're an atrocious liar."

"Ahem. Well, anyway, I know someone. Lemme see what I can find out about this nut job before he does any more harm."

With another bear hug, he saluted playfully and marched down the walkway toward the horse lot. Jimmy was a great guy, and she was thankful to have this burden lifted from her shoulders. She knew the threat from Gordon was real, but crossing the Texas border uninvited was no easy task. Border patrol forces for both countries possessed high reputations for defending either side of the Texas fence line.

Having crossed "find Jimmy" off her to-do list, Cora jetted over to the pharmacy to pick up a few first aid supplies. Nash Wainwright, third generation pharmacist, ordered provisions for Cora on a regular basis since she was still new to the area. Nash was the same age as Cora, 30, and they could have passed for cousins. Both were red-haired and slightly freckled. But where Cora was curvy and of average height at five foot seven, Nash was a lanky six foot two. He looked up from his viewscreen at the back counter when the doorbell tinkled her entrance, a smile lighting his face.

"Hey, Cora! Didn't expect you in 'til Thursday. Only one of your orders is in, the muslin strips and the cotton."

"No worries, Nash. I was in town to see Jimmy and thought I'd stop in. How's your dad?" she asked as she walked to the rear of the store.

"The cold's better, thanks." He bent behind the counter, brought out a plain brown cardboard box, placed it in front of him. "Here ya go."

Behind her the bell announced another patron and Nash said to the customer, "Be right with you."

The customer rumbled, "Take your time."

His voice. Ben's voice. She'd never forget the tone, a kind of gravelly timbre that spoke of late nights and thirsty mornings. Cora took a deep breath, turned slowly around.

"You!" he exclaimed. "Why can't I go anywhere in this dinky little town without running into you, woman? I've had enough!"

As he spun to exit the pharmacy, Cora darted past him, blocking the door. With one hand on her hip, she pointed at him. "No! This stops now, Ben Tucker. What are you, seventeen years old?"

Ben's eyes widened and he spluttered. "Agh! Woman, you make me so – so – agh!" He threw his hands in the air and pleaded, "Nash? Come on! Isn't this harassment or something? Can't you do anything?"

Nash laughed. "Man, you want me to protect *you* from that little ole girl?" Nash snorted, shook his head, and disappeared into the aisles of shelves lined with bottles.

"Enough is enough, Ben. You stormed out of my house, half-doped on opium with a bloody chainsaw wound on your arm and a concussion. You left your horse, for goodness' sake! Do you know think he just showed up at your grandmother's house on his own? No! And all this because I believe something different than you do. Well, excuse me, mister high and mighty," she railed. "I guess it's impossible for two people to occupy the same space and not think exactly the same way about things."

Ben had gone from a bright shade of crimson to a deep purple by the time she finished lecturing him.

"Breathe, Ben."

He glared, sighed, and reluctantly took a deep breath. "Look, Cora." He paused, and she raised an eyebrow.

She waited. And waited. Finally, she said, "Ben. Let's start over. I think we can be friends, but we'll have to accept we are different. I've had experience with grudge-holders. They chew on their feelings until madness takes over. I refuse to be like that. Can we forget it and move on?" She stuck out her right hand. "We'll even shake on it."

Of course he grumbled, and shifted his feet, scuffing up Nash's floor with his work boots. He towered over her, his sandy brown hair disheveled from running his hands through his hair. Finally, he mumbled something, but Cora couldn't make it out.

"What?"

"I'm sorry, okay!" Then more quietly, "I'm sorry. I don't know why I reacted the way I did. Well, I do, but it's not your fault. I handled it badly."

"None of us are perfect, Ben. How's the head? The arm?"

Nash had occupied himself across the store, alternating between stocking shelves and flicking glances their direction. Cora took pity on the pharmacist and raised her voice, saying, "It's okay, Nash. We're not going to kill each other after all." With a grateful smile, Nash returned to the pharmacy counter behind them. Cora and Ben moved away from the front door as another customer entered. They stood near a rack of peppermint sticks, the bright red and white twists smelling like Christmas.

"The head's okay. Felt like a mule kicked it for a few days. The arm is healing. Itches like crazy, but it'll do. Doc McMullen did okay, for an old fart. Definitely not as easy on the eyes as some," he said around a grin. There was the mischievous boy again. She relaxed even more, confident the worst of the storm had passed with them.

"Guess I better head home. I've got patients scheduled this afternoon," Cora said, hitching her backpack on her shoulder. "Do you need any meds for your arm?" She nodded at the bandage wrapped around his massive forearm.

"Naw. I'm good. Thanks, though. Hey, um, listen … you want to catch a movie in the park Friday night? I'd like to make it up to you, maybe start over again? What do you say? I promise not to act like a butt again."

It was Cora's turn to be surprised. Her sensible brain lectured her. *No, you can't go. He's your patient. He drives you nuts.* "Sure. Why not?" Sensible Cora groaned to herself.

"I'll meet you there."

His smile lit his eyes, green fire flashing. Sensible Cora growled silently. Impetuous Cora kicked up her heels in delight.

She nodded and said, "Well, 'til Friday." She walked past him, and as she did, he said "Lilac."

With a questioning look, she turned. "Lilac?"

"Your hair. I remember it, from when I was hurt. Like lilacs in late spring." He flushed crimson, and cleared his throat. "You know, like in the woods and stuff."

Cora blushed and ducked her head, covering a smile. When she was down the sidewalk a dozen paces, she turned back.

He stood filling out the pharmacy door, arms crossed in front of him, watching her as she walked away. Ben raised one hand in a small wave and grinned, and then ducked his head as he ran the upraised palm through already tousled hair.

On the ride home, a slow fire kindled deep in the hidden caverns of her stomach. She puzzled over blazing emerald eyes and a sly smile, and ignored Mae's warning to guard her heart.

9

The witch should have gotten the letter by now. He smiled, a slash across his face that froze below his eyes. He glared feverishly at the calendar on his mahogany desk. The number 14 pulsed at him, seeming to rise from the sheet of paper. October 14, the day she died. His Missy.

A knock on the glass pane of the door annoyed him. "What?" His voice was a whip.

Nancy, the secretary and full-time dispatcher scowled back at him. "Hettie's on the phone. Wants to know if you'll be coming over for Will's birthday party tonight. Said you keep ignoring her calls and emails." Her eyes flicked to the disconnected intercom, but she held her tongue.

Gordon growled under his breath, raked his hands through his salt and pepper hair. He needed a haircut, but it was the least of his worries. He didn't have time for all this drama with his former mother-in-law, either. Couldn't the woman take a hint?

"Fine, put her through."

"Don't bark at me." She rolled her eyes, smacked her gum, and turned, but before she walked through the door she gazed at him over her shoulder.

"Look, Deputy. I know what day it is. We all do." Nancy softened her tone. "You're not the only one who misses her, Gordon."

He finger-combed his hair, rubbed his hands across the stubble on his jaw, and took a swig from the flask concealed beneath the desk. He switched on the viewscreen, waited for the ring of the transferred call.

Hettie's face filled the screen when he punched the accept button. She held his son on her lap.

Gordon cleared his throat. "Ha – Happy birthday, William. How's my boy?"

The chubby one-year old smiled and waved his hands, reached out to touch the viewscreen on his end, but Hettie gently guided his hand away.

"Gordon. Can we expect you tonight? Will's looking forward to seeing his daddy. It's been a few weeks since the last time you visited, you know." An admonishment, but she tempered it with visible patience for the baby's sake. Her smile looked forced.

Guilt gnawed at his belly. He loved his son, but not easily. The gurgling baby bouncing on his grandmother's lap had jet black hair and bright blue eyes, just like Missy's had been. Every time he looked at his son he saw his dead wife. Then he saw the witch standing over her and pounding on her chest, reaching out to close Missy's eyelids for the final time before the paramedics wheeled her away. Anguish ripped through him, fueled by the hatred he harbored for the woman who killed his Missy.

"Gordon?"

"Uh, yes, well, I'd love to come and see the little guy. There's this case here at work, though, taking up a lot of my time, and …"

William babbled and drooled, grabbed his grandma's hand, shoved it in his mouth.

Her tone sharpened. "He needs you, Gordon. Whether I like it or not, he needs his father in his life. Look at him! Can't you even look your son in the eyes? It's his first birthday, for crying out loud!"

Gordon jerked his head up, his eyes boring into the screen. "I know what day it is." He enunciated each word through gritted teeth. "Why today, Hettie? Why not tomorrow? Missy died today!"

Anger flared in Hettie's face. "You selfish man! I know today is the anniversary of Melissa's death. She was my *daughter*! How could I not remember?" Her voice gained strength and volume. "And she didn't die today, she died a year ago! When are you going to accept it? When are you going to understand that a part of her lives on in your son, her son?"

The chair squawked as he shoved back from the desk. He leaned over and jabbed at the screen. "I see her every time I look at him! I can't look at my son without seeing Missy!"

William whimpered, tears welling in his eyes. His lower lip quivered just before the cry erupted in a wail.

"Now you've done it!" Disgust painted Hettie's face. "Come or don't come. I'm past caring."

The image flicked from the call to the home screen in the blink of an eye, the county seal graphic replacing the angry visage of his former mother-in-law.

Gordon kicked the chair into the wall, and raging, picked up the framed picture of his son and hurled it across the room. Glass shattered on impact. Within seconds Nancy raced through the door, her eyes wide and head swiveling.

"Out!" His bellow echoed off the four walls of his office.

He snatched the jacket off the back of the leather swivel chair and shoved his arms into it, checked his holster, pocketed his badge. The door rattled in its frame as he slammed it shut behind him. Thrusting a finger in Nancy's direction he growled, "Direct all calls to Scallion and Holt for the next two hours."

He floored the pedal of his issued all-terrain cruiser, reversing carelessly and leaving black tread marks seared into the pavement, then gunned it down the street. He needed to get away, clear his head. Glancing at his watch, he noticed it was close to the time of the meet anyway. He'd get there a little early, fire at a few targets, blow off some steam.

Once past the city limits of Bee Tree, he eased up on the throttle, taking the curves faster than he should but not at breakneck speed. Sunlight flashed through the trees lining the highway, creating a distracting strobe effect. As he reached out to grab his sunglasses, a deer darted out in front of him. Gordon swerved, fishtailing wildly, but quickly regained control. The whitetail flitted across the road, disappearing into the opposite tree line with a flash of white.

Breathing heavily, he pulled over, put the vehicle in park. Close. Too close.

He closed his eyes, inhaled sharply through his nostrils. In his mind's eye he saw Missy lying on the bed, his newborn son at her breast smiling as he nursed. The deep sigh of relief, of bursting joy, awe at her strength and the miracle of new life. And then, blistering reality shattering it all, Missy's blue-tinged lips gasping for breath while he clutched their son.

His knuckles whitened around the steering wheel of the cruiser. A cry threatened to escape his lips, but he clutched his jaws together, refusing to release it. He exhaled and leaned over, opened the glove compartment and snatched the water bottle. The harsh burn of vodka singed his throat and he reveled in the pain, welcomed the fire.

Gordon didn't know how long he sat parked on the side of the road before his jaw unclenched and the knots in his shoulder loosened their grip on his back. Lately, only the alcohol helped. Helped release him, numbed the ache.

Ten minutes later, he turned left off the highway onto a rural route, a compacted dirt path barely qualifying for the term "road". Through the trees he wove, for two miles, until he pulled to the side. This is where the guys from the office came to blow off a little steam, kill a few cans, jars or melons with weapons not set on stun, away from the simulation room at the precinct.

It was also where he was scheduled to meet with Grub.

Grub dipped his filthy hands in a dozen black market outfits, deftly playing them against one another for his benefit, and his slimy reputation preceded him. It was said he got his name from being able to dig up anything a man could ask for. Gordon's skin crawled at the thought of using the lowlife, but use him he would.

The deputy killed targets until the clop of hooves sounded behind him. He turned slowly, holstering the sidearm.

Grub dismounted, loosely tied the sorrel to a nearby sapling oak. He stood beside the horse, about a dozen paces away from Gordon.

"You got the money, Lawman?"

Gordon eyed him stonily. "If you have it, yes."

Grub snorted. "'Course I have it. Why you want it?"

"None of your business. Bring it here."

Grub shrugged, his scrawny shoulder brushing his oily brown hair. He reached into the saddlebag, fished out a brown paper-wrapped package.

"Took a little while longer than I expected. Not many lurking around, know what I mean? Them being *illegal* and all." He snickered at his own joke.

"I have a legal interest in antique firearms which no longer function."

Once again, Grub shrugged. He stuck his hand in his pocket, jangled his fingers. Withdrawing his hand, he displayed a dozen cylindrical brass rounds, the light reflecting and glinting gold against a grimy palm.

"This is extra." The informant's crooked grin showed crooked brown teeth. "If you're interested. Coincidental-like, happens it's the same caliber as your newly acquired Colt."

Gordon wasn't expecting ammunition, but it was a definite plus. He nodded, reached into his own pocket, and pulled out a handful of glitter. Gold, silver and copper disks shone in the filtered sunlight. He selected one gold unmarked coin, payment for the pistol. "How much more?"

"Couple silvers oughta do it."

"One silver. And I don't drop any hints to Dog that you've been skinning him."

Grub shifted his foot in the dirt and bit his lip, but he nodded, spitting on the dirt near Gordon's foot. He reached out a smudged hand, pocketed the money.

"Not a word, Grub. I'll know."

"Whatever, Lawman. See you around."

When the sound of hooves had faded, Gordon unwrapped the package. An early century Colt .45 gleamed in his hand. Heavy, surprisingly so. But it felt … right.

Finally, things were looking up.

10

Cora waved to her young patient as the wagon trundled down the dirt drive, one hand shading her eyes from the mid-afternoon sun. Little Billy Walker flapped his newly casted arm in her direction, bouncing in the buggy as he and his mother drove away. A sudden gust of wind teased a curl away from her face and kicked up the dust thrown by the departing wagon into a swirly dust devil. Bruised and heavy clouds multiplied on the horizon, an autumn storm brewing to the north and west. A faint rumble sounded in the distance, like the deep bass drum of a far-off orchestra. She hoped the rain stayed away, though they needed it badly.

If it stormed, Movies in the Park would be cancelled, and so would her date with Ben. Huh. A date. Not something she had planned to happen five months after moving in, and yet, something that intrigued and excited her. Butterflies leapt and fluttered beneath her sternum even as thunder growled in the distance. Flickers of light danced between thunderheads.

It was ridiculous to contemplate anything more than friendship with the man, she knew. And yet, she couldn't help but feel like a teenage girl when he settled those fiery emerald eyes on her face.

74

Heat blossomed in her cheeks, the screen door clattering as she let slam shut behind her. She strolled back to the treatment room to clean up the debris from casting Billy's arm. Cora gathered bits of plaster-coated nylon, swept up a small pile of crumbly dust that had fallen to the floor. One of the surprise welcome gifts offered to her by the city council had been a hand-held radiography wand, and it had been well-used in the short time since she had called Cotton Springs her home. The other gift went hand in hand with the wand – an ultraviolet rapid setter. It cut the drying time in half for casting broken limbs. She remembered opening the door to her new home, her hands shaking with excitement, and walking into the bare living room, only to find a plain white box adorned with an enormous red bow. The two medical tools nestled in the padded box made her feel more at home than a mess load of furniture ever would.

Cora smiled at the memory as she closed the last cabinet door in her exam room. Once the chart for Billy was complete, her assessment and treatments documented, she locked her viewscreen and stowed the flexible keyboard in a narrow drawer. Now that her work was complete for the day—fingers crossed—she could concentrate on not panicking for her date with Ben Tucker.

***

A warm breeze fluttered the hem of her dress. Even though the temperature was in the high seventies, she was grateful for the lightweight sweater she wore. The dress was feminine; cream colored with tiny blue flowers scattered all over, like she had gathered handfuls of bluebells, tossed them into the wind, and they settled on the delicate cotton. It skimmed below her knees, flirty and elegant. Cora always felt like such a girl in this dress. It was one of three in her possession, since most of the time her career dictated her wardrobe. Strappy sandals adorned her feet, and pearls dipped and swayed from her earlobes. Dangly earrings weren't incredibly practical when treating patients, especially young children, so it was a treat to get all decked out for her night on the town.

She stood at the back of her house, facing the stables and small fenced paddock where her horse, Rusty, lazily nibbled at the fringes of a hay bale. The movie was scheduled to start in about an hour. Prior to getting dressed for the evening she had come outside, and harnessed Rusty to the little buggy she used now and then. Not for the first time she longed for a motor vehicle, but it was out of the question. Even if she had the money to buy one, she'd rather put the funds toward an investment into her practice. Cora had always gotten by with either a bicycle or horse for most travel, except for the move to Texas. That trip involved horses, steamship, solar rail, and wagon train, in that order.

Rusty lifted her head and flared her nostrils before Cora even heard the sound of hooves coming from the drive on the other side of the house. Her horse neighed a welcome, and another answered her enthusiastically. Curious, Cora strode around the side of her home.

Ben had one boot in the saddle and the other on the ground. He smiled when he saw her.

"Hey."

"Hey, yourself. You get lost? Town's that way." Her finger pointed south.

"Funny girl, huh? No, I'm not lost. Checking to see if you wanted company on the ride into town. Looks pretty ugly on the horizon."

He had his hand shading his eyes against the sun. Cora was framed from behind in the fading western sunlight, so she walked toward him and the porch. She didn't want him to go blind staring into the sunset. As she rounded the front of the horse, she flushed beneath his following gaze. His eyes grew wide.

Ben cleared his throat. "Well, Doc. You, um, sure clean up nice."

She grinned. "Thanks. It's not often I get out like this, so it's fun."

He nodded at her feet with his chin. "Planning on riding in those shoes?" His voice held a skeptical note.

She chuckled. "Not at all. I hitched my buggy up a little while ago, and Rusty's ready to head out. She's grazing over by the paddock."

"Hmm." He scratched his chin. "Well, I suppose I could still ride beside you on the way in."

"Why don't you ride in the buggy and leave your horse here? I mean, he *is* a horse, right?" she joked. The beast was huge. "You can either stable him, or let him graze in the pasture. It's not terribly big, a few acres, but he's welcome to it."

Ben had a mischievous look in his eye again, and a sly grin plastered on his face. "I think I can get on board with your plan. I'd never turn down an opportunity to ride into town sitting next to a pretty lady." The rascal.

"But, I think I'll stable him. If it does storm, he'll be sheltered."

Cora nodded. "Good idea."

On the slow ride into Cotton Springs, with the buggy squeaking in protest in the rougher spots under Ben's massive frame, they discussed generalities. The weather, how Ben's arm was healing and itching like the dickens, how his grandmother was faring. She felt comfortable sidled up to him, her head barely reaching his shoulders. He had insisted on driving, and she agreed. She found she enjoyed letting someone else take control, even for something as trivial as the reins to the horse. Off in the distance, thunder rumbled, but above them clear skies dominated. Thankfully, there were no other buggies in front of them to kick up dust.

The Indian summer breeze kissed Cora's cheeks, blowing curly locks of hair back and over her shoulders. The wind alternated between a sigh and a gust, fitfully teasing them with hints of summer's departure and the coming coolness of autumn. As they made their way into town, Cora was once again enthralled with the charm of the downtown sector of Cotton Springs. Gaslights lined both sides of the road into town, and branched off to light the main arteries of the business district. In the failing light of day, the posted lamps burned bright. Though, she supposed, the term *gaslight* was more sentimental in name than accurate in function. The lamps, like all lights, were solar. And yet, they didn't lose their old-world charm.

They pulled into the carriage lot across from The Square. Ben tied Rusty to the hitching post, and came around to Cora's side of the buggy to hand her down.

"Your grandmother would be proud of your manners, Ben," Cora teased.

"Darn right, she would. If I didn't behave myself, she'd pop out from behind a tree or a building, and somehow snatch my ear and drag me off for a spanking like she did when I was a kid."

Blankets were scattered across the green grass of the park. People lounged and ate from picnic baskets, chatted animatedly with each other and watched over children scampering on the playground. Couples leaned into each other, smiling and conversing softly. There were easily over a hundred townspeople scattered about.

Cora spotted an empty blanket on the fringe of the park near a stand of trees, and pointed it out to Ben.

"Who puts out the blankets?"

Cora shrugged. "Oh, different people. Some have been donated to the city, so there are those. Others are brought from home and spread out for neighbors to use. I've brought a couple in the past."

They made their way across the green, weaving in and out through the patchwork. Both found themselves saying hello and waving to a few people, Ben more so than Cora. Of course, he had grown up here, and knew everyone. After they settled onto their little cloth viewing seat, Cora raised an eyebrow. "Didn't they do this when you lived here?"

He shook his head. "Naw. Must have started this while I was away."

"How long were you gone from home? I'd think even a bounty hunter would get homesick."

Ben leaned back, his arms outstretched behind propping him up. It was like watching a skyscraper relaxing against a neighboring building.

"I was in the army before I was a tracker, remember. Fifteen years a soldier, in fact."

Cora chuckled under her breath.

"What? Something funny about the army?" he asked congenially.

"No," she grinned. "I was trying to imagine someone finding fatigues and boots to fit you."

"Ha ha. Everyone's a comedian."

The gaslights dimmed, leaving the crowd surrounded by the darkening canopy of sky above, the dying sun hidden by storm clouds in the west. The white brick façade of Wainwright's

Pharmacy lit up, and the movie began. Cora loved the old classics they showed, films that transported her to a strange time and place, similar to her own but at the same time, completely alien. Tonight's picture was *Night at the Museum.* The audience cheered, and quieted as the movie began.

Clouds scooted across the sky, joining their stormy friends in the north and west, obscuring stars and hiding the cautious half-moon. Light from the movie flickered across faces, illuminating laughter and smiles. Cora lost herself in the story, and didn't notice when she rested her head against Ben's arm.

***

Ben noticed. The breeze blew the scent of lilac into his nostrils. Stray curls the color of fire tickled his arms, and occasionally his neck, when the wind picked up. He inhaled the smell of Cora, earthy and sweet, a little spicy. The crowd around him laughed in unison, but he had lost interest in the movie. Thunder rumbled in the northwest, an echo to the pulse coursing through his body.

The film would end soon. People in the audience would cheer their approval, and it would be time to drive Cora home to her house in the woods. But for now, for this moment, he sat on a blanket in the middle of a park, with the weight of one of the most frustrating and intriguing people he had ever met resting against him, and he was content to sit.

And breathe.

11

Raindrops spattered the glass panes, and through the windows Cora watched the storm whip and bend saplings, sway the tall oaks and the magnolias. Though it was nearly noon, dark skies lingered, the storm blotting out the sun with bruised and battered clouds. Lightning flickered, and a few seconds later thunder rumbled. She felt it in the floorboards, heard it reverberate in the walls.

She sat behind her desk, viewscreen alight with a patient's records, the keyboard patiently awaiting her fingers. Try as she may, she couldn't concentrate on charts. Her thoughts drifted to a blanket in the park, the woodsy smell of Ben's shirt as she leaned on his arm, the quiet ride home in the dark while lightning sparked in the distance and in the space between them. She knew better than to consider him as anything other than a friend. What was she thinking? Guilt and desire warred within, her heart as tumultuous as the squall outside.

An abrupt crash came from the living room. Cora sprung from the desk and rushed out of the office, expecting to see the front door blown open by the storm. The door was open, but standing inside was a woman, soaked completely through. She stood in a massive puddle of rainwater, brown hair plastered to her skull, not an inch of dry clothing to be seen. A ragged and torn umbrella hung limply from her hand, its metal bracing twisted and broken, the fabric torn and punctured.

Cora snatched the throw blanket from the back of the couch, and hurried over to the woman.

"Are you okay?" Cora hastily skimmed over her drenched visitor, who nodded vigorously. "Good, let me fetch some towels. I'll be right back."

The woman tucked her chin, the corner of her mouth turned up, shy eyes downcast, and thanked her quietly. Cora retrieved two large bath towels from the hallway linen closet, and presented them to the soggy stranger.

Cora sized her up. "Start drying off. We're about the same size. I'll get some of my clothes, and you can wear something dry, okay?" The woman nodded. When Cora returned with a folded stack of clothes in her arms she found the woman toweling off, but she hadn't moved a step. The shredded umbrella lay discarded at her feet.

"I'm sorry for barging in like this on a Saturday." Cora waved her off.

"Don't worry about a thing, honey. Take these to the bathroom down the hallway, and put them on. We'll get you dry."

With a small smile, the woman nodded her thanks, and briskly walked down the hall, a trail of water snaking behind her.

Cora sat on the arm of the sofa, puzzled, but patient. A few minutes later, the woman returned, dry in Cora's clothing, hair towel-dried and damp, her cheeks flushed with embarrassment.

"I, um, draped my wet stuff over your shower rod. Hope it was okay. I'm Beth, by the way. Well, Elizabeth, but everyone calls me Beth. Winslow."

Cora held out her hand. "Cora Thomas. But I'm assuming you already know my name?"

Beth smiled, nodding her head in return. "You're probably wondering why I'm here, huh?"

"The thought had crossed my mind, but usually people drop in for medical care." The unspoken question lingered in the air.

"I want to have a baby. Well, we – my husband and I – want to have a baby. We've tried for a year now, and no luck. I was hoping you could offer some advice, maybe do an exam? I never expected the storm to hit like it did."

"I'm happy to help however I can, Beth. Would you like to talk here or in the office?"

"Here's good, for now. Oh, who am I kidding? I feel utterly ridiculous. I should just leave. I should have called first, or waited until Monday."

"Nonsense. Just relax. I'm a good listener, so spill it."

This morning Beth had told her husband she was headed to Cotton Springs for a little shopping. The skies were steely, not overly threatening, but she grabbed the umbrella anyway before going out to hitch up the horse to the buggy. Hoping the rain would hold off like it did yesterday, Beth drove the five miles into town. At the post office, she casually struck up a conversation with the clerk, and learned Cora's address. When she walked out of the building onto Main Street, lightning flashed closer and thunder rumbled in answer. She hastily unhitched the buggy, and raced the last mile on horseback. About halfway to Cora's home in the woods, the torrent broke, soaking her in seconds. The umbrella was destroyed in the amount of time it took to get from the stable to the front door. Cora nodded her understanding, encouraged Beth to go on.

Beth gave a small chuckle, "Don't know why I bothered with the thing. I was already drenched." She shrugged her shoulders. "I don't usually keep things from Ronnie – my husband, but I don't think he'd be comfortable with me seeking a professional's help right now. We've tried so hard for the past year and still no baby, but he urges me to be patient. We've only been married a few years, he says, so there's no hurry. I'm afraid something is wrong with me."

Beth's lip trembled a bit. Cora sensed there was more to her story, a weight hanging heavy in Beth's heart, and she needed time to feel comfortable enough to unload her concerns. She began to ask questions about Beth's monthly cycles, any current medical problems she may have, symptoms that stood out to her as a potential problem with conceiving. Beth answered the questions in a mechanical voice, but wouldn't meet Cora's eyes.

Cora sighed. "I'll be honest with you, Beth. There's only so much I can do without performing tests, getting blood samples, ultrasounds. To have a complete picture, we'd need Ronnie to participate in the testing. We need to know his motility count. But," she said carefully, "I get the feeling there's something you're not telling me."

The woman on her couch wrung her hands. Tears leaked down her cheeks, and she sniffled as the lightning flickered through the window. Beth answered in a hesitant whisper, but a peel of thunder rumbled, frustrating Cora's hearing.

"I'm sorry, honey, but I didn't understand."

Beth whispered, barely audible with the storm raging outside the windows. "I feel like I'm being punished."

"Punished? For what?"

Sobs wracked Beth, doubling her over in painful anguish. All Cora could do was rub her back, wait for the torrent to subside.

When the tears had abated, and Beth was able to speak again, she took a deep breath, but kept her eyes on her lap.

"When I was eighteen, I got pregnant," she began. Hesitantly at first, but steadier as she spoke, voicing the ghost of a memory rather left buried. "My boyfriend and I had been together for about a year. We had been so good, abstinent, for so long, and we thought we'd be together forever. Or, at least, I did. So we did it. Heat of the moment, you know? We stopped fighting it, let go. Two months later, my period hadn't come and I took a pregnancy test. It was positive."

She continued the tale, explaining how she went to her boyfriend's house to tell him, in person. The ride over to his home a few miles away gave her time to think, time to clear her head to choose her words wisely. She wasn't prepared for his reaction.

"He threw up on my shoes," she said dully. "Not quite the reaction I was hoping for. Honestly, I don't know *what* I was hoping for. Anyway, after he wiped his mouth, he looked up at me and asked what I was going to do about it."

Beth had been flabbergasted. They were young, yes, but they loved each other. Surely he wanted to get married, start their family. But no, he didn't.

"He said, 'Get rid of it,' and turned and walked away, leaving me staring at his slumped shoulders. When he came back he had a handful of coin in his hand, shoved it at me," she said. "Like the baby was nothing but an inconvenience."

For weeks Beth anguished over the decision, what to do with her baby. She was eighteen, unwed, at the mercy of a family she would shame. What choice did she have?

"I knew it was wrong," she cried. "But I did it anyway. I had an abortion. I killed my child."

Beth rocked back and forth, crying silently, hands gripping one another in her lap. Cora felt her heart break for the woman in front of her. In her profession, this was, sadly, a common experience. Because of her faith, she knew abortion was murder, but her soul ached for the suffering the women endured in making that decision, in living with it. Cora had never performed the procedure, and she never planned to; but it did not stop her from sympathizing with the woman in her living room who had come to her for help.

Cora chose her words carefully. "Beth, please look at me. Honey, what's in the past can stay there. I can't imagine the burden of your choice, and I'm sorry you were at a place where you felt you had to. I know there's nothing I can say to make the hurt go away. I imagine you think about it every day?"

When Beth only nodded, tears slowly streaming down her face, Cora continued. "From a purely clinical standpoint, I need to reassure you the chances this is related to your current inability to conceive are slim. I can examine you to be sure, but I feel confident it is not the reason."

Because her heart ached, Cora leaned in and hugged Beth. She held her tight until she felt the woman breathing more steadily.

"Who do you think is punishing you, Beth?"

Timidly, she answered, "God."

Cora expected the response. "Do you want my personal opinion?" Beth nodded. "God is in the grace business, in the forgiveness business. We've all made mistakes, some small, some crazy big. The Bible teaches that all sin, the bad things we do, is the same to God. I don't know where you stand in your faith," she continued. "But I do know none of us are good enough for God, and we never will be."

"But I don't know how to get past this!" Beth exclaimed. "The guilt … it consumes me. And every month I get a period, I think, this is my punishment. I deserve this!"

Cora slowly shook her head. "Honey, I don't think the problem is God not forgiving you. His grace is a free gift. This a matter of forgiving yourself."

She stood, walked over to the bookcase in the corner of the room, and slid a small book from the shelf. Cora held it in her shaking hand, and flashed back to the day she handed Missy a wrapped Bible, to the look of hatred on Gordon's face as he held his newborn son and watched the paramedics wheel Missy's body away. She gathered her confidence, banished the memory, and took a deep breath.

"Do you have a Bible?" she asked Beth.

The woman shook her head no. Cora laid one in her lap. "Now you do," she said with a smile. "Read about God's mercy. We'll schedule an exam appointment for you if you'd like, but I think you should talk this over with your husband. Wait," Cora said, when Beth's eyes grew large like saucers. "The decision to tell him about your past is yours, and yours alone. I'll never say anything to him. But you will want him on board for fertility testing, if it's what we're going to pursue."

"Thank you, Cora. I can't … I can't tell you how much this means to me."

"I'm always here, even if it's a quick chat. And if you have questions," she nodded in the directions of the Bible, "I'll do my best. There are a few believers in town, which is quite a new thing to me coming from America. There's even a small church, but I'm sure you knew that." Beth nodded. "Maybe I'll see you there?"

Beth smiled. "Maybe so."

"Looks like the rain has eased off a bit." Through speckled glass panes, Cora watched as gusts shook the trees, but the downpour had transitioned to a spitting rain, and the skies above showed slips of blue behind the gray.

"I'll get your clothes back to you soon," Beth explained. "Promise. But I guess I should get going while I can."

Cora walked Beth to the door. "I'm here if you need me."

The storm was breaking apart, fizzling out. Cora waved to Beth as she rode down the drive and turned onto the main road. She hoped Beth, and her husband Ronnie, would find their way back to Cora's house soon, though she knew Beth had a storm of her own to endure in the days to come. She whispered a prayer that God would comfort Beth and bolster her spirit, and Beth would let God through the chinks of her walled-away heart.

Cora faced her own ghosts as the storm rolled to the east. Missy's face was there before her, eyes closed in death. Her best friend, gone, never getting to know the son she loved from conception. Thinking of her new patient, Cora desperately needed a happily ever after.

12

Dry, brown oak leaves skittered across the deer path, the crisp northerly wind cartwheeling piles of the shed foliage through the trees. They came to rest on mounds of pine needles, creating a rusty red and dull russet blanket in the forest surrounding Cotton Springs. A weak and watery morning sun peeked through the tall trunks of pine and oak, barely warming the autumn air still moist from the rain the day before. The front had cooled the land, dropping temperatures thirty degrees overnight. Squirrels chittered and frantically searched the ground for acorns, tails twitching as they excitedly chirped at one another. One second they were pawing through leaves searching for treasure below, and the next, heads jerked erect as footsteps in the woods signaled their retreat.

The squirrels chastised Ben from the branches above. His boots barely made a sound in the soft undergrowth. Rainwater had soaked the ground quickly, and despite the inches filling the water gauge, only a few puddles dotted the forest floor. Ben stopped and stooped. Two feet off the rugged footpath used by the local wildlife, a tuft of soft honey-colored hair dangled on a snapped branch. Two small markings imprinted the soft mud between leaf piles. He was on the right track.

Two hours had passed since he had gotten the call from Linda Murdock seeking his help. The Murdocks lived a few miles outside of town on a small holding, about ten acres of mostly wooded land which butted up against the Angelina Forest, a national forest that retained its name from pre-Republic days. Linda's dog, Mable, a much-loved poodle, had been missing since the evening before. Linda and her husband, Wally, searched their land well into the night with no success. It was no secret Ben was back in town, and he was well-known for his tracking skills. Never mind that the prey he usually stalked walked on two legs rather than four. Calling him in had been a no-brainer for the Murdocks, or so the said. Ben was happy to help. To be honest, any excuse to get his mind off a certain curvy, sassy redhead was welcome.

Cora had clouded his head the last day and a half. How the little woman had sunk her hooks into him he had no idea, and it chafed. He had no time for a relationship, wasn't looking for one. His grandmother would be her old active self before long, and he would return to work, accepting tracking or bounty contracts. He certainly didn't need to be wasting time with a female who put stock into ridiculous myths and closed-minded fallacies.

But when he closed his eyes at night, he saw brilliant blue eyes staring back at him, and smelled lilac in the air. Infuriating woman!

Ben was so involved in berating himself that he nearly missed the cougar track on the edge of the deer path. The cougar track overlapped the small dog's, clipping the canine impression along the bottom of the footpad. Mable had a stalker. Unsettled, Ben quickened his pace and refocused his attention to the task at hand.

At first glance, the evidence of the big cat's presence looked like that of the poodle, except for the size. But Mable's prints left the slight dip of claw marks near the toes, and the cougar's did not.

Because the cougar left tracks more than twice the size of the canine, he also knew he was dealing with a fairly large wildcat.

As if it were ripped from the earth itself, the scream of the cougar reverberated through the trees, and the barking growl of a dog answered in kind. Ben swung his rifle to the ready, and followed the sounds north and slightly east, forgetting the tracks on the ground, following his ears instead. Birds squawked and launched themselves into the air. Squirrels fled in haste up towering bark-covered trunks. Ben's long legs made short work of the run as he dodged shrubs, stumps and trees. The fight continued audibly, the big cat hissing and screeching, the dog continuing her snarling assault. Over a rise Ben thundered. He topped the straw-covered knoll, and found the fight at the bottom, near an immense fallen oak, its root ball in the air.

Mable the poodle had her back to the moss-enshrouded roots, growling and barking menacingly with bared teeth. The sable-colored cougar darted in and out, hissing and swiping with powerful paws, claws digging into the forest floor, sweeping the air as it lunged.

Ben halted and took aim, his breaths evening out. He switched the rifle from stun to lethal with a click, then pulled a breath deep into his lungs. On the exhale, the sights aligned and he squeezed the trigger. The cougar dropped with a cough in mid-lunge. Mable retreated beneath the fallen oak. The cougar remained motionless.

With a soothing croon, Ben approached Mable, though he could only see her eyes gleaming from within the tree-turned-cave. He withdrew a treat from his pocket, tossed it in her direction, then sat back on his haunches as he waited for her to decide whether he was friend or foe. The wait was short. In less than a minute Mable wagged her tail enthusiastically as Ben scratched behind her ear, but the threat of a fight had clearly drained the poor animal. With a quiet yip, she edged to the security of the fallen tree's root ball. Ben followed her, curious as to why she would want to remain.

He knelt down, peered inside, and was surprised to find Mable laid on her side, with three newborn pups pawing at her in hunger. The puppies were dry and clean, obviously a few hours old. Ben sat beneath towering trees and watched as the youngsters suckled, their mother relaxed with eyes closed.

An hour later Ben presented a jacket-wrapped bundle to an overjoyed Linda Murdock.

"Ben, I don't know how to thank you." Linda beamed as Mable lathered her face in doggy kisses.

He ducked his head and smiled. "My pleasure, Mrs. Murdock. But I won't lie. Mable had unwanted company. A cougar tracked her. It was attacking when I found them."

Linda gasped, hand to her throat. "Oh, my baby!" Ben didn't understand much of what was said after, as she goo-gooed to the wiry-haired squirming dog.

"Looks to me like she was out exploring yesterday, found it was time to deliver these pups." He glanced down at the bundle in his arms.

"Honestly! I had no idea she was even pregnant! Wally thought she was getting fat and lazy. Oh, aren't they the sweetest things ever?"

He thought they looked like moles, to be honest. But Ben smiled and nodded his head. "They're something, all right."

"Let me go in the house and get my purse."

"Please, it's not necessary. On the house."

"You do your grandmother proud, you do. Thank you, Ben. Ever since the kids up and left the house, Mable's been my baby,

92

until we get those grandkids. She wouldn't be here, it sounds like, if it weren't for you. Now we have grandpups!"

Since Linda had her hands full of wiggling mama dog, Ben carried the bundle of puppies into the house. He eased his way out of the house, leaving sounds of yippy happiness behind him. After he mounted his horse, he tipped his hat while Linda waved from the porch. His stomach rumbled, reminding him it was lunch time. A burger from Dixie's Café would be just what the doctor ordered.

And thinking of doctors ordering things brought to mind red curls blowing in the breeze, and playful blue eyes staring up at him. Ben groaned.

Infuriating woman!

***

"Hear you helped Mrs. Linda find her pooch." Dixie slid the plate in front of him.

Ben stared at her in question. "Now how in the world do you know? I left her house and came straight here as fast as Goliath could bring me."

"Now that is one appropriately named horse. Everyone in town has made a remark about your beast. What is he anyway?" Dixie tilted her head to the side when she was curious. But she also nibbled her lip when she was nervous, and she was chewing away.

What had her so agitated? "Percheron-Thoroughbred cross."

Dixie flicked her attention over his shoulder to a booth behind him, so quickly that he barely registered it. Her teeth snagged her lip again, but in a blink she was smiling in his direction again.

"How's that burger?" She bent over to grab some napkins from beneath the bar.

He grunted his approval around a mouthful of juicy beef, picked up a fry and held it in reserve, swallowed the bite of burger. "Great as always, Dix. You've got a gift." He winked at her playfully.

"Oh, stop it, you big flirt. Everyone knows you've got your sights set on a different target. You're not fooling me." She laughed and wiggled narrow eyebrows at him.

He rapped his chest and coughed.

Dixie batted her eyes, lashes fluttering. "Food go down wrong?"

He grunted again in reply, set about demolishing the food in front of him. She chuckled and flicked a towel at him, had moved down the bar to serve another patron when the ding from the kitchen sounded. Between bites, he watched Dixie.

He had known her since freshman year of high school, when she moved to Cotton Springs from Houston. Big city girl turned country gal, she fit like a glove in the small community. She worked at the diner when it was the Cotton Café, after school and for years after graduation, earning tips and saving her money religiously. When the previous owner died, Dixie snapped up the restaurant the minute the heirs put it up for sale. She'd been churning out delicious grub for ten years now, and still looked like she did the day she tossed her graduation cap in the air. Though she was beautiful, blonde and leggy in denim, their relationship was platonic, more siblings than anything. His time in the army, and after, tracking bounties, hadn't diminished the friendship, despite the years away. Any potential suitors knew they had to pass Ben's inspection first. It both soothed and irked Dixie to no end, he knew. He was probably a little overprotective. His own sister had complained about the same thing countless times.

It was because he knew Dixie so well that he noticed the chewed lip and the eye flicks across the room when she didn't think Ben was watching. Time to get to the bottom of this.

He wiped his mouth, kicked back on the bar stool, put his hands behind his head and sighed loudly. "Outstanding as always, Dixie." His praise rumbled louder than necessary. Down the bar a little ways she straightened, eyed him suspiciously. Ben turned around to the booth behind him, in the direction of her nervous glances..

He eyed the stranger. "Isn't that the best food you ever had, now?" From the corner of his eye, Ben saw Dixie nibble on her lip, her attention half on the customer she was serving, and half in his direction.

The man, mid-thirties, wore a tattered red and black checkered flannel shirt, and well-worn denim jeans that frayed at the hems around scuffed leather boots, the soles thin with wear. He nodded as he stood, threw some coins on the table, and shoved his hat on his close-cropped head.

Without speaking, the stranger walked out the door. The bell chimed in his wake. He didn't look back.

Dixie finished up with her patron, and stalked over to Ben. Hand on her hip, she glared at Ben. "Nice performance. Want to tell me what you're doing?"

Ben raised an eyebrow. "You can't hide anything from me, Dix. Why did he upset you? Did he say something before I got here?"

She rolled her eyes in response, but sighed all the same. "Can't put my finger on it, Ben. He's not from around here." She waved her hands in exasperation. "I'm probably making a big deal out of nothing."

"What?"

"He was friendly enough. Talked a little funny, like he was from up north somewhere. But he asked where to find Doc."

"Doc McMullen's across the street. You can see the sign from here."

"Not Doc McMullen. Doc Thomas. Cora."

"Dixie, what *exactly* did the man ask?"

She tapped her finger against her lower lip in thought. "Well, it's like I said. Asked where he could find Cora. Called her by name, even knew what she looked like. I don't know, Ben. There's something *off* about the guy."

"What did you tell him?" Ben's eyes flared dangerously.

"Hey, cool it, Ben. I didn't tell him a thing. Told him, yeah, there's a new doc in town and she fits the description. But I didn't like the way he looked, so I didn't tell him anything else. Changed the subject real fast, asked how he knew her. He didn't answer." Dixie held a hand up. "Went back to eating his food. Occasionally he'd look up at me and stare. But you walked in, and he backed off."

"Was he on foot? Horseback? What?"

"Didn't see a horse hitched out front, and you saw as clearly as I did he walked out and kept on walking."

Ben brooded a bit longer with his sweet tea in hand. He laid his coin on the bar top while Dixie was across the restaurant bussing a table. On his way out, he grabbed the fork and knife the nosy stranger had used, wrapped them loosely in a napkin.

The bell announced his departure, and he waved at Dixie through the plate glass window. He walked two doors down, turned the knob and sauntered into the sheriff's office. He nodded to the secretary, Betty.

"Afternoon, Ben. What can I do ya for?" Her drawl made it sound like she said *far*.

"Jimmy in?"

She hooked a thumb over her shoulder. "Back in his office. I'll let him know you're coming."

Ben said his thanks, and walked down the well-lit corridor to the glass-paned door. "Deputy James Wilson" was etched on the glass. He rapped on the door, and entered when Jimmy barked. "Come in!"

"Ben." The deputy edged around the modest desk, extended his hand in greeting.

"Jimmy." Ben answered with a firm shake. "We got ourselves a problem."

He relayed the scene in the diner, adding his gut feeling to the telling, and all the while Jimmy scratched his chin. When Ben laid the napkin-wrapped utensils on his desk, Jimmy's eyes opened wide.

"Now, look, Ben." Jimmy backed in retreat, hands held high. "I know you're worried. Frankly, I am too. But I can't run a guy's prints or DNA without probable cause or a warrant. You've worked with enough law enforcement to know."

"I'm asking this as a favor. I don't know why this guy would be asking around after Cora, but I don't like it."

"Well, it makes sense to me. After the threatening letter she got, I mean. Didn't expect the guy to be so tactless, though."

"Wait a minute." Ben glowered at the deputy. "Hold up. Letter?"

"Uh – Cora didn't mention it? Well, yeah, maybe you should ask her about it. I just figured, since you guys are dating and all ..."

Ben blinked. "Dating?"

Jimmy laughed. "You know. Like going on dates with one another? Like, say, to Movies in the Park on a Friday night?"

"We're not dating! We're friends!" Ben exhaled heavily, grunted. "And don't change the subject." Ben pointed a finger at the deputy. "Now, what letter?"

Jimmy reluctantly told Ben about the day Cora found him in the park, asked him to look into the matter for her.

"And I have, as much as I could," Jimmy said. "I'm also keeping tabs on her family in Missouri. Covertly."

"I know all about your covert guy. The whole county does. Heck, the entire country knows by now."

Jimmy's cheeks colored. "Yeah, well, the guy's got skills. Hasn't been caught, has he? Unlike our sloppy stranger asking around about Cora." The deputy scratched his chin again. "All right, fine. I'll run him. But if anyone finds out, well ..."

"Don't worry. No one ever looks at search requests from little towns."

Jimmy grunted, ran a hand through his hair. "I'll let you know what I find out. Question is, what do you want me to tell Cora?"

"Don't you worry about it. I need to have a talk with the Doc myself."

13

Early in the morning, with a steaming mug of coffee in hand, and a belly-full of egg and toast, Cora tromped down the porch stairs to the stable to feed and check on Rusty. Frost coated the grass, and her breath misted in front of her face. The sun wouldn't rise for another hour or so, and the land was peaceful, sleeping. Stars winked in the darkness. Rusty nuzzled her hand through the wooden fence, and snorted softly as Cora patted the mare's head.

With the horse fed and watered, Cora strolled back inside her home, briskly rubbing her arms after she shrugged out of her jacket. Two days into autumn temperatures, and she craved the summer heat. She exchanged her muddied footwear for fuzzy slippers, set her boots neatly outside the door on the porch. Then, she swapped tee shirt and plaid flannel pajama pants for sweats and running shoes.

The early-morning two-mile jog cleared the remaining fog from her sleepy brain, got her blood pumping instead of slugging through her veins. Texas was warmer this time of year than Missouri. She idly wondered as she reached her turnaround mark – a stand of willows drooping over a middling sized cattle pond a few feet from the horse path – whether snow had fallen yet on her family's spread. Cora smiled as she imagined her brother roaring and spluttering as he cleared snow, could smell the fresh bread her mother baked when the temperature dropped, envisioned her dad with his feet propped up on the ottoman with the almanac in hand, a cup of coffee steaming on the table beside the chair near the front window. The crisp Texas wind buffeted her face, but she could almost smell the snow, so vivid was the image.

But this was home now, this quaint little town with its charm and appeal. Her shoes slapped the hard-packed earth in a steady rhythm, her breathing labored but steady. She watched the sun come up as she turned at the mail box at the end of her drive. Enough time to shower and dress remained before the day began in earnest.

Before Cora knew it, Monday morning had blurred into Monday afternoon. Her schedule was packed. Yearly checkups for three youngsters, a gynecological exam, a monthly pregnancy progress check for a woman in her seventh month. Add in a case of tonsillitis, a stomach virus, a sprained ankle and a sports physical for basketball season, and Cora found herself exhausted at two o'clock in the afternoon. Her stomach rumbled in protest. The egg on toast and a glass of orange juice at six o'clock had since burned itself out, and she had neglected to eat lunch. Not that she had the chance. Her stomach rumbled loudly again, more insistent.

She made a hasty ham sandwich, grabbed some chopped carrots, and slammed a cold shot of coffee for a much needed jolt. In the mood for a little music, she turned on the radio and tuned it to the local station out of Lufkin. A little bluegrass would pick her right up. If only her charts would update themselves. She sighed, headed down the hallway to her office.

The afternoon sun flooded through clean glass panes, and fluffy white clouds chased each other across an azure sky. The wind had died down, and the thermometer attached to her window read sixty-eight degrees. Cora stood by the window and nibbled her sandwich, completely at peace. Tired, but content. She sat behind her desk, put the bowl of carrots on the desktop within reach and powered up the viewscreen, rolled out the flexible keyboard. A flashing envelope icon at the bottom of the screen indicated she had a new email.

She grinned from ear to ear. It had been weeks since she heard from her brother, John.

Sis,

Sorry for taking so long to write to you again. You know how it is here, always something happening and never like you thought it would. We had put to put Sally's mare, Jewel, down a couple weeks ago. There was a mudslide after the last bout of rain, and she slid down the short canyon in the east pasture. Wasn't much we could do, broke her two front legs. Sally was distraught for days, but she seems to be doing okay now. Ma took a tumble too, but she's fine now. Gave Dad quite a scare, for sure. Don't be upset because I didn't tell you sooner, but I didn't want you to worry. She broke her collarbone in the fall. Says it was the darndest thing. She was up in the barn tossing down hay, got halfway down the stairs and missed one. Knocked her out, but no concussion. I think it messed with her memory a little, though, because she swears someone pushed her. I searched every inch of the barn and didn't see anything out of the ordinary. I think she just slipped and fell.

Sally says to tell you hello, and she wishes she could see you. If we can arrange a visitor's pass, we'll try to come out in the spring. The boys are as rambunctious as ever and growing like weeds. They miss their Auntie.

Take care of yourself, sis. I try not to worry about you, so don't give me a reason.

Your brother,

John

Cora wiped a tear from her cheek, her lunch forgotten. Her mother fractured her collarbone? And she thought someone pushed her down the stairs! No, John had to be right. Had to have been a result of the fall. Don't worry, he says. Cora growled at the screen in frustration. She should have been there to help. Frustration and anger threatened to overwhelm her. Resentment verged on hatred for what Gordon Wilkes had done to her, to her family.

She shoved back from the desk, stomped down the hallway, and raced out the front door. She flew down the steps and ran to the barn, where she let out a blood-curdling scream, exasperation erupting from deep within. Mice skittered away in fear, and Rusty whinnied in concern from the pasture. Cora's fists were knotted, balled-up in her stomach as she doubled over, screamed some more. When that didn't help, she lashed out, punching the rough-hewn beam nearest her. With a gasp, Cora clutched her injured hand. Tears streamed down her face.

Ben burst through the door, nearly knocking Cora down as he launched himself into the barn. He turned his head left and right, his eyes alert and his fists at the ready. Cora stood dumbfounded, her throbbing hand temporarily forgotten as she tried to process his large and imposing presence.

"Where is he? What happened?" Ben scanned the dim interior, a frown on his face. "Are you okay?"

Cora nodded, wiping the tears from her eyes.

"You're crying. Why are you crying? Did someone hurt you?"

She shook her head. "I'm fine. No, I'm not fine. I'm mad."

Ben stared at her blankly. "You're mad?"

"It happens." She tried not sigh, and failed miserably. "Not that I'm not happy to see you, but what are you doing here, Ben?"

The tension in his shoulders relaxed noticeably, like a balloon deflating. "About the time I rounded your house to stable Goliath, I heard crying in the barn, and a hellacious scream. I dropped the reins and ran in here, thinking you were in trouble. What did you do to your hand?"

"I hit the pole."

"What did the pole do to you?"

She chuckled in spite of herself. "It was there. I was mad. So I hit it." Cora shrugged. She realized her anger had dimmed drastically, and she was left with a puffy face and a stinging hand. She sniffled.

He nodded at her hand. "Let's go get some ice on your knuckles."

"Well, gee, thanks doc. Never would have thought of it."

"Don't pout. And there's no need to bite my head off, Cora. I'm trying to help."

She stormed past him, embarrassed and frazzled. He followed her into the house, and sat at her dining table as she got an ice pack out of the freezer. Now that her tantrum was over, she felt ridiculous.

There he sat, a hulking giant with one arm resting on the round white table, his feet outstretched and crossed at the ankles. His eyes twinkled in amusement, which rankled her, but she couldn't fault him for it. She flounced into the dining room and flopped down into a ladder-backed chair.

"Here, let me see your hand." Ben reached over to remove the ice pack. He sucked air over his teeth at the abrasions on her knuckles. "Remind me never to get on your bad side, Doc."

"Hmph."

"Want to talk about it?"

She sighed. "No. But you're not going to let it go, are you?"

Ben shook his head. "Nope."

"Didn't think so." Cora told him about the email, the news from her brother, her mother's fall and broken collarbone. "It's exasperating to be hundreds of miles away and helpless! I should have been there."

He sat quietly, lost in thought. Then he looked her in the eyes, held her gaze until she looked away from the penetrating green irises boring into her head. He leaned forward over the table, closing the distance between them.

"Why are you here, Cora?"

She looked down at the cold compress on her hand, avoiding his eyes. They unsettled her with their intensity. "What do you mean?"

He whacked the table, cracking the air. Cora jumped, eyes wide. "I mean the reason you left Missouri."

"Because I had to!" she yelled. "He was coming after me, after my family. I had to get away, Ben!"

"Who? Who was coming after you?"

She clenched her jaw. "Gordon Wilkes. A deputy sheriff."

"And why was a deputy after you?" Ben's voice softened.

"Because his wife died! There was nothing I could do, Ben. She was my *best friend*. She wanted a baby for ten years, and she died minutes after delivering him!"

Cora stood, began pacing the floor. Her damaged hand forgotten, she told the story, gesticulating wildly in parts, motioning calmly in others.

"I didn't want to leave Missouri. My parents, my brother and his family, my career … they were all there. But Wilkes wouldn't stop, wouldn't leave us alone! He blamed me for Missy's death. Still does!"

Her anger spent, she collapsed at the table. She was exhausted from work this morning, from the fury of learning of her mother's injuries, even from Ben's sudden and unexpected arrival.

"There was an inquiry. The board convened, examined the case, turned my life inside and out. Missy's autopsy confirmed what I suspected had happened, a pulmonary embolism. I was cleared to continue my practice. But Gordon wasn't finished with his persecution. Oh, no." She couldn't keep the caustic bitterness away. "First he attacked my practice. He went to the papers, presented his 'case' against me even after the board's judgment was passed. The press ran with the story, calling into question my wisdom, intelligence, you name it. But, you see, he was a respected deputy. A fine upstanding citizen." Cora snorted. "No one questioned him, and my patient load dropped to nothing. I was forced to go back home from St. Louis. My family has a little spread east of Imperial, not too far from the Mississippi River. Twenty-eight years old, my best friend dead, my career in shambles.

"But Gordon wasn't finished with me. Even though he lived miles north, up in Bee Tree, he tormented us. We know it was him, even though we never saw him. A few neighbors said they saw a sheriff's cruiser in the area a time or two, but they couldn't say whether or not it was him. My parents' fence line was destroyed in three places, our horses scattered. My brother's house was defaced, paint thrown all over the front. Bright red paint, the word "murderer" scrawled on the door. My nephew's dog was killed. The word "witch" was burned into the front yard of my parents' home, and it's only by sheer luck we were able to put out the fire before it burned the house down. My dad had gotten up for a drink of water, saw the flames."

Cora took a deep breath, rested her head in her hands, elbows propped on the table. Ben sat silently, waiting for her to continue, but anger flared behind his eyes. His jaw clenched and unclenched repeatedly, like he was chewing rocks.

"So we had a family meeting, and I told them I was going to find another place to live. They didn't like my decision, especially my brother. John's quite possessive of me. I was at the library the next day and picked up the newspaper, looking for ads for a midwife in the surrounding area. I wasn't concerned for myself, just my family, you see. I opened the paper, and staring back at me was an advertisement for a small Texas town seeking young professionals." Cora gave a small laugh, remembering the uproar the little breach of security caused. "I stole the page, by the way. I knew there was no way the state authorized it. I heard the next day the governor was in a tizzy, sacked dozens of state employees trying to douse the fire. And come to find out the ad was planted by Jimmy's friend."

"So this Wilkes guy loses his wife, blames you, and terrorizes you and your family? And no one can prove he did any of it?"

"Pretty much."

After seeing the ad and snatching it out of the library, Cora had made an appointment at the Republic of Texas embassy. The asylum request was filed after she presented her case to the ambassador.

"I think I would have been granted asylum without the added propaganda, but it did help ice the cake. Not to mention my professional credentials are always in need in small towns. The Texas government accepted my certification without requiring me to take the boards here."

A day after receiving approval to reside in Texas on a permanent basis, John had escorted Cora to the remote port call of Ferret Landing, eight miles southeast of Imperial on the Mississippi.

"Two weeks of travel and I found myself here, in Cotton Springs. Jimmy knows the whole story, and so do the Crocketts." She nodded at Ben. "And now you. I've tried to leave my past in Missouri with few here the wiser."

"Except he found you. Wilkes. Didn't he?"

Cora pulled the elastic band from her hair, and ran her hands through her tousled hair, red curls entwining around her long, slender fingers. A burnished halo surrounded her head. Man, she was tired.

"Sounds like you've already talked to Jimmy, Ben."

He walked to the kitchen and opened the cupboard, taking out a glass tumbler and filling it with water from the tap. The glass gave a dull clunk as he sat it in front of her. Cora smiled her thanks, took a few swallows.

"Gordon sent a letter, a threat. I'm tired of running away. Can you understand? I moved to an entirely new country to get away from that maniac, and he's still on his quest for vengeance. Did you know he truly believes I'm a witch? The Satan-worshipping, ritual performing, curse-spewing witch. Which makes no sense because he claims to not believe in any of it." When Ben's eyes widened, she went ahead. "Yeah, he thinks I cursed Missy, caused her death. The man thinks I killed my best friend. He's insane, bent on vengeance. All because I was praying aloud for her at the end, when there was nothing left to do but pray for a miracle."

When the steel hardened his countenance, she forestalled him with a look. "I won't try to convert you, Ben. But Gordon's fixation centers on my belief. Whether you like it or not, it's who I am." She pressed a hand to her heart. "In here."

Ben eyed her cautiously, and stood up, his long legs eating up the short distance between the dining area and the living room. Hands tucked in his pockets, his head down, he stomped back and forth, and stopped short across the room in front of the fireplace. Cora watched him as she would a wolf, cautious and leery.

What she wouldn't give to know what was going on in that thick skull of his. His eyes locked on hers as he sauntered over, reached out a hand. She hesitated, tense, but when he cocked his head and grinned she placed her smooth hand in his leathery one. She couldn't resist.

"Let's get outside, take a walk. I need some air."

The recent rain tamped down the red clay driveway. After weeks of choking on dust clouds, Cora breathed in clear, crisp autumn air without coughing. Ben held her hand hostage as they wandered around her property, through the skeletal oaks and the reddening pines. Little bursts of electricity seemed to flow from his hand to hers. Her heart quivered, and it terrified her. This wasn't supposed to happen, being drawn to a man who denied her God. She was a ship with billowed sails, blown to the edge of a whirlpool.

They walked in silence. She took two steps for his one, crunching over brittle sticks and moldering leaves beneath a woody canopy. Clearly Ben was thinking. She had seen the same expression on her brother's face, the one that meant he was carefully and deliberately arranging words in his head. She peeked at his face, nearly a full foot above her own. His jaw worked, the ropy muscles flexing and pulsing.

"Ben?"

He cast his gaze down. "Hmm?"

Cora halted, the tether of their linked hands pulling him back. Worry wrinkled his eyes, but the jaw muscles relaxed visibly. The corner of his mouth pulled up in a crooked grin.

"Was there something you wanted to talk about? You seem a little tense."

He sighed, looked at the slip of blue sky overhead. "I won't pretend, Cora. I can't. You know how I feel about religion. Can we move past it? For now? There are other, more pressing, matters to deal with."

Cora studied the worn toes of her leather boots, took a few deep, cleansing breaths. God whispered to her, a booming murmur. *Do not yoke yourself. Trust my timing, child.* She closed her eyes, heart torn, and pushed away the insistent voice in her head.

She looked up at Ben, read the question in his face, the worry. "For now."

He nodded, measured and deliberate. "There was a man in town today, at Dixie's place, asking about you. Mid-thirties, worn and ragged, like he'd been traveling a long time. Asking where the lady doc lived, what Dixie knew about you."

Caught off guard, Cora gasped, a hand covering her mouth. "What?! No!" Not again. "He can't do this to me! He has no right."

"I hate to tell you, Doc, but vengeance isn't a rational emotion."

Reluctantly, she dropped his hand. The empty air between them begged for the prior connection, but instead she paced the forest floor, hands shoved in the pocket of her jeans. Her fingers itched for his touch.

"You went to Jimmy." It was more a statement than a question. He nodded and shrugged, like a schoolboy caught with his hand in the forbidden cookie jar. "Good. Would Dixie describe the guy to the sheriff, maybe work up a sketch with their software? Or you could. You saw him, right?" Surprise and relief suffused his face, but just as quickly he looked away. Was that embarrassment? The man was a study of emotions today. Why did that pull at her so?

"I didn't even think to ask. I, um, sort of took the utensils he left behind. Jimmy's going to run the prints and DNA on the down-low."

Cora snorted, ran a hand over her face. "Jimmy's a good guy. I don't want him to get into any trouble."

"Trust me, unless this idiot is a major bad guy somewhere, Jimmy's search won't even blip on the higher-ups' radar."

"I thought this was over, done. Then the letter from Gordon, this guy asking questions about me. Why can't it just go away? Vanish."

Cora crossed her arms in front of her, chilled more from the situation than the brisk breeze. She didn't hear him come up behind her. She jumped when his arms slid around her, pulled her close. When she tried to pull away, Ben tightened his grip. His arms were muscled tree trunks wrapped around her, shielding her. She felt herself falling, melting. She told her brain to shut up, and acted with her heart's instinct instead, relaxing into his embrace. The warmth of his breath bathed the top of her head, his chin a comfortable weight. Minutes passed with only the sounds of nature serenading them. She wished it could go on forever, this feeling of hope, security. Hysteria lurked in the shadows.

"What is this, Ben?"

Belatedly, she realized she had whispered it aloud, and tensed. Four breaths, five passed, then he released his hold, turned her around. Cora craned her neck backwards to look him the eye, despite the knot twisting deep in her stomach. His sandy brown hair needed a trim. She wanted to run her hands through it. She wanted to run away from him. He had no right to do this to her.

Green eyes bored into blue. Her breath caught in her throat as he stopped inches away. He smelled of hay and horses, musk and diner, saddle leather and mint. Though he towered over her, she didn't back down. He reached out a hand, gently ran his thumb along Cora's jawline. She shivered.

His whisper blended with the wind, tossing and twirling mottled leaves around their feet. "I don't know what this is, Cora. But I'm here. And I won't let that man touch you."

Ben's forehead rested on the top of Cora's head, her face nestled in his chest. She breathed him in, closed her eyes.

Quietly, he added, "I promise."

14

Mae sighed in contentment. "You have magic hands, Cora m' dear."

Cora sat angled next to Mae on the older woman's faded plush sofa, the large upholstered flowers fading into the background of her homey living room. Cora massaged the oil into Mae's wrinkled, leathered hands. Applying gentle pressure in circles with her thumbs, she focused on the gnarled joints, easing the compression from a light rub to a deep penetrating knead at the base of each finger and thumb.

"Nonsense. No magic. Only the good stuff given to us by the Creator to heal your aches and pains. It's just my job to mix 'em together."

Mae's free hand reached up to grip Cora's shoulder lightly. "You're a sweet girl, Doc. Thanks for bringing this over. Dab's out on a job, but he could've gone by your place this evening."

"I had to run to the post office and bank this morning anyway, so no worries. How does that feel?"

"Warm. And tingly, in a good way. The old stuff worked fine, but I like the way this heats up my creaky old joints."

Dust motes glittered in the morning sun streaming through the windows of the little blue house on Main Street. Through the glass Cora watched people walking and riding, not a heavy crowd, the usual hustle and bustle of downtown Cotton Springs. At this end of town, cottages flanked the main thoroughfare. Postage-stamp yards dotted either side of the paved street. In the mottled green-brown grass of the Crockett's front yard was a sign for their business, Crockett 7 Construction. The shingle-style sign swayed to and fro on its chains, the gusty wind giving it a life of its own. Across the street and three doors down, just out of sight, sat Annie Hayes' home. Cora rubbed Mae's right hand, and idly wondered if Ben was planning to visit his grandmother today. Maybe she could stop in, check on her patient. Her decision made, she nodded to herself. Mae cleared her throat, and waved her free hand in front of Cora's eyes.

"Earth to Cora."

"Hmm?"

"I asked, dear, what was in the new stuff. But you seem to be in a different place right now. Wouldn't have anything to do with our resident giant, now would it?"

Mae's eyes sparked when the massage came to a swift halt, but quickly resumed in vigor.

A flush crept from Cora's neck to her cheeks, inflaming the scattered freckles and making them stand out in contrast. She cleared her own throat. "I don't know what you're talking about."

Mae laughed, a guffaw that ricocheted off the beige walls. "Dog-gone, girl! I may be sixty-five, but I know the look a woman gets when she's thinking about a man." She wagged her finger at the younger woman. "I told you to watch out for him. You listen about as well as my own children, bless their rebellious hearts."

113

"The rub." Cora looked down her nose at Mae, mock-stern before cracking a smile. "The rub is a vitamin E and coconut oil base, infused with peppermint, eucalyptus, camphor, and oregano essential oils. All are excellent for inflammation and pain. Oregano and peppermint add the extra warmth. I'm thinking of tinkering around with capsaicin, the chemical in hot peppers like jalapeno. It's also good for pain, but you don't want to play around with a pepper, and accidentally rub your eyes."

"Play with fire and you'll get burned."

"Not going to give up on it, are you?"

"Nope. I'm an old woman. Don't snort, dear. It's not lady-like. Maybe I'm not *that* old. But I could use a little romance to brighten my day. Lay it on me."

"I hate to disappoint you, but we're just friends. And don't snort. It's not lady-like."

If she were being honest with herself, though, she'd admit she didn't know *what* they were. Since the day at her home over a week ago, Cora had seen Ben every day. The day after she stupidly assaulted the barn pole, Ben dropped by to retrieve the hat that had flown off his head in his haste to rescue her. The brown felt western hat was on the ground near the barn doors, blown by the wind into the shadows. He stuck around for half an hour, chatted while she fed and brushed the mare during a break in the patient schedule. And though he kept a decent distance, his overt hungry stare made her feel craved, devoured.

The following day she spotted him at the feed store while she was out for a late morning jog. She waved, and he gave her one in return, but she continued to pound the pavement in front of her. After a long, heated stare, he turned back to his conversation with the two old-timers parked on the bench by the loading dock.

Some days they encountered each other in town and stole a few minutes from their busy schedules.   They joked and laughed, shoulders brushing against one another, invisible sparks flaring brightly as they strolled down Main Street.   Other days Ben made a point of riding to her house for one reason or another.   They had lunch twice at Dixie's place, where more than a few eyes followed them in speculation.   His hand brushed hers across the table, his gaze lingered on her face over the menu.   Their friendship had deepened, bloomed, a brilliant cluster of chrysanthemums exploding in the cool autumn air.   The anticipation of their next encounter, the breathlessness of the next touch, the earth shifting when he tilted his head a certain way and winked at her.   It was a continuous battle, to ignore the nagging voice speaking to her soul.   She complained about the dilemma to Mae, who clucked in sympathy.

"Well, dear, maybe it's for the best you remain friends, considering his rather obstinate viewpoint on God.   I know it's not what you want to hear, though.   I can see it in your eyes."

Cora clenched her jaw in frustration, even as her thumbs continued in their circular massage on Mae's arthritic hand.   "Why does it have to be so hard?   It feels natural when I'm with him.   From the first moment we spoke, it's been...like we've known each other forever.   Does that make sense?"

The older woman's eyes drew down, her compassion evident. "Maybe the timing is off.   Trust God, dear.   He's got your best interests at heart."

Definitely *not* the advice she desired.   She coveted Ben's company, but overlooking the physical chemistry between them was nigh on impossible.   The air was as electric as the skies during a hot summer storm when they were together.

Cora finished the massage on Mae's other hand, and passed the rest of the time gossiping about trivial rumors. As she was gathering her things and stuffing them in her ruck sack, she glanced out the front window.

A man stood, hands in the pockets of his worn jeans, on the sidewalk adjacent to the Crockett's home, staring into the window straight at Cora. The hair on the back of her neck stood on end. Hastily, she continued packing the bag and covertly snuck a lidded peek through the glass. There he stood, intent.

"Mae?" Cora turned her back to the window. "Casually come over, give me a hug or something, and look out your window."

Puzzled, the older woman complied, gripping Cora in a tight squeeze. She mumbled in Cora's ear, barely moving her lips. "What am I looking at?"

"Is there a man staring at us?"

"Yes, but he turned. He's walking away pretty quick-like."

"Do you know him, Mae?" Cora's shoulders tensed.

"Not personally, but I've seen him before. He came by last week, asking Dabney about hiring on as a laborer. Poor guy looked pretty ragged, said he was new to town and looking for some work. What's the matter, honey?"

"It's nothing." She didn't enjoy lying to Mae, but she didn't want to alarm her friend. "He looked like he was watching me. Gave me the creeps."

"Probably trying to work up the nerve to see if Dab had made a decision." She patted Cora on the arm. "Don't worry your pretty little red-head, Doc."

Cora left the new tub of ointment with Mae and accepted the muffins and pumpkin bread as payment. Not wanting to squash them in her pack, she juggled them briefly until she had the goods cradled in her arms. She looked up and down the street, searching for the watcher, but he had disappeared. Discarding her earlier plan to visit Annie, she decided to walk down to Dixie's Café instead.

A few minutes of conversation and pecan pie later, Cora's suspicions were confirmed. Dixie said the man matched the description of the traveler who was in her restaurant the week before. She walked out of the café both vindicated and confused.

She had one stop remaining before heading home, and she had a hard time not looking over shoulder and around every corner. At the library, she fished a couple of books out of her bag to return, and checked out two new ones, a mystery set at the turn of the century and a history book.

The clerk, Stella, nodded to the non-fiction selection. "Good one for Texas history, sugar. You won't find any socialist propaganda all the American books tend to throw in."

"You have American-published books here?"

"Well, sure. We have books from a variety of nations around the world. Couldn't exclude our idiot neighboring country." She winked at Cora, smacked her gum, and turned around to pull books out of the return drop box. "Will we see you at the Fifty-Year Celebration, Doc? Should be a blast!" The inventory scanner blipped with each book the librarian scanned with one hand, while her other snatched a paper from a display rack.

Cora looked at the flyer Stella scooted across the counter. Live music, games, food and drink, and fireworks after dark. She smiled. "This looks like fun! October thirty-first? I don't see why I couldn't go."

"I hear a certain bounty hunter might compete in the lumberjack games." Her white smile all but covered her face.

Cora rolled her eyes. "Et tu, Brute?"

Stella threw her head back and cackled.

"We're just …"

"… Friends. Yeah, I get it. Mm-hmm. You keep telling yourself that, sugar."

"Stella?"

"Hmm?"

"How long have you lived here, if you don't mind my asking?"

The woman tapped a finger to her lip, pulled her glasses off her nose and chewed on the end of an ear piece. "I'm thirty-eight, moved here with my parents when I was eight. Left for a few years to go to college, and came back after six … so, twenty-four years? Why do you ask?"

"You probably know darn near everyone around here, right?"

She nodded, her blonde hair brushing her shoulders.

"Ever seen a guy about six feet tall, short brown hair, kind of rough looking? On the grungy side, soles worn nearly through on his boots?"

"Not from around here, you mean? Because you described half the population of Angelina County. Guy came in on Saturday, mostly fits the description, I guess. Never saw him before. He looked through the back issue papers for about an hour and left. Didn't say a word."

"Do me a favor, will you? If he asks about me, don't tell him anything."

"You got it. Know the guy? No? Well, he won't learn anything from me."

The door to the library slammed open, the glass shaking in its panes, but thankfully, remaining intact. Cora gasped. Stella swore under her breath.

"What in the name of thunder, Nash?"

The wiry pharmacist was agitated, his red hair sticking out in tufts, his eyes wired. "Oh, thank goodness. Quick! Cora! You have to come now. There's been an accident. It's Dabney."

Cora abandoned the books and baked goods on Stella's desk and ran.

15

Cora trailed after Nash's bobbing red head. His gangly legs churned down the sidewalk, the green of The Square a blur as she kept pace with the long-legged pharmacist. Nash looked back as he rounded the corner onto Main Street, but Cora was hot on his heels. Her pack thumped against her back to the rhythm of her steps. She only had a rudimentary field kit with her, and she prayed the accident wasn't serious. Cora motioned to Nash to keep running, and he needed no more encouragement. She heard him struggling for breath, but he didn't slow. Her quads burned, unaccustomed to the added weight of her leather boots, and yet she maintained the pace.

Two blocks south of Main, off Beech Street, Nash turned the corner. Cora saw the red and blue emergency strobes illuminating the siding of homes from a block away. Spurred by the sight of the sheriff's vehicle at an angle in the middle of the street, she pushed her legs nearly to their limit, passing Nash in her haste to reach the site.

Doc McMullen's white head stood out as he leaned over a man sprawled on the ground in front of a little red brick home. Neighbors had flocked to the scene and stood grouped in twos and threes, quietly talking and gesturing. Two deputies interviewed bystanders, their tiny lapel cams capturing the statements and relaying the video feed to the station. Jimmy Wilson had his arm around Mae, and was walking her to his cruiser parked at the curb. Tears streamed down her lined face as she caught Cora's eyes, and she reached out a hand in Cora's direction. She had aged years in the hour since Cora had seen her. She desperately wanted to comfort Mae.

Instead, Cora knelt beside the doctor. "What've we got, Doc?"

"Oh, good, Cora. I'm glad Nash found you. Ambulance is in route and should be here in less than five." The grizzled doctor leaned back, rested his weight on his heels. "I've gotten Dabney stabilized, but I need you to check on Buck." The physician jerked his china at a young man sitting a few feet away, his arm cradled in his lap. "The x-ray wand is in my bag, sitting on top."

Dabney was unconscious. Judging from the backboard and head stabilizers, they were most likely dealing with a fall. Doc McMullen confirmed her suspicions when she asked. Cora focused on Doc's voice as she retrieved the bone scanner, noting as she looked up that Dabney's left ankle was clearly broken. The joint was swollen to twice its size, red and purple bruising already marring the skin. The foot flopped at a ninety-degree angle to his leg.

"The homeowner, Robyn Fuller, heard glass breaking while she was in the kitchen making lemonade for the boys out here. Dabney and his crew were hired to work on the roof, but when Robyn came running, the ladder was through the window. Dab and Buck were on the ground." Doc jerked a thumb over his shoulder. "You've got your recorder?" Cora nodded, flashing the combination watch and voice recorder her brother had given her two Christmases ago. She activated the device before she forgot. "Good. Make sure you get Buck Newlin's exam on record. We'll need it for both our records and the police report." The white-haired doctor handed her a lapel cam, too. "For video, just in case."

Police report? She had assumed the sheriff's office was the first to respond because of the proximity, but when she considered it, there were more than a few brown-uniformed men walking around the area who were not emergency responders. Besides Jimmy and the other two deputies, she now noticed another placing evidence markers near the fallen ladder and taking photos with a holographic camera.

Still more than a little puzzled, Cora duckwalked over to the young man, Buck Newlin. She had yet to meet him, but there were a lot of people in the area she still had not become acquainted with in her short time in Cotton Springs. Buck was a fit-looking man, in his early twenties. Bronzed neck, face and hands testified to many hours working in the sun. His light brown hair was mussed and on the long side, and his head was bowed as he hunched over his injured arm. He was in obvious pain, his eyes squeezed shut, the muscles in his jaw knotted visibly. His left arm was supported by the right, the uninjured hand cupping the elbow of the other. When she placed her hand on his back, he jerked and groaned. She smiled reassuringly. "Easy, Buck. I'm Cora Thomas. All right with you if I scan your arm?" The man tugged his chin down once. "I'm going to have to extend your arm as straight as I can. Where is the worst pain?"

"Wrist." Buck's lips barely moved.

"Okay, thanks. Easy now. Here, you help me out as much as you can, and let me know when I need to stop."

Cora gently manipulated the young man's arm, stopping at the hissed intake of breath, and continuing once he gave the okay to go ahead. She looked left and right, trying to find something she could rest Buck's arm on. As she reached around to pull off her pack, someone handed her a soft, folded blanket. Shading her eyes with one hand and looking up, Cora said, "Thanks. You're a lifesaver."

The woman's face was grim, but determined. "No metal. Those buckles on your pack might interfere with the x-ray."

"That was thoughtful of you, um——."

"Robyn."

Cora gingerly wedged the soft cube between Buck's elbow and his side, so it both supported the elbow and the wrist. "This is your home?"

She nodded. "The guys were repairing the leaky roof that I've been neglecting. I feel awful."

"None of this was your fault, Robyn. Accidents happen. Everything will be okay." Cora smiled and powered on the scanner, waited for the display to indicate it was ready to accept a new image. She hollered over her shoulder. "Doc? You saved Dab's scan, right?"

"Yeah, such as it is. Angelina Regional confirmed the upload. Radiologist thinks it's a surgical case. They'll do the 3-D imaging at the hospital." Cora heard rather than saw the crinkle of the thermal blanket opening behind her. Doc McMullen was treating Dabney for shock.

The green light flashed on the wand, and she began the x-ray, starting at the shoulder. Slowly and steadily she hovered two inches above the arm as she worked her way to the wrist. It was a tedious process, but the technology was amazing. To think, in the old days they required giant machines and lead-lined rooms for this procedure. In less than thirty seconds, Cora viewed a high resolution image of the bone structure beneath Buck's skin. She dictated the findings aloud.

"Patient is Buck Newlin, laborer for Crockett 7 Construction. Date of birth is?"

Buck gritted the words past his lips. "September 7, 2074." Twenty years old, younger than Cora guessed.

"Thanks. Patient indicates pain in the wrist of his left arm. Field scan indicated two breaks, one complete fracture of the ulna, approximately one centimeter from the junction of the ulna and the pisiform bone. The radius shows a hairline fracture approximately three centimeters from the scaphoid bone. Transmitting wirelessly to radiologist for confirmation and a more detailed analysis."

Sirens sounded in the distance, the wails bouncing between the buildings and homes, faint but growing louder as the ambulance closed the distance.

"Buck, we need to send you on to the hospital in Lufkin to get this arm set. It's more complicated than I'm licensed to handle, and a radiologist needs rule out surgery. Do you have any other pains I should know about? Abdomen, back?"

"No, just the arm. Thanks, Doc."

The siren wailed closer as the ambulance approached. "What happened, exactly?" Cora splinted and wrapped Buck's broken wrist.

Robyn hovered as well, situating herself between Doc McMullen on the left and Cora and Buck on her right. She knelt down to hear the story. "I'm interested, too. I heard the window shatter and came running."

Cora cradled Buck's splinted arm, the borrowed blanket supporting the wrist in the young man's lap. As she unslung her pack and dug into her field kit for a mild painkiller, Buck began his story. Behind him, deputies continued marking evidence and taking pictures.

"Dabney asked me to come down and get the flashing from his truck. Mrs. Fuller's chimney was the source of the leak, and we were going to replace the flashing and re-shingle. Already had the roof deck fixed and the solar skin laid. Anyway, I came down the ladder and walked over to the truck. The guy was standing there, near the toolbox, so I asked him what he needed. Shady looking guy. Said he needed to talk to Dabney about a job."

Alarm bells sounded in Cora's head.

"Told him Dab was on the roof, and he couldn't talk right now, but he was welcome to wait a little while until he came down. I got the metal and shingles out of the back of the truck, and I heard the guy behind me over by the house, hollering up at Dab. Dab was looking down at the guy, talking to him. I turned around to close the tailgate. Next thing I knew, Dab was on the top of the ladder and it was swaying, he was yelling, and the guy was running off across there." He pointed to the row of lawns next to the Fuller home. "I ran over to try to push the ladder back against the house, but I was too late. Dab tried to jump off the ladder when it got closer to the ground, but all that did was land him and the ladder half on top of me, and the other half of the ladder in Mrs. Fuller's front window. I tried to break my fall with my left arm, but Dab was knocked clean out, his ankle turned out all funny."

Buck grew quiet.

"Did you see the man do anything to the ladder, Buck?" When the man shook his head no, she pressed him. "Could you describe him to Jimmy?"

He thought he could, he said. Cora thanked him, and gently patted him on the shoulder, letting him know she'd check on him soon to see how he was doing.

Cora turned to Doc McMullen and Dabney. Her friend's eyes fluttered open as the ambulance turned the same corner Cora had raced around only a few minutes before. Paramedics piled out of the rescue vehicle, grabbing their gear and jogging over to where Doc and Cora knelt by their patients.

As Doc gave his report to the EMTs, Cora searched for Mae and Jimmy. The older woman sat sideways in the cruiser, her legs hanging out of the open door. Doc McMullen waved them over, and Mae ran to her husband's side.

He looked up at his wife. "Mae? What happened?" His voice was a gnarled whisper.

"It's okay, Dab. You're going to be fine. Doc and Cora are going to take good care of you, but first, you have to go on the ambulance to the hospital. They'll make sure you're okay. You took a fall off the ladder. Doggone it, honey, I told you to stop crawling on roofs and leave that job to younger men!" Mae's shoulders shook with wracking sobs.

Jimmy pulled her back and Cora stepped aside as the EMTs lifted Dabney onto the stretcher.

One of the paramedics addressed Mae. "Ma'am, you can ride with us to Lufkin. We'll take him to Regional. He needs a deep body scan to make sure there are no internal injuries we can't see in the field." She nodded, squeezed Cora on the shoulder. Cora enveloped her in a tight hug.

"They'll take good care of him, Mae, don't worry."

Cora briefed the EMT on Buck's condition. Jimmy said he'd take the young man and follow the ambulance to the hospital. He turned to Cora. "I'll need a copy of your field notes and exam when you get a chance."

"Doc gave me a lapelcam, so it should already be over at the station. Jimmy, I don't like the sound of this."

He looked her in the eyes. "Neither do I."

Soon, both the ambulance and Jimmy's cruiser were out of sight, and the echoes of the sirens faded. The music of chirping crickets took their place. Cora and Doc McMullen stood in Robyn Fuller's lawn, their shadows extending across the browning yard. Neighbors returned to their homes, and the deputies talked quietly near their vehicles.

Robyn appeared next to Cora and Doc, handing them both a glass of lemonade. "Someone should get a glass of this." Her mouth remained turned down in a frown. "I can't imagine anyone wanting to hurt Dabney. Can you?"

Cora shook her head.

Doc McMullen stretched his back and rolled his shoulders. "There is no evidence that says this stranger had anything to do with it, only hearsay. Dab could have lost his balance. We'll know once the sheriff and his boys have had a chance to look at the evidence, put together any witness statements."

"You sound like you've had a lot of experience with this sort of thing." Cora's brows lifted in surprise.

The aging physician grunted. "Not a lot, but some years in Houston as a young resident taught me a lesson or two about crime. We don't see nearly as much of it as my grandparents did, but there are still bad people out there."

Sadly, Cora knew the salty old doctor spoke the truth.

16

For months now, Gordon had dogged every patient in the witch's confiscated records, searching for someone–anyone–holding a grudge against the woman. Not a single, solitary citizen had a complaint about her. Further proof to him she was unnatural. Every nurse, doctor or lab tech he knew received a complaint as least once. Investigations had brought him in contact with numerous medical professionals over the years. Some of his best sources were doctors and nurses. Coin persuaded all kinds.

The federal insurance company and medical board both dropped the case, saying they could find no wrongdoing. Gordon spat. Her wealthy brother greased some hands. Had to be it. The doctors tried to explain all the jargon to him, but it made no sense that his previously healthy wife could die so fast. Unnatural. And it all came down to the witch.

He sat on a wrought-iron bench at the southeast corner of Lakeway Park. The jogger's path was empty. The frigid wind and drooping gunmetal clouds deterred the exercise junkies. In the distance, the playground stood abandoned. Good. He hated coming here. It reminded him of William, and his gut knotted up thinking of his son. Gordon had missed the birthday party.

He uncapped the bottle sitting next to him. Three swallows later, his stomach burned, warmed him up from the inside. Gordon stood, stomped his feet to wake his toes, and checked his watch. No sooner had he read the time than he heard leaves crunching on the path behind him. He turned, eyeing the woman in front of him.

"You the lawman?" Her was voice raspy, like nails across sandpaper. Smoker's lines grooved ditches around her mouth. A thick layer of makeup caked her face, a paltry attempt to conceal pockmarks and blemishes.

"Natasha?"

She nodded.

"Let's take a walk. It's too cold to sit around and chit chat."

"Whatever you say, boss man." She chuckled. It sounded like a bullfrog laughing. Natasha, if that was her real name, barely reached his shoulders in height. She was thick through the shoulders, narrow in the waist. Not fat, not skinny either. He eyed her sideways as she pulled a smoke out of her purse.

"Those things'll kill ya." He did nothing to disguise the sneer on his face.

"Lots of things kill people."

"Grub tell you what I need?"

She nodded, inhaling the cold air and the heat of the cigarette. Exhaling, she waved her hand. The bitter tang in the curling smoke told Gordon it was drug-laced, most likely the narcotic known as Happy. She had guts, smoking that junk in front of an officer of the law.

Natasha winked at him. "And you're gonna take care of the little incident back in August sitting on my record?"

"Yep. But you perform first." Gordon stopped beneath a soaring sycamore. He pointed at her. "You don't, and you'll regret it."

"Hey, lighten up, Lawman. I'll make your *statement*. Tell me what I need to know, the deets and all, and I'll come in and make it good. I used to be an actress, you know." Natasha grinned, and he noticed a gap in the top row of yellowed teeth.

He doubted it. "All right. First thing tomorrow, I expect to see you in my office downtown." He handed her a sheet of paper, the information she needed typewritten. "Memorize it. Now. You can read, right?"

She snorted and rolled her eyes. He looked around the park as she read. The list detailed the information she needed to make an official complaint about Cora Thomas. He had to get the case reopened.

"Got it." She wagged the paper in his face. Gordon raised an eyebrow, and held out his hand.

"Borrow your smoke?"

Natasha took a long drag on the cigarette, blew smoke in his face. He yanked the butt out of her hand, touched the corner of the paper. It flared, the curling black edge bleeding into brown, the orange-red tongues licked the air. Gordon dropped the Happy-laced smoke on the ground, smashed the butt with his boot.

"Hey!"

He ignored her ungrateful outburst. He was doing her a favor. "The dates are important. If nothing else, remember those."

The woman glared at him, turned on her heel with a practiced pout. Over her shoulder, she winked at him. "See you in the morning, lawman."

At nine o'clock the next morning, Gordon sat in his office, pretending to read the stack of warrants, staring at wanted shots of criminals. His head snapped up at the sound of the front door slamming shut, and he smiled to himself when he heard Natasha's throaty voice. Over the intercom, Nancy's voice squawked. "Gordon? Got a woman out here who wants to make a complaint about a lady. You want to take her statement?"

He paused for effect, shuffled some papers. "I'm swamped at the moment, Nancy. Have Scallion take it."

Half an hour later, Deputy Scallion poked his head into Gordon's office.

"Got a minute?"

Gordon nodded and motioned to the chair on the other side of his desk. It sat a hair lower than his own, a power play technique learned from a mentor. "Whatcha got, Scallion?"

The younger man scratched his head. "Not sure how you're gonna take this, but thought you should know. Woman came in and made an official statement about a doctor she felt had acted unprofessionally, possibly criminally." Scallion slid the paper over the desk.

Snatching it up, Gordon scanned the document. He let himself appear surprised. "Cora Thomas? But we interviewed everyone we could find when Missy died." *This is almost too easy.*

"That's the thing, Wilkes." Scallion sat forward in his chair. He pointed to the end of the statement. "See here? She says Thomas treated her *off* the record."

Gordon scratched his chin. "I don't know, Bud. Think she's legit?"

Bud raised a shoulder. "Got me. But all these months after it happened? I don't know. Lady said she was scared to come forward,

131

something about voodoo and all." Scallion gave half a laugh. "Gotta look into it, though, right?"

Perfect. "I guess you're right, Bud. Let's keep this on the up and up, though. Thomas is now wanted for questioning, but she's been granted asylum in The Republic. Guess we'll have to petition for extradition papers."

Way too easy. It took all the bearing he had not to smile.

17

"Hop in, Doc." Deputy Wilson patted the front passenger seat.

A bitter gust of wind bit the back of her neck, but she was glad she had twisted her red mop into a hasty bun. Otherwise, she'd look like she was wearing a hornet's nest on her head by the time they got to Lufkin. Normally, this early on a Thursday she would be seeing her first patients; today was an exception. Cora had cleared her calendar and rearranged patients so she could visit Dabney Crockett.

"Appreciate the ride in, Jimmy." Cora sidled onto the smooth seat. "Not many folks in these parts with cars or trucks, and those clouds don't look horse-and-wagon friendly." She leaned forward, searching the skies through the windshield.

The deputy confirmed her suspicion. "Front coming in. I hate to see the warm weather go, but it won't be gone long." He winked at her. "Give it a day or two."

"I normally check the forecast every morning, but I've forgotten lately."

Jimmy sneaked a glance over. "Can't imagine what's got you all worked up."

She caught his grin out of the corner of her eye. Cora flicked a playful hand at him. "Stop it. I've been busy with patients."

"Um-hmm."

She felt the heat creep up her cheeks, like the sun rising in the morning sky. "Well, maybe I've had some other distractions, too."

Jimmy barked a laugh. "Wouldn't be the first time Ben Tucker had been called a distraction."

She rolled her eyes, and settled in, admiring the smooth ride of the police cruiser. The dash panel fascinated her, with all the lights and flashy buttons, the on-board touchscreen encompassing a good majority of the center dash and console. The wan morning sun strobed between tall yellow pines flanking the small two-lane highway. Jimmy deftly maneuvered the vehicle around bends and curves in the road. They passed a dozen riders and two wagons on the horse path. She shivered at the thought of riding today.

"Now that we have time to ourselves, I need to update you on a few things." He lowered the volume of the scanner. "Sorry, the console can be distracting. Anyway, the letter from Wilkes you turned in?"

Cora perked up, alert concern edging past her resolve. "Has anything happened to my family?"

"No, no, that's what I wanted to tell you. Not a peep, all's quiet. And my source hasn't picked up anything on his radar either. I'd like to think Wilkes was venting. It happened near the anniversary, right?"

She nodded. "Yes, it was. I don't know, though. He sounded pretty ominous in the letter."

"We're not dropping the investigation, so don't worry." He skimmed his eyes over to her, then back to the road. "We didn't find anything suspicious going on in your family's neck of the woods."

She sighed, relieved. "Thank God. My mule-headed brother wouldn't say anything to me if it *was* happening. He waited weeks to tell me about my mother's fall ..."

Cora grew quiet. "My brother John wrote my mother claimed someone pushed her down those barn stairs. You don't think--?"

He ran a hand through his shaggy hair. An agitated scowl marred his face. "Your brother never requested someone come out and take a look around. Said he didn't see anything out of place, no trace anyone had been there other than your mom." He shrugged. "Too late now to do anything about it."

"I guess you're right. It's just, I've never known my mother to imagine things. She's very down to earth. Maybe it was the fall."

"Could be. Most likely the injury caused memory problems."

They rode in silence for a minute, but Cora had to ask. "What about our stranger in town? The one asking about me, and maybe the same one who was there before Dabney fell?"

Jimmy turned his head a fraction in her direction. "First DNA scan and fingerprint scan were clean, as far as Republic records go. I've got in a request for international, but it's low in the priority pool. I couldn't flag it urgent because I didn't want any undue attention. Know what I mean?"

"Gotcha. Look, I don't want you to get into trouble. You've helped me out a lot already, honestly."

He waved his hand. "Don't worry. I'll take care of myself if anything rebounds."

Five miles north of Cotton Springs, the homes grew more abundant, like clumps of dandelions flourishing in summer. A subdivision here, a ranch there. What was once a small city a hundred years ago, according to Stella at the library, had exploded into an area housing more than 150,000 citizens. Surrounding towns and communities had been gobbled up as the State of Texas prepared for war with America. The Second War of Secession lasted only a year and a half, but in that time, folks living in the metropolis cities of the state fled to outlying small towns, to avoid being in strategic target areas. Lufkin, one of the leading lumber and paper producers in the area, had swelled from about 35,000 inhabitants. New towns popped up overnight, like a fern sending out runners.

Cotton Springs was one of those "runner towns", as the locals like to call them. The entire Big Thicket area of the Republic appealed to Cora on a variety of levels. The Pineywoods engulfed the whole of eastern Texas, a snug cocoon shutting out the glaring, ugly world and nestling its people in a home that spoke of security, of deep roots not easily displaced. Granted, there were those who couldn't wait to grow up and get out. But more and more city slickers found their way back behind the pine curtain. Cora felt at peace here. Home.

The two-lane Farm Road 58 expanded to four lanes as they entered the city limits. More vehicles traveled the streets, mostly public transit buses; but sedans, trucks and vans merged together, creating a flow almost like blood coursing through arteries. The southern side of Lufkin was mostly residential, but businesses and shopping centers dotted the highway as well. Cora noted, however, the hustle and bustle of the urban environment did little to dissuade horsemen. She saw dozens of horses with reins looped casually around hitching posts outside shop fronts, or riders guiding their massive animals on parallel horse paths.

"You come up often?"

He shook his head. "Not as much as I used to, and mostly just to the courthouse and jail. Pitiful." Jimmy chuckled as tree-lined roads sped by the windows. "My great-grandmother had an old photo album she would dig up every time we came to visit. This was back before the Collapse, you know."

Cora nodded. Her great-grandparents talked about the good old days too, when the United States was whole and strong.

"Pictures of my granddad's family at the zoo, Independence Day photos, family reunions." His wave took in the highway in front of them. "Strange thing was that there were a ton more cars on the road then. Gas-guzzling beasts. Can you believe almost every family had one, two, sometimes three? A car was in almost every one of those old pictures of Nana's."

"My grandmother had a photo she treasured, too. It was a picture of her parents and their car with 'Just Married' written all over the back glass, and cans tied to the bumper with ribbons." The memory tugged at her heart.

"See the foundry over there? Reclamation Industries?" He pointed out her passenger window. She nodded. "My granddad was one of the first employees there, a few years after the Collapse, when people began picking up the pieces. Former junk yard turned industry. All the metal from the broken down automobiles was scrapped and reclaimed, turned into useable materials."

Cora was impressed by the ingenuity, saddened at the necessity. Her grandparents told horror stories of living in the Collapse era, nearly a decade of abject poverty, rampant crime and struggling to survive. Entire families were wiped out, either starved or murdered for food, clothing, or gold. The shattered remnants of the government were thrown together piecemeal by a few surviving Congressmen, and they determined that a democratic republic was no longer sufficient for the need of the people. Unified Socialist America emerged from the shambles of what once was the United States. Two years after the unification, Texas declared her independence, and the Second War of Secession rocked an already battered populace. Rumor had it Texas had been biding her time, preparing to secede for decades, stockpiling food, weapons, and ammunition. No one in the Republic ever denied the veracity of the rumor, either.

With the nation broken, in shambles from economic collapse, the younger constituency faced the enormous task of rebuilding two countries. All citizens struggled to find their place, fought to accept new laws and governing bodies. With that acceptance came the drive to improve, sustain and secure a future for their children and generations to follow. Cora was born American, and transplanted a Texan. Despite the hardships, she thought she could grow to love the new life God provided.

Outside Lufkin, main highways converged in two loops around the city, the outer – newer – bypass, and the older loop built back in the twentieth century. Jimmy navigated through interchanges and traffic lights, emerging in the downtown business district which was the heart and soul of the city. Antique stores, eateries, and a long-standing theater bumped hips with bookstores, coffee shops, cable cafes, and hologame rooms. A feed store on the corner stood opposite a general store on Pineland Avenue, and down the way on Hickory Street was the restaurant district.

They made their way past Jet's Barbecue and The Little Buddha, Times Square Eatery and Lupe's Cantina. Dozens of cafes, delis, and restaurants flanked the narrow street for three blocks. At this time of year the outside bistro tables stood forlorn and vacant, but people flocked in and out of doors, single and in groups.

"Have you been to The Rooftop?"

He whistled. "Phew, too expensive for my wallet."

"I've wanted to go there since I moved here. Everyone's always talking about the food and the view of the lights of downtown at night." Cora imagined sitting at a bistro table on the roof deck, a sultry summer wind caressing her shoulders as she and Ben nibbled on mouth-watering food under the stars. He would reach across the table, stroke her hand lightly with his thumb. Goosebumps raised on her arms as the corner of her mouth turned up. Then, he would lift her hand to his mouth, kiss the back of her hand ...

"We could pick up some take-out after we visit Dab, if you'd like. Oh, hey, sorry. Did I startle you?"

For the second time since she got in the police cruiser, she blushed a spectacular crimson. Cora cleared her throat. "Sure, maybe some Lupe's?"

Jimmy nodded. "Sounds like a plan. I'd say you could get Rooftop, but they don't open 'til the evening. Snooty."

Cora laughed, and people-watched as they drove through the downtown district. A few men tipped their hats to the deputy's cruiser as they passed, but most rushed from shop to shop, bags full of loot bumping their legs, in their haste to get out of the cold October wind.

"So you grew up here, right?"

"Yep, not too far from the hospital, actually. Mom was a nurse for thirty years, most of those at Angelina Regional, where Dab's recovering."

They slowed as the paved street turned to cobblestone, and before them lay the jewel of the city. Three hospitals sprawled in a roughly triangular layout, with Angelina Regional Medical Center being the largest. The other two points of the triangle were The Specialist Center, where award winning specialty doctors practiced; and Point of Grace Women and Children's Hospital.

One of the first excursions outside her new home had been to ride to the city, and introduce herself at all three of the hospitals. Point of Grace dazzled her with its modern technology. It had a comforting and nurturing atmosphere; and it was, by far, Cora's favorite health center. How could a midwife *not* adore hallways lined with canvases portraying families, mothers, children and babies, or the numerous corkboards with newborn photographs pinned in proud display? The facility prided itself on numerous national awards, and the technology in use behind those walls exceeded most American hospitals.

As much as she'd love to stop in at the women's hospital, today was about Dabney and checking in on Mae. She had prayed for them almost non-stop, every time they crossed her mind.

Jimmy checked his mirrors, turned into the hospital parking lot. "I called in before we left. The charge nurse said Dabney was awake and doing well. In a lot of pain, but I guess you don't fall off a roof and walk away scott-free."

He parked the cruiser in one of the law enforcement slots near the front. She muttered, "Thank you, Lord," under her breath as they exited the car, and scooted across the parking lot to the front doors. The wind had fangs!

A whoosh of warm air greeted them as the doors glided open. The heated gust thawed her cheeks and killed any pathogen present on their bodies. Jets of ozone were emitted upon entry into the vestibule, one of the many advances in medicine she often took for granted when working in a hospital, but missed practicing in the country.

Jimmy marched to the nearest bank of elevators, punched the number three. A short ride up, and they turned right. At the nurses' station, they were directed further down the hallway and around the corner. Jimmy briskly knocked on room 323, and led the way when Mae's voice bade them come in.

Dabney rested in the bed, the head of the motorized bed raised, his left leg casted to the calf muscle and suspended in an immobilizing sling. Mae was walking over to them as they ducked in the door.

Her watery eyes flared to life. "Cora! Jimmy! Oh, it's so good to see you. Look, Dab. Look who's here."

Dabney's eyes fluttered half open. "Hey, Red, Jimmy. How y'all doing?" His dry voice croaked and skipped, but it brightened her day to hear it. Happy tears welled, but stayed put in her eyes.

"The better question is how are *you* doing, Dabney?"

"Doctors say I'll live." He cleared his throat, coughed. "I feel like I was on the losing end of a bullfight."

Jimmy snorted. "The only bull I saw was a bull-headed man who should have listened to his wife's advice to stay off the roof."

A laugh rumbled out of the older man's chest. "Ow. That hurts." He rubbed his chest.

"He's black and blue all over," Mae supplied. Obviously, the ankle is broken. He bruised a kidney, cracked a rib, and has a concussion as well. The orthopedic doctor was able to realign the bone without surgery, praise God."

Cora exhaled, relieved that Dabney's injuries were not as serious as they appeared at the Fuller home.

"How's Buck? I think I landed on him."

"Broken wrist." Cora squeezed Dab's hand when he groaned. "Hey, don't worry about him. He's young. He'll bounce back. Jimmy brought him home last night."

The deputy nodded. "Yep, brought him back high as a kite, as a matter of fact. He was singing at the top of his lungs last I saw him. He's crashing at his folks' house."

Jimmy toed the white tile floor, hooked his thumbs in his belt loops. "Dab, I hate to ask, but you know I've got to." Dabney nodded a hair. "The man talking to you before you fell. You ever seen him before?"

"Yeah, a few days ago he came by looking for a job. Said he was new in town, had experience in building. I told him to let me look over my jobs and I'd get back to him in a few days." He coughed and winced, coughed again. "Mae, get me some water, will ya darlin'?" He sipped a swallow from the straw. "Thanks, honey. Anyway, I asked him where he was staying, and if he had a way for me to call him. Said *he'd* find *me* in a few days."

"He was outside Mae's window about an hour before the accident." Jimmy's eyebrows raised in question. "I was giving her a therapeutic hand massage. I got up to leave, and while I was packing up my stuff, I noticed him staring at me through the window."

"Didn't think to tell me this before?" Jimmy's eyes rolled to the ceiling as he ran a hand over his face, frustrated.

She understood Jimmy's angst, but give a girl a break. "Not with my friend lying injured on the ground, and a patient in front of me. No, I thought he was watching me, that it was the same guy asking questions about me in town. I never would have thought the man would hurt Dabney."

"Hurt me?" Dabney's thick eyebrows rose and met in the middle of his forehead. "Naw. I told the fella I didn't have enough jobs now to justify hiring on another laborer. He got all huffy and ran off. I tried to come down to talk to him, and I lost my balance." He took a deep breath, cleared his throat again. "Now, what don't I know?"

Cora and Jimmy exchanged glances, and Jimmy shrugged, put his hands in the air. She owed at least some explanation to her friends. "The guy looking for work? Well, he's been asking questions about me in town. We think it could be related to the reason I sought asylum in Texas." Cora sighed. "I thought I had left the drama behind me."

Jimmy looked at Dabney. "So you've got no clue where we could find the guy, huh?"

Dabney shook his head slowly, painfully. "I wish I did."

"It was worth a shot. Guess now I've got to get back to town, track the guy down the old fashioned way."

The door behind them whisked open with barely a sound. Cora looked up, and up some more, until her eyes found two fiery emeralds staring back at her. She couldn't breathe. The man had no right to make her chest flutter so.

"Don't bother, Jimmy." The rich timbre of Ben's voice released butterflies in her stomach, but she worried at the grim half-smile on his face. "I found him. But you're not going to like where."

18

Jimmy shifted on his feet, hooked a thumb in his belt loop. "You've got our attention, Ben. Spill it."

Cora's gaze drilled into his head, held his thoughts hostage. The way her cheeks flushed made her freckles stand out even more. Who knew freckles could tug at his stomach, twist it and turn it all which-a-way? She had piled her crazy hair up in a messy topknot. He wanted to unwind it, tangle his fingers in those bright red curls.

"Uh, Ben?" Cora cleared her throat, her face beet red.

Why was everyone looking at him cock-eyed? "What?"

Jimmy chuckled. "You were saying how you found our suspect?"

Oh, yeah. He was, wasn't he? Dang woman. Ben jutted his chin in the Crocketts' direction. "How much do they know?"

"All of it. I trust them. They're the first friends I made when I moved." She shrugged. "They're family."

Mae enveloped Cora in a hug.

Ben exhaled, ran a hand through his own sandy hair. "I got to the Fuller house after everything died down, took a look at the footprints in the yard left by our mystery man. Robyn told me you were at the sheriff's office, Cora, giving a statement and copying them on your field notes. So I rode out to your place to have a look around, see if our guy had been nosing around."

He glared, daring her to make a sound.

Cora opened her mouth, like a fish gulping air, but she closed quickly. "Well? I take it you found something?"

He pulled his wallet-cam out of his back pocket, unfolded it until the four squares snapped together seamlessly. Tapping the display button, he turned the screen to his audience. A rough campsite, a blackened ring of rock surrounding a pile of charred coals, a shelter built into the tangle of briars nearby. Another image of a boot print with an onscreen ruler showed the size reference. The prints were an obvious match to Ben's keen eye.

"Where?" Cora's mouth was a grim line. The light in her eyes was blue fire, anger suppressed but ready to ignite. Goodness, he admired her spirit. From sweet to saucy, at the flick of a switch.

"On the back edge of your property, near the creek running into the national forest."

She paced the confined room, three steps across and back. She was cute when she chewed her lip. Cute? He groaned. He never used the word *cute* to describe anything.

"Cora, stop pacing." Dabney's bark was like gravel crunching beneath hooves. "You're making my head hurt."

"Sorry, Dab." She looked up at Ben. "What now?"

Jimmy raised a brow in question as Ben raised his hands. "Considering our deputy here, I'd say the lawful thing to do is turn over this evidence to his office. I've sent you a copy already."

"Well, it explains why the guy wants a job."

Mae nodded. "Getting cold out there. Can't be fun living in the woods in this weather."

Cora voiced his own thought. "I hope this won't make him desperate."

Jimmy chewed on a thumbnail. "Okay, with your permission, Cora, I'll set up surveillance cams around your house. With any luck we'll get an image we can use. The results from the international sweep of the DNA and prints should be back in two, maybe three days. Cora, you'll need to come in and make a complaint about this trespasser so I can legally put those cams up." She nodded. "Good. We have a plan. Let's give Mae and Dabney some time to rest. Mae, you need anything before we head back?"

She shook her head no. "Food's pretty good here. Doctor said another day or two to monitor the concussion and the swelling on the foot. Pretty sure there's nothing to worry about with his hard head, though."

"Hmph," Dabney grunted.

Cora laughed, squeezed Dabney's weathered hand. "As eloquent as ever, old man." She leaned over, pecked him on the forehead. "Don't overdo it, you mule."

"Hmph."

"Hmph back at ya. Mae, call me if you need anything," Cora added with a hug.

In the hallway, the three stood silently. Ben stared at Cora and clawed past the urge to grab her and pull her in close, smell the lilac in her hair. He jabbed his hands into his pockets. She smiled shyly at him, her bright blue eyes flickering between him and the deputy. Finally, Jimmy cleared his throat. "Um, well. I'll go, uh, warm up the car."

"Jimmy, hold up." Ben stalked after the retreating lawman, turned to see Cora watching them curiously. He winked at her, and she rolled her eyes.

"Mind if I take Cora home?" he asked.

Jimmy narrowed his eyes. "Isn't it a bit nippy for horse travel?"

"I've got a truck outside."

"Honestly?" The deputy's eyes rose in surprise. "When did you get it?"

"Day before yesterday. Walt had it, fixed one of the solar skins on the back." Walt owned the garage on the outskirts of town. Ben lifted a shoulder in a what-are-you-gonna-do gesture. "Got a good deal on it, thought I should modernize a bit."

Though he topped Jimmy by half a foot, the deputy squared his shoulders and lifted his chin. He reminded Ben of a hound, sniffing new ground. "I hear the talk in town. So lay it out for me. What's going on with you two?"

This was an interesting twist. "That's a question I wish I knew the answer to, and that's the truth. Am I stepping on toes, here, Jimmy?"

The man's eyes widened as he shook his head. "No, nothing like that. Cora's like a sister to me. I know she's only been in town a few months. Given her circumstances, I can't help but look out for her. Keep her safe." He rubbed the back of his neck in a quick motion, rolled his head. "Look, I know the two of you…agh! Just, don't hurt her, Ben."

Ben looked him in the eyes. "I'll do right by her, Jimmy. You have my word."

"Hell-ooo?" Ben turned around to find Cora tapping her foot, an eyebrow raised, hands on her hips. He knew that pose.

After a firm handshake, Jimmy waved to Cora. He turned down the hallway, disappearing into the bank of elevators.

Ben ambled over to Cora, amused at the question and indignation in her eyes. She was flickering fire, and he ached to touch her. At the moment, however, he knew he'd be singed. She narrowed a stare at him. "And what was *that* all about, Ben Tucker?"

"Clearing the air. You know, man stuff."

"Oh, for heaven's sake. Men! Why is Jimmy running off? He's my ride!" She threw her hands in the air and walked down the hallway.

Two nurses in blue scrubs whispered together behind the half-moon desk, casting entertained glances in their direction as he followed the red bounce of her topknot. "Cora, wait!"

She turned, arched an eyebrow. "Yes?" Ouch.

"I, uh, sort of asked Jimmy if I could give you a lift home."

She planted her hands on her curvy hips again, tapped her foot. "I'm not in the mood for a twelve-mile long horseback ride in the cold."

He laughed. "How about riding three hundred horses?"

Her foot tapped. He laughed. "I've got a truck, Cora. Don't worry. Nothing but the best for my lady friend."

She rolled her eyes. "Fine, Mr. Big Shot. Let's get out of here."

"Ever been to the zoo, Doc?"

***

Cora snagged the wool scarf Ben tossed her. She wrapped the coarse, solid black strip of fabric snug and tucked the ends into her fleece-lined leather coat, slipped her hands into the soft pockets. Her bare neck shivered in gratitude.

Animal dung and buttered popcorn assaulted her nostrils, an olfactory memory of childhood trips to the St. Louis Zoo springing to life in her head. Outside the entrance, a small lake sparkled in the sunlight. Red, white and blue streamers fluttered in the wind, hung from rafters and trees, slung between rooftops and draped higgledy-piggledy across branches far overhead. Buntings adorned the high fences.

"Gosh, it's been years since I've been to the zoo." She waved toward the streamers. "Looks like they're getting ready for the Independence Day festivities."

"Haven't been here since I was a kid. Last time, there was a bit of a misunderstanding between me, some mud, the crocodiles, and my grandparents."

She giggled. "Why am I not surprised?" Giggled? What was she, seventeen years old again?

The clerk at the window had to bend down and look up through the glass. "My, my, you're a big one, aren't you?" The middle-aged woman eyed Ben up and down with a wink. He paid the fare, and snagged the tickets the lady scooted through the slot below the window. "Y'all enjoy." The clerk clicked long ruby-glossed fingernails on the steel countertop.

As they walked through the turnstile, Cora could hear the woman yelling, "Daisy, git over here and look at this feller. He's huge!"

Cora stifled a laugh and snuck a peek at Ben, only to find him smirking down at her. "Happens all the time."

Sidewalks branched like limbs on a tree, snaking their way through a multitude of exhibits. Solar-powered heaters were spaced every ten feet or so, warming the walkways for the patrons. A variety of animal houses broke the harshness of the wind. Native bushes, miniature palm trees, and creeping ground covers flanked the concrete paths. Ahead of them, a peacock strutted, stopping to spread his iridescent tail and calling to a peahen nearby. Birds chittered and cawed, held tweeted conversations in the trees above, while barks, grunts and growls filled the air around them. In the distance a lion roared, sending birds flocking to the sky.

"I've always loved the zoo." Cora rubbed her hands together to create some friction, blew on them to warm them up. "When I was a little girl, my grandfather would ride me around on his shoulders at the one in St. Louis. I felt like I was on top of the world! After we spent hours looking at all the animals, he'd buy me and my brother cotton candy and let us ride the little train all around the grounds."

"The reptile house was my favorite. All those wiggly snakes and lizards with their tongues sticking out. Scaring my little sis was easy as pie."

Ben ducked under an overhanging limb, nearly bonking Cora on the head. She didn't mind. It put him closer to her.

"You never talk about her, your sister."

He shrugged. "We're not as close as we were. Sort of drifted apart after I enlisted in the army."

"She live around here?"

"A few miles west of Cotton Springs. She moved back with a husband in tow about three years ago. They breed cutting horses."

"And does she have a name?" Like pulling teeth with this man.

"Nina," he said absently. "Hey, let's go see the lions."

They ambled and wandered around the enclosure, reading placards about the animals, ducking when the occasional parrot flapped low above their heads. Cora found herself walking closer to Ben, seeking warmth. Okay, maybe there was more to it. Her skin tingled and butterflies pounded her stomach every time their arms bumped. Without thinking, he leaned down to speak to her. She thought it had to be ingrained in him, living most of his life taller than the average person. Yet, despite his colossal size, Ben was gentle, careful. Cora wasn't petite, at five seven, but she felt tiny, miniscule next to him.

An hour flew by, and still they walked, stopping to point at a majestic eagle swooping to capture a mouse, laughing at the antics of the ring-tailed lemurs. Cora was disappointed when the exit loomed around a bend. She wasn't ready for the day to end.

"They have a train," Ben said, mischief in his eyes. "How about a ride?"

Cora clapped her hands like she was nine years old. "Yes!"

Excitement turned to speculation when they arrived at the station. The "train" was hardly larger than a model.

"You think you can fit in one of those?" Cora pointed at the tiny compartments.

The conductor obviously had his doubts, too, as he ogled Ben up and down.

"No problem. But I think we'll have to take separate seats."

There were few children on board, mostly toddlers and parents holding babies. Ben sat at the caboose, and she snagged the seat in front of him. The whistle blew and the bells clanged, and they were off. The pint-sized train puttered along the track, rocking back and forth, picking up speed, but by no means flying down the rails. Children clapped and babies cried. Cora was enthralled. Even the frigid wind did nothing to dampen her spirits.

Through the African exhibit the train trundled, enormous gray elephants snagging limbs from high trees near the edge of the field, keeping them company. With an ear-to-ear smile, Cora turned to Ben to thank him.

And found his smoldering gaze on her face. Her cheeks flamed, but she held steady. The grin slid from her face as butterflies turned to eagles' wings, pounding inside her chest. Ben reached out a hand, cupped her chin.

Entranced, she dared to move forward. Slowly at first, but growing braver as he leaned in. His lips touched hers hesitantly, questioning. She grabbed his head and pulled him in tighter.

Fireworks exploded in her head as the kiss deepened. A dull roar deadened all sound, like the pounding surf of the ocean, and the only thing she felt was Ben's lips on hers. Heady and sweet, the smoldering fire threatened to consume her.

She lost herself in the kiss, and for a small moment in time, the world around her vanished, and there was only Ben.

19

The remainder of Thursday was a blur to Cora. She rode a wave of happiness throughout the day, until it glided to the shore of her front porch that evening. She and Ben had eaten ate a mountain of fajitas and enchiladas at Lupe's Cantina, toured the antique shops, and watched a matinee in the restored theater. What was the title of the movie? She had no idea, and couldn't care less. Cora soared.

A fiery bulbous sun sank to the west as they drove home. Though it was nothing fancy, Cora was grateful for Ben's truck, as the temperature dropped with night creeping in. The pickup spun dust clouds as it pushed down her driveway and slowed to a stop. Ben jumped out of the driver's side and hurried to her door, opening it chivalrously with a flourish of his calloused hand.

"My lady."

Cora laid a hand on her heart. "My hero."

"All right, enough nonsense. Let's get you in the house. My teeth are chattering."

He held her hand as he walked her up the porch stairs. So simple, the contact of one hand to another. His was rough from hard work and outdoor living; hers, softer, but not from a life of luxury. Her skin tingled as he rubbed a soft circle on the top of her hand with his thumb. Such a little gesture, igniting a bonfire deep within. She never wanted this feeling to end.

Reluctantly, she turned to say goodnight. Chin up, he nodded to the door. With a raised brow, she unlocked the door. Before she could step into the house, he pushed past her. Cora rolled her eyes heavenward, as Ben slipped into macho mode. Looking left and right, he searched each room, opened every closet, peered under every bed. Even the kitchen cabinets weren't safe from his inspection.

"Anything out of place?" he asked quietly when he returned to her.

She shook her head side to side. Cora inhaled deeply, hesitant. "You could stay a little while." What was she saying? It was though her mouth had a mind of its own.

The intensity in his eyes threatened to overwhelm her. "As much as I'd want to, I need to head home."

Deflated, but also relieved, she walked him to the door, stood on the porch in the cool autumn chill. He brought their hands to his chest, grasped their knotted hands with his free one. He planted a lingering kiss on her forehead.

"You are a puzzle I can't solve." The wind swirled around them. The sun was a red smudge across the horizon, and the purply blue of the sky was dotted with early stars.

"I'm a simple person. Not much to figure out."

He shook his head. "I had a good time today, Cora. But there's one thing you should know, that I forgot to mention. About the visitor on your land?"

She shuddered, not wanting fear and uncertainty to cloud her high.

"I messed with his campsite, after taking the pictures. Made it look a cougar had been there. A few slash marks in the right places, a well-placed track here and there. There was a little food stashed inside the shelter, so I scattered it about. Wiped my prints from the area. And installed one of my own security cameras in the trees nearby, so I could see who this jerk is." He reached out, cupped her chin, angled her face up to his. "He is not going to hurt you."

Cora believed him.

"He's bound to be spooked, if he's got any sense. Maybe it will make him sloppy. Well, even sloppier than before. I get the feeling this guy isn't a pro. Which, to be honest, confuses me."

He enveloped her in a hug. His smell filled her head. Leather and earth, musk and freshly laundered shirt, like it had been hung on the line in a bright summer sun.

"Thank you. For today, I mean. I had an incredible time."

She shivered as a gust blew around the house. An owl hooted nearby, and Rusty whickered in the paddock. "Shoot, I need to feed the horse."

"Go inside, get warm. I'll take care of Rusty."

"Sure you don't want to come in, at least for some coffee?"

His eyes blazed with unbridled desire. Then he blinked, tamping down the emotion. "Trust me, Cora. It's better I go, mainly because I want to come in so much. I'll see you soon."

Cora shivered, not from the cold, as she closed the door and whispered good night.

She slept soundly, dreamlessly, waking energized before the alarm could sound, and well before the dawn sky unfolded. Cora dressed in cotton sweats, laced on her running shoes. Humming a tune, she stretched, her thoughts bouncing around like the ball in the game machine they fiddled with at the antique store yesterday. What was it called? Oh, pinball. Yes, her thoughts skittered like a pinball, memories of Ben's lips on hers thumping around her brain. Muscles warmed, and she couldn't hardly wait to get her run on. She needed to expend some of the verve coursing through her veins.

One mile in, her feet thumped the ground rhythmically, breaths measured. At the two mile mark, she felt good. Solid.

Liquid gold erupted on the eastern horizon, highlighting the fog of her warm breath that misted the cool air. Despite the bitter winds from the day before, this morning held the promise of a warmer day. Her feet pounded to the beat of her heart, shoes on pavement striking like a metronome. Birds twittered a symphony, and squirrels chittered at her as she ran beneath the forest canopy.

By the time her mailbox came into view, cotton candy clouds dotted the azure sky and her stomach rumbled in protest. Four miles today. Not too shabby. Her shoes clunked on the wooden boards as she dropped them outside the front door. She made it to the kitchen with more huffing than she would have liked, wincing at a stitch in her side. Maybe she had pushed a little too hard after all.

A tall glass of cold orange juice, two scrambled eggs, and some bacon later, with the coffee maker burbling, she reviewed her schedule. Glancing at the clock above the mantle, she grimaced at the lack of time between now and her first appointment. She gobbled the last of the bacon and washed it down with the remaining shot of citrus, checked to make sure the front door was bolted, and headed to the shower.

In record-breaking time she was dressed in scrubs, her still-damp curls twisted and secured on top of her head. She hustled down the hallway to prep the examination room and make sure all the necessary tools were laid out and sterile. A quiver of excitement shot through her as she worked in the clinic addition, the room still smelling slightly of paint and new wood. Cora prepped the tray, and slid it into the little oven-like sanitizer. She liked to call it the "zapper". Had a nifty ring to it. No sooner had the green light flashed ready did she hear the knock on the front door.

Out of breath, she rushed back to the front door, remembering she had engaged the lock before her shower. She opened the door, and greeted her first patient of the day.

"Beth! I'm so glad you're here. Come in." She ushered the young woman in. "Have a seat. Want some coffee?"

"Gosh, yes, I'd love some. I was running late this morning, and didn't get a chance to have my cup of motivation."

Cora laughed. "Sounds like we're kindred spirits. Sit tight."

She returned with an outstretched mug, steam rising from the black surface. "Is your husband on board?"

Beth nodded. "After a lot of cajoling, finally. But he doesn't want to, you know," she said, wiggling her hand in the air, "*do anything until my tests come back.*"

"I understand totally. A lot of men find giving the sample to be embarrassing. If he'd like, he can go through Doc McMullen, and I can get the results from him."

The other woman sat back against the plush couch cushions. "What a relief." Beth adopted a gruff, manly tone, "'I don't want no woman messing around with any of my stuff' he claims."

Cora grinned at Beth over her coffee mug. "If you don't mind me saying so, you seem more at peace today."

She shrugged, a smile on her face. "I am. Since my last visit here, I've done a lot of soul-searching, a lot of reading the Bible you gave me. Thanks for that, by the way. And a ton of praying," Beth smiled, a light shining from her face. "I'm a child of the Savior now, Cora. And I know He's forgiven me. The hard part is letting it go. The shame, I mean. The guilt. I've held on to it for so long."

Cora put her mug on the coffee table and wrapped her arms around Beth, gave her a squeeze. "Welcome to the family, sister."

"I've never had a sister, before," Beth mused. "I think I like it!"

"Letting go gets easier. Kind of like running, you get better with practice."

Beth sat silently, sipping her coffee. "I suppose you're right. I'm learning to be a patient person, but it's not all that easy." One last gulp, and she placed the mug on the table and grinned. "All right, Doctor Cora. Let's get this exam over and done with."

Cora laughed as she led her down the hallway. Beth *oo*ed and *ahh*ed at the clinic addition, complimented her on the paint color and the finishes. The examination took about fifteen minutes. Cora sat at her desk, entering her observations and other data in Beth's file. Three vials of blood and a test swab in a sterile sealed tube sat on the tray near the exam table.

"Based on this initial assessment, you appear to be in excellent health." Cora consulted her notes. "All of your girly parts are in the right places, no obvious lumps or bumps in the wrong places. We'll see how your blood work and PAP come back, and go from there. Should take a few days. Doc McMullen and I use a courier service and have it taken up to Lufkin. They're pretty fast on the turnaround."

"So now we wait."

"Hey, seriously, everything appears in order. A few more questions, and we'll be done."

Cora outlined how she wanted Beth to keep a calendar, take her basal temperature, and note any significant events which occurred over the next month. "If you notice twinges, pulls, cramps out of the ordinary, write it all down. The more information we have, the better, and it helps you to know more about what's going on with your body. And now, the part your husband won't like. He has to save up until ovulation day."

Beth crinkled her face, perplexed. "Save up?"

"Yep." Cora's mouth pulled up in a sideways smile. "The men don't like this part. If you *practice* conception too much, sperm levels decrease. Saving up for ovulation days increases the sperm count, making it more likely one of his swimmers will get through to your egg. In this case, practice doesn't make perfect."

Beth groaned, a hand over half her face. "Can you be the one to break the news to my husband?"

"Not a chance." Cora laughed at the look of utter despair on Beth's face.

Later, on her way out, Beth turned, her hand on the door knob. "Will you be at the church meeting tomorrow?"

Cora smacked her head. "I forgot the meeting was moved to Saturday because of the Independence Day festivities on Sunday. Yeah, I should be there. I've got no impending deliveries, and Doc's on-call this weekend."

Beth reached out to hug Cora. "Good. I'm glad I'll get to see you there. It'll be my first day, and I'm nervous."

Cora squeezed her new friend. "Don't worry. None of us bite."

Beth walked out the front door, and Cora followed, nearly toppling over her as Beth stopped short.

"I'm so sorry!" Cora threw a hand out to steady herself, and heard Beth and Ben's voiced intertwined in surprise.

"What are *you* doing here?" they asked simultaneously.

Cora looked from Ben to Beth, and back again. "I take it you know each other?"

"Of course, we do!" Ben replied, exasperated. "What are you doing here, Nina?"

"Nina?" Cora asked, bewildered. "Who's Nina?"

Cora swiveled her head between Ben and her patient.

"This," Beth replied with a pointed finger jabbed at Ben, "is my bull-headed, mule of a brother."

20

"Well, this is awkward." Cora looked from Ben to Beth, and back again.

Ben's and Beth's—or was it Nina's—horses nuzzled one another at the hitching post in front of Cora's home, oblivious to the confused angst of their owners.

"Well?" Beth scolded her brother with a hand on her hip.

"I'm here to see Cora, Nina." Ben rubbed his face, made a quick sweep through his windswept hair.

"Oh, come off it. Why would you come to see her? In need of a midwife?" Beth spat a caustic laugh into the air.

Cora held her hands out in supplication, helpless. "Do you two need some time? Maybe to figure out identities?"

"Oh. That. He's always called me Nina. I can't seem to get him out of the habit."

"Because it's your name," he replied through gritted teeth.

"Elizabeth. I go by Elizabeth, or Beth," she said, nodding to Cora. "Nina Elizabeth Tucker Winslow."

Ben dismounted his equine monster, slung the reins over and around the post. He stood on the ground, Beth on the porch, and they were nearly at eye-level. She stared him down, hands on hips. This close together, she could see the resemblance. Same hair color, both had green eyes, though hers were a softer shade. Her cheeks were flushed, anger and embarrassment flickering over her features.

"Were you following me, tracker?"

Ben's brows rose to his hairline. "Why would I follow you? You have your own life, I have mine. You're an adult now, Nina."

"Wait, please. Just wait." Cora closed her eyes, took two deep breaths, and then looked at Ben's sister. "Can someone please tell me what I should call you?"

"Beth, please. I'm sorry. My brother and I have a strange relationship. It's … complicated."

"No, it's not. I left home and you disowned me, no matter how many times I've begged for forgiveness. It's pretty simple."

"Agh! Men!" Beth gripped her hair with both hands, rubbed her palms over her eyes. "Cora. I'm sorry. I'm behaving badly. He took me off guard." Cora watched as Beth inhaled and exhaled, each breath measured, eyes closed as if meditating. She glanced at Ben, to find him drilling her with those eyes of his, seeming to plead with her for understanding. The intensity of the stare caught Cora off guard, and her cheeks flared to life.

Cora saw the realization dawn in Beth's eyes, which were as wide as saucers. "You? Him?" She looked back and forth between the two. Cora could almost see the connections fusing in her brain.

"We're …" Ben began.

"…Friends," Cora finished. The half-smile on her face seemed lame, even to her.

"More than friends." Ben pinned Cora with a heated stare.

Cora's cheeks flamed. She threw her hands up in the air. "I don't know what we are!" she growled.

Well, that shut the bickering siblings up. "Beth, I'll let you know in three or four days what I find out." She held up a hand, forestalling Ben's obvious question. "Ask *her* if you want details. Don't forget to do the chart. Ben, inside," she said curtly, paused. "Please."

Beth rolled her eyes, and he snorted. They passed on the stairs, but as they were almost clear of one another, Ben reached out, took his sister's arm gently. "Nina, I'm sorry. It's good to see you. You surprised me, is all."

She stared up at her brother, and back at Cora. "Trust me, you weren't the only one surprised. Cora," she said looking back with a small smile, "I'll see you tomorrow."

Ben and Cora stood on the porch and watched his sister ride into the sun, the glare filtering through the pines and the oaks. She sighed, turned to him, laid her head on his chest. "What is going on?"

He rubbed small, slow circles through the knitted sweater she wore. The air had warmed into the fifties, and the breeze was warmer, not the brazen cold from the north as it was the day before. This westerly wind held the promise of a warmer weekend, proof that Texas weather could, and often did, change at a moment's notice.

"Let's go inside. I'll tell you about Nina—Beth—whatever she wants to be called. I need a shot of caffeine."

Once inside, he made himself at home, stalking over to the cabinet, rattling dishes, pouring coffee into a white ceramic mug. He turned and leaned against the kitchen counter, although he was practically sitting on the stone surface.

Idly, he turned the mug in his hands. "After I graduated high school, I was restless. Got into a lot of fights. The last one—the worst—happened when this jerk started in on us because we lived with my grandparents. Most of the time guys would try to take me on, to prove they could knock the big man down. This time, though,

163

the kid went too far. So did I, in the end. The kid spent a night in the hospital.

"After the fight, I found myself at the cemetery, visiting my folks. The parents of the kid were going to press charges, and I was looking at possible jail time. Eighteen years old," he said, shaking his head. "So I went to the cemetery to clear my mind, talk things over with them, even though I know they couldn't hear me."

He looked so sad, forlorn. Lost. With a questioning look, he gestured to the pot. Cora shook her head.

Ben sipped the coffee, two, three, four gulps. "The sheriff had talked to the judge, and to the parents of the kid I hurt. Explained the situation from my point of view, how my parents died, and the reason my sister and I were sensitive to ridicule. Anyway, Mae found me that afternoon in the cemetery. She tried to console me, but I was so angry, so full of frustration, hate. I barely remembering speaking to her. I had made up my mind to take the deal the judge offered. Enlisting in the army. The next day I was gone, on the way to basic training. Never looked back.

"And I didn't say goodbye to Nina—Beth. Whatever, she's Nina to me, and always will be. It was like …" he paused, eyes closed, "like I couldn't say goodbye, because I couldn't face the disappointment in her eyes. She always depended on me, and I let her down."

Cora eased up beside him, bumped him gently with her hip. "Beth seems like a levelheaded woman. I know if you talk to her you'll work things out."

"If only it were that simple. Look, I don't know how much you know about my past."

She laid her head on his arm. "Mae told me about your parents."

"Hmm. I wondered. You seem close."

"She's like an aunt to me."

He nodded. "After my first enlistment ended, I came home on leave, took some time to decide whether or not I wanted to re-up. I was at Moody's having a drink, when I heard a couple guys yacking, mouthing off about this girl one of them was dating. Except the name caught my attention. Never saw the guys before; they hadn't grown up here. He didn't know me, didn't know he was talking about my sister."

Ben balled his fist, pounded his thigh with a thunk. "The things he was saying about her ... I couldn't believe what I was hearing. Not my sister, my Nina. Thankfully, my time in the army had cooled my jets, taught me some bearing. Otherwise, I would have killed him on the spot."

"Oh, Ben, how awful."

"Yeah, and I made it worse. I marched straight over to the house, slammed open the front door. Startled the mess out of Nan and Papa. Nina was in her room, curled up in bed reading a book. What was she? Twenty? Twenty-one?" he said bitterly. "She hadn't seen me in five years, and the first thing I do was stomp in the room and accuse her of lewd behavior, sleeping around."

Cora remained quiet, pensive. She took his hand, led him to the living room. The clock above the mantle showed she had about twenty minutes until her next patient was due to arrive. They sank into the cushions of her plush sofa, and she fell into him because of sheer physics. Cora tried to edge back, but he wrapped an arm around her, held her close. Her heart beat faster, a thump-whump against her ribcage. She felt her pulse throb beneath her chin, a hot wave of anticipation sweep from her fingertips to her ears. Her skin was ablaze under his fingers. He stilled, and cleared his throat, shook his head. Cleared his throat again as a small smile turned up the corner of her mouth.

"Hmm. Yes, well. This all happened twelve years ago, or thereabouts. My whole life I sheltered her, protected her, because my parents weren't there to do it. And in my arrogance, my self-righteousness, I crushed her instead. The look on her face. I can't begin to describe it." Ben ran his hands through his hair, gripping hard and pulling, mussing the already messy mop. She ached to comfort him, hold him.

"But I was too proud to admit I was wrong." Anguish pulled at his eyes. "So I ran. Again. Enlisted for another five, and then another. I came home on leave when Papa died. Nina refused to speak to me. Everyone was calling her Beth by then. Nan wrote pretty regularly, and I kept up with things back home through her letters and emails. Two years before I retired, Nina got married. She didn't want me there. Retirement came, and I packed it up and came home, determined to make it right with her.

"She heard me out. Finally. Accepted my apology, introduced me to Ronnie. But she was still cold, distant, and to be honest, I couldn't blame her. Who would? I was a jerk."

Cora decided he needed a kick in the pants. Since they were sitting, she punched him in the arm instead.

"Crap! Why did you hit me?!"

"Snap out of it. What matters is what happens today. Let the past stay there. Build on the present. Beth, Nina, —whoever—your sister seemed surprised to see you today, but she didn't shun you or shut you out. Don't give up. I know it will work out."

"We've talked a few times since I've been home with Nan." He scooted to the edge of the couch, elbows resting on his knees. "Forced to, after Nan's stroke. I've gone out to her place a time or two, to try to mend fences. I'm wondering why she thought I had tracked her down today."

"A misunderstanding. It'll pass. Trust me."

"So, she was here to, um, see you in a professional manner?"

She nodded. "Yes, and that's all you'll get from me."

He put his hands in the air, don't shoot style. "Gotcha. You have more patients coming in?"

"In about ten minutes or so, but I still need to prep the room."

Ben stood, stretched his back. It was like watching a mountain perform yoga. "I guess I better scoot. Are we still on for the movie tonight?"

"I can't wait. You picking me up in your fancy truck?"

He laughed. "Only the best for my special lady."

At the door he turned to her, a slow burn igniting his green eyes. Now that she thought about it, a foot wasn't too much height difference. She was close enough to see a sparkle of gold here and there, flecking the iris. "Cora?"

"Hmm?"

His mouth edged near her ear, stopping short. His breath was warm on her cheek, tickling her earlobe. She closed her eyes, thrilled with the closeness, electric with anticipation. Ben whispered, "Wear your hair down tonight?"

Gently, he laid a kiss on her cheek, lingered a moment. He smoothly closed the door behind him.

Cora slid to the floor, a helpless pile of girl-goo. She was breathless, quivering, smiling from ear to ear. She had never been happier.

21

Downtown, at the sheriff's office, Deputy Wilson stared at Ben in disbelief.

"You did what?"

Ben spoke slowly, a little ticked off, enunciating his words as though speaking to a toddler. "I. Bugged. The. Campsite."

Jimmy snorted. "I heard you, but I couldn't believe it came out of your mouth." The officer motioned Ben to the chair on the other side of the hardwood desk.

The office suited Jimmy. Traditional, austere, but with a homey touch here and there. Ben rapped his knuckles on the desk. "Oak?"

"Maple. My granddad built it when he was a young man. Rather have his desk than the issued metal one. And stop changing the subject."

Ben chuckled. "Don't worry, Jimmy. I gave our unwelcome guest a little scare. Made him think a cougar had been at his pitch. And I put a minicam in the tree nearby, camouflaged. It's motion activated and has an alert system tied to it, with a one-mile range. We both know how long official proceedings can take."

"Let me guess." Jimmy leaned back in his chair. "You did a little camping out yourself last night?"

"Yeah, but I slept in my truck. Parked it over at Walker's abandoned barn next door to Cora's place. The guy didn't show, Jimmy."

"And what would you have done if he had, Ben?"

Ben ran a hand through his hair, scrubbed his face. "He's not going to hurt Cora. I will not allow it."

"We don't know *who* this guy is, what he wants. So far, all he's done is ask questions and try to get a job. Now don't," Jimmy said, holding a hand up, "argue with me. You know it's true. The only offense he committed is trespassing, and we're taking care of that today."

"Cora knows about the minicam. I told her last night. I didn't tell her the only thing it recorded was a couple of deer, an owl and some squirrels. Went over there this morning, but sort of ran into my sister, and my brain got fried with female emotion."

Jimmy steepled his fingers in front of his chin. "I heard."

"Heard what?"

"You, Beth, blow-up, boom."

The rumor mill impressed and annoyed him simultaneously. "How?"

"Shelby."

"Shelby? What does *your* sister have to do with this?"

"Beth stopped by the grocery store, and Shelby was working. Beth vented. Shelby came in, spilled the beans to me. Sounds like things are getting serious with you and the little Doc."

"I don't know what we are. Except the town's favorite gossip topic."

Jimmy cleared his throat, sat forward abruptly. "We'll go to Cora's place, clear out the site. Confiscate whatever's out there and bring it in for evidence. And I won't press charges against you for tampering with a crime scene, either."

Ben barked a laugh. "Like you would. Come off it, Jimmy. What are we going to do about bringing this guy in?"

"*If* we find him, all I can do is give him a warning."

"That's bull, and you know it!"

"I didn't say we couldn't watch him, keep tabs on him. Apply some creative pressure. If he shows back up. You know how fast gossip flies around here. He probably caught wind something was up, and bolted."

Ben hated to admit it, but the scenario seemed probable. Shelby, was known for a flapping tongue, and in small towns, gossip was a respected art. Those in the know, knew. Shelby wasn't the only one with the gift of gab. Maybe there was a way to use the grapevine to their advantage, drop a tasty morsel here and there, and hope their prey would bite. Because make no mistake about it.

The hunter had become the prey.

***

Hair up? Down? Cora analyzed her hair in the mirror, twisting rowdy curls this way and that, dropping the mess over her shoulders in a fiery mane. Ben wanted it down, she mused. But it drove her nuts when she left it unbound. These curls had a mind of their own. Ugh, the things she'd do for the man.

The evening was cool, but not cold. One day she'd acclimate to this fickle weather. For tonight, she dressed in khaki corduroys, a white button-down cotton blouse, and a denim jacket over it. She fussed and fretted over footwear. Girly stuff was not her forte, she admitted. Most of her women friends had a closet full of shoes, a pair for every occasion. Her collection consisted of leather work boots, two pairs of sandals, some chunky slides, running shoes. Tonight she zipped up the blister-making heeled ankle boots. She would suffer for three extra inches of height. The things she did for love.

Whoa, wait a doggone minute! Love? She froze, one hand on the zipper, sitting on the edge of her bed, the eyelet duvet cover squished under her. No, no. No way was she thinking *love*. She liked Ben. Like, get the shivers thinking about him, about those little lines at the sides of his eyes, and man, those emeralds sitting in his face. Quivered thinking of those few, precious kisses they shared. The way he smelled, all man of the earth, leather and horses. How safe she felt when his arms surrounded her. She mentally slapped herself across the face.

No, absolutely not. Cora zipped the boot so hard she pinched her finger. She sucked her finger, wincing at the sharpness of the pain. Ouch! She growled under her breath. Guard your heart, Mae warned. Ha! So much for that happening. But she was not in love.

Fuming, she stomped to the living room. A sharp rap on the front door halted her. She glanced at her watch. He was early, but she was ready, so no big deal.

Wiping the frown from her face, she shook out her hair, smoothed the jacket over hips. Beaming, she whipped the door open. "Couldn't stay away ... Jimmy?"

"Hey, Cora."

"Don't take this the wrong way, but you're not who I was expecting. Still," she said, ushering him inside, "make yourself at home."

He stood by the front door, barely over the threshold, twisting his western hat. "Wish I came bearing good news."

"Jimmy, you're scaring me." She caught her lower lip with her teeth, anxious.

"Well, I guess I have *some* good news. We gathered up all your unwelcome visitor's gear from his makeshift campsite. If he comes back, he'll know we're on to him. I decided to leave Ben's minicam in place, and we added a couple more to the area. If he shows up, we'll get a good shot of his face. I've also got Shelby lined up to place some choice words about the guy into the town rumor mill. We're hoping to spook the guy, shake him up a little. At least until the scan results come in."

"But it's not why you're here, is it?"

"No. After I got back to the station, I found Betty on the phone. She waved me down, transferred the call. Do you know a woman named Hettie Meadows?"

"Yeah, she's Missy's mom. I met her once or twice. Why?"

"She called in a tip, of sorts. She's friends with Nancy, the secretary in the sheriff's office in Bee Tree, Missouri.

"The word is someone came in and filed a complaint against you. Said you performed some unethical procedures, treated her off-the-books, and so on. Investigators have been out asking questions, and Hettie was re-interviewed about Missy's delivery and death."

Cora was furious. "Never! I never treated anyone off the record, not with my license on the line. What is going on?"

"Sounds like trouble to me, if I'm being honest. Mrs. Meadows knew something was fishy. The officer questioning her wouldn't give her any details, so Mrs. Meadows called up her friend, Nancy, in the office and got the low-down. Nancy also confirmed Wilkes has been missing a lot of work, and when he's there, he's like a time bomb. Mrs. Meadows, Hettie, called our office with all this. She thought you'd want to know."

Cora narrowed her eyes at Jimmy. "There's something you're not telling me."

He sighed, head down, fiddling with his hat again. "Listen, I don't think they'll make a case. But … they're talking extradition."

She felt the scream building pressure in her sternum, a steaming geyser rolling and pushing to the surface. It erupted in a vicious howl, like the haunting shriek of a cougar. Cora threw back her head and let it all go. The frustration, the hurt, anger, confusion, and yes, fear. The whites of Jimmy's eyes shone against the tan of his skin, open wide in surprise and disbelief. "Why is all this happening?"

He hesitated, patted her back as he would a skittish horse. "Keep thinking positive thoughts. You better believe whatever happens, we'll fight it."

"Fight what?" Ben stood glowering, looking from Jimmy down to Cora.

Ben filled the open doorway, his shoulders nearly spanning the width of the frame. He gripped the trim in one hand, his hat in the other. "What's going on?"

"It's starting, all over again. Wilkes and his psychotic witch hunt. He's relentless. And I'm tired. But I will not sit idly by and let him ruin my life again!"

Ben laid a hand on her shoulder, tried to pull her into his warmth. It was so tempting to fall, surrender into his protection and comfort. But right now, she needed some space, to work through all the emotions raging and exploding in her head. She said so to Ben, who retreated a step with a worried frown.

Cora told Jimmy to fill Ben in on the situation, and she stormed out the front door and down the front steps. She paced in circles in front of her house, wishing she could hit something, but remembering how her hand felt the last time she assaulted an inanimate object. Her heels protested the friction, but she told them to shut up, too.

She thought of the distance she had traveled to escape Gordon's misplaced fury, both in miles and in healing. Months of doubting herself, wondering if she could have done anything more to save Missy's life; and finally, at long last, finding peace, a new home. Then, acceptance, knowing she performed all measures to save Missy's life. It was her friend's time to go. Instead of regrets, she thanked God Missy had found salvation before that dreadful day. At the touch of a hand on her shoulder, Cora spun. And found Ben waiting. He smiled, and the knots in her chest loosened, her hands unclenched. Pacing no longer seemed necessary.

Jimmy stood on the porch, watching her with a worried slant to his eyes. He leaned against the porch column, content to wait until her fiery anger had gone from bonfire to slow-burning coal. She shuddered into Ben's arms, drank in his strength, and pulled back. She took him by the hand and led him up the wooden stairs to where Jimmy stood. The deputy held out his hand.

"Look, I know this might be hard, but Hettie wanted you to have this. She emailed me the file. It's a photo." A baby grinned back at her, teddy bear clutched to his chest. Coal black hair and bright blue eyes, so much like his mother's it made Cora's heart ache. She turned the photo over, saw the name William Wilkes printed on the back in Jimmy's square hand. Happy tears welled up in red-rimmed and swollen eyes, but she refused to let them drop. No, she was finished feeling sorry for herself. Anger and determination kicked the vulnerability away.

"Thank you, Jimmy." Cora stood, wiped dry her face. "I'm sorry I broke down, but it won't happen again. Ben, you ready to go to the movies?"

Eyes wide, he shrugged. "I'm ready if you are. Sure you want to go out? I understand if you want a rain check."

"Gordon Wilkes will not control my life any longer," she spat, fire in her voice. "I will not give him the satisfaction. Let his little spy see it, just let him watch."

Ben chuckled, swept her into his arms. "That's my feisty red-head."

She held on tight, inhaling his scent. Her heart beat rapidly against his chest. His eyes held hers hostage, her still wet lashes barely blinking. She nearly purred at the possessiveness she saw in Ben's face. *His* red-head, huh?

Jimmy cleared his throat. "Um, well, I guess I'll mosey back to the precinct. You'll keep an eye on her?"

"Won't take my eyes off her."

22

Cora hummed as she rode to church, Rusty's iron shoes clip-clopping along the asphalt of the town street. Overhead, the sun played hide and seek with fluffy silvery clouds, but for now, the yellow warmth bathed her back. She almost didn't need the sweater and light scarf she wore, but the faint breeze tickling her neck and ears made her happy for them nonetheless.

If I Only Had A Brain seemed a fitting song to keep her company. Dorothy, Toto, and all her friends in Oz entertained them last night at Movies in the Park. The chill in the air had given her the perfect excuse to snuggle into Ben's thick arms, although she burrowed more than snuggled. Would she ever grow tired of his smell, his laugh? A magical night culminated with his capable hands twisted in her curls, and him kissing the brain right out of her head, standing in the moonlight beneath the stars, while lightning bugs flickered and danced at the tree line. When Ben kissed her, she felt as though *she* were the one caught up in a tornado and whisked away to an enchanted place, where colors were bolder, more vibrant, and the impossible became likely. Life was a black and white movie out of his arms.

Rusty whickered at the line of horses already hitched at the little church on the corner. It was a modest sized building, traditional, with a steeple at the front, and wide double doors to greet the congregation. Maroon and gold chrysanthemums popped against the white of the wood siding, while low holly bushes with dots of red berries flanked the front steps. A small wooden sign announced Living Waters Church, the name carefully and professional hand lettered in black lacquer paint against a creamy white background.

There were no churches in America, not in the traditional sense. There were buildings designated for people to gather, for those who chose to follow the collective faith programs approved by the State. Individual churches conforming to any one particular denomination had been outlawed at the reformation of the country, post-Collapse. "For the good of the people" the government proclaimed. Their rationale was if a person chose one faith, it might be offensive to others. Therefore, citizens could either choose to worship all gods in a joint community gathering place, or choose to worship none and go about their lives within the confines of government regulation, owing no allegiance to any deity whatsoever.

Cora had bucked the system when she became a covert Christian, and toed the criminal line the day she handed Missy a Bible. At least here, the Republic and its territories were allowed the religious freedoms of the old United States. Sadly, though, many churches had closed during the time of the Collapse, reformation, and subsequent War of Secession. The people had lashed out at one another, blaming race, genetics, and religion. Such a dark time in history. Cora was grateful to have been born after the dust had settled, and a semblance of normalcy had returned.

She left Rusty in the company of three mares and a gelding. Cora rubbed her horse's long nose, scratched behind Rusty's left ear, and gave her half a carrot to munch. She laughed at the soft velvet lips snuffling the vegetable out of her hand. Two more people were headed her way, their horses quickstepping the closer they came to the other animals. Soon the line of horses would be swishing tails and stamping feet, whinnying and nibbling at one another.

Cora entered the church, allowed her eyes to adjust to the dimness of the interior rather than the bright sky. Wooden pews gleamed, and a fresh floral arrangement adorned the alter table in front of the pulpit. There were about twenty people, gathered in clumps of twos and threes, chatting away the minutes until the service began. Several people looked her way; but before she could finish waving, they were whispering to one another, shooting a glance or two surreptitiously over their shoulders. How odd. She felt an uneasy itch along her spine.

She liked to sit near the front, a few rows back from the preacher. Their group was so small they rarely used the choir loft snugged behind the podium. She laid her Bible on the pew, tucked in the corner near the aisle. Mae was there, dabbing at her eyes with a handkerchief as she talked with Nash Wainwright, the pharmacist. Nash's wife, Cindy, and their two young daughters stood with Mae, the little girls squirming and wiggling and giggling.

Cora passed a group of acquaintances on her way to visit with Mae. As she walked by, the previously animated conversation halted abruptly. One of the older ladies nodded her head briskly, and turned to the group, her hunched back to Cora. The itch between her shoulder blades flared. She didn't like the feel, the vibe, but she was probably being paranoid. It had been a hard few days lately. Before she reached Mae and the Wainwrights, the doors opened. Sunlight and Beth Winslow filled the tiny entry. She smiled, beaming, and waved to Cora, who changed direction to welcome Beth to the church.

"I'm so happy you've come!" Cora said, excited. Then with a laugh, "I wasn't sure you would after yesterday morning's drama out at the house."

Beth waved her hand in a shooing motion. "I'll admit it was a bit of a surprise, seeing Ben there. And I behaved badly, if I'm being honest," she confessed. "How did I not know you two were an item? The grapevine is prolific around here!"

"Not sure if 'item' is the right word, but maybe. We're still working on defining our relationship."

"Judging by the way Ben was looking at you, you're an item. Like a lion eyeballing a gazelle." Beth's smile touched her twinkling eyes.

"You two need to talk," Cora replied seriously. "Fences need to be mended."

Beth nodded, her eyes pensive. "And I plan on it. Soon, trust me. I have some forgiving to do, and we need to work things out. I can't go on, holding on to this grudge. It's too heavy, you know?"

"Yeah, I get it."

Beth looked around the small auditorium. "I know I'm new here, but why is everyone staring at us?"

"I don't think it's you. Something's going on, but I don't know what."

The young preacher cleared his throat, and people made their way to the pews.

Pastor Dean spoke about building one another up, and not letting strife divide Christ's people. Cora admired how seamlessly the youthful minister wove scripture into the lesson, without sounding judgmental and condescending. Truth shone from the pulpit. Cora basked in it, her spirit lighter than it was earlier. It was as if the apostles Paul and Peter were there, speaking to their church in

Cotton Springs rather than the early church, encouraging and gently admonishing God's people to care for, nurture, encourage and support one another, as only those who belong to Jesus could. He cautioned against backbiting and gossip, warned of the irreparable damage sustained when family members hurt one another.

After the message, the congregation sang one hymn together and departed, filing out of the auditorium in a gaggle of laughter and smiles, pats on the back and bear hugs. Mae found Cora and pulled her aside as they exited the church. The sun peeked through the clouds in fits and bursts, radiant beams streaking through the billowy clumps.

As Mae opened her mouth to speak, though, John and Angie Walker stepped up, and John laid a hand on Cora's shoulder. Their son, Billy, peeked around Angie's full denim skirt and waved his casted arm.

"And how's your arm doing, little man?" Cora asked with a grin, stooping down to his level. The scamp giggled and hid himself in a fold of blue cotton.

Angie laughed and said, "You'd never know anything happened, Doc. He's doing fine. We'll be out to your place in a few weeks to have you take the cast off, and not a moment too soon."

Her husband, John, a reserved man, spoke quietly, cryptically. "And so you know, Doc, we don't believe a word about what's going around. Don't worry yourself. We'll be here if you need us." Angie nodded her agreement, and they were off with a wave. Cora stared after them, puzzled.

"Mae, do you have any idea what that was about?"

Bewildered, Mae shook her head slowly. "Not the faintest, dear, but then again, I got home late last night. Can you believe it?

Dabney gets to come home tomorrow! The swelling in his ankle is under control, and the rest of his injuries are healing well."

Cora gathered Mae in a tight hug. "I'm so happy for you!"

"Things are going to have to change around our place, with my stubborn man recuperating. So if you know of anyone who can run jobs and not take flack, you let me know. We'll need a foreman to take Dab's place for a while."

"I'll certainly keep an eye and an ear out."

Cora kept a smile plastered on her face, made herself wave to friends as she hurried to Rusty at the hitching post, even though a good majority of those folks barely managed a grim nod in her direction. No, she didn't like this feeling. Surreptitious looks, whispered conversations when she was near, open stares. They reminded her of the fallout after Missy's death.

Beth caught up to her as she mounted the horse. "Phew! Those sure are some friendly people inside! Thought I'd never get free."

"I'll take your word for it, today," Cora mumbled.

"Hmm?"

"Aw, nothing. Thinking out loud, is all. What's up?"

"You going to the Freedom Festival tomorrow?"

"Wouldn't miss it! Ben's playing lumberjack, and I absolutely have to see that."

"Ronnie and I will be there, too. I was, um, hoping maybe we could sit together, eat some barbecue. You know ... us, you and Ben?"

Cora leaned down over the horse and said, "I think it's an excellent idea."

Beth nodded briskly, her honey-brown hair swinging over her shoulder. "Well, it's settled. See you tomorrow!"

As she swayed back and forth with the horse's gait, Cora pondered the lukewarm reception at church. Her thoughts moved to the town's celebration tomorrow. The food and the games, getting together with the people of Cotton Springs as they spilled out into the streets. She imagined loud music and laughter, the sweet tang of barbecue sauce in the air, Ben swinging an axe and running the log roll. Naturally, she wondered how Ben would accept the lunch date with his sister and her husband.

Cora hoped the only fireworks she'd see were the ones at the conclusion of the Freedom Festival.

23

Barnum Pond glittered, a sun-struck sapphire blazing across the field. On the east side, a clump of three droopy willows dipped their long weepy arms in the water, teasing the surface with wispy fingers. The five-acre body of water was more than a pond, but less than a lake, a favored swimming and fishing hole for the local teens. Today, a modified buoy system enclosed a large rectangular area filled with massive cut logs, set aside for the logroll event, or burling, and the boom run. She didn't envy the lumberjack contestants. It was about 75 degrees and sunny, but the water would be frigid.

Wooden picnic tables dotted the field adjacent to the pond, most of them donated by townsfolk over the years. Red and white checkered tablecloths covered the rough pine planks. Platters, bowls and plates buried most of the festive fabric. Adults and children alike swarmed the tables like ants. Late arrivals were happy to spread a blanket on the ground nearby. Shouts, laughter, and the buzz of continual conversation ebbed and flowed, echoed off the pond, and bounced back to the baseball fields where Cora had positioned her canvas lawn chair.

Jimmy Wilson sat across from her, his bubbly date, Sandy, next to him with her arm looped around his. An empty chair waited for Mae, who was at home getting Dabney settled into bed, probably listening to his moaning at missing all the fun. Beth and Ronnie were due to arrive any minute. Ben's cowboy hat occupied his seat while he was gearing up for the lumberjack games. Hundreds of people swarmed the sports complex, filling both baseball fields and the football field with picnickers and party goers. School buildings rose nearby, with all grades located on this one campus. Ah, how Cora loved the small town life.

She tuned out the squeak of Sandy's relentless voice, thinking back to Independence Day celebrations in Missouri with her family. America celebrated in July, a much hotter month than October to be sure. Cora thought the cooler temperatures of autumn were nice, but it also felt strange, foreign, to see the dulled russet colors of fall on the deciduous trees rather than the verdant green of summer. Instead of the American flag with its red and white stripes and forty-seven stars, the Lone Star flag of the Republic flew en masse, the blocky red and white stripe to the side of the blue star-emblazoned field on the left, repeated in intervals along the fence line of the ball fields. Little hands waved tiny versions of the standard as they darted and ran, weaving around group after rowdy group. Not so different, after all. Cora leaned back in her chair, sipping the cool sweet tang of lemonade. She closed her eyes and let the warm autumn sun shine muted behind her shuttered eyelids. With the bandstand hopping, the banjo and fiddles dueling strings, she could almost imagine her family there beside her. Even Sandy's shrill tongue faded to a buzz. For a little while, she was home.

She jerked forward and jumped clear out of her chair as an ice cube slid down her shirt. She spluttered, gasped and yelled, dropping her glass of lemonade on the grass beside her in her haste to reach the ice before it melted and soaked her shirt. Laughter infected her small circle and a deeper voice joined in from behind her chair. Ben loomed, his glass empty except for the ice, and a grin smeared across his face. He didn't even have the decency to look ashamed.

"Ben Tucker, I'm going to get you!" Cora cried as she chased Ben. He tossed the remaining chunks of ice from his glass at her. "Agh! Stop it! That's it. This means war, buddy!"

She laughed as she raced after him, and the crowd cheered her on. She didn't have a chance. Those long legs of his ate up the ground. She was nimble and quick, but wow, he was fast. Much faster than a man his size should be, if you asked her. Ben led Cora on a merry chase, in and out of picnic blankets, around the bandstand, and ending up at the elementary school. He rounded a corner past the library, leaving the gathered crowds in their red clay dust. She tucked around the building, close on his trail.

It was like ramming into a brick wall, running into Ben. She *oofed* and bounced back, but he caught her as she stumbled, pulled her close. Breathing heavily, she looked up into his deep green eyes, saw the amusement lurking; but also saw the heat, the intensity, like he had sprung a trap laid for one of his bounties, and he was about to collect the reward.

Cora gulped, her chest rising and falling rapidly from the excitement of the brief sprint, but more from the nearness of Ben. They were in a narrow alley, a corridor stretching between the elementary building and the cafeteria. Shadows and darkness hugged the walls and corners.

Cora gazed up at Ben as he swept a curl away from her face. "Here," he said, "let me help you."

He gently untied her hair from its topknot, dropped the elastic band on the dirt at their feet. Softly, his fingers combed the curls away from her face. His face leaned toward hers, his voice a whisper. "I keep telling you to wear it down."

"Why?" she murmured.

"So I can do this." His fingers wrapped around the red locks and pulled her in tight. His lips possessed hers and her face ignited. Heck, her whole body was on fire, flames dancing at her fingertips. A bonfire roared in her belly. She had no idea how long they stood there, only that when they came up for air, all she wanted to do was immerse herself back in his kiss. Her fingernails raked across his chest, the fabric bunching beneath her hands. This time, she grabbed him, nipping at his bottom lip playfully, possessively. He belonged to her, and she to him.

The sound of a foghorn startled them apart. Where the horn ended, his groan continued. "Great. Fantastic."

"Time to saw some logs?"

He growled, picked her up and brought her to eye level, as if she were as light as air. He thoroughly kissed her again, and plunked her back on the earth, leaving Cora breathless.

"Yeah, let's get back over there. Saved by the horn."

She elbowed him in the side. "Funny guy."

Hand and hand they strolled through the throng of people meandering toward the little clearing set aside for the lumberjack competition. The mayor, Willis Stiles, stood on a platform built of hay bales stacked four high. At his side stood a young lady, late teens or early twenties, in a sparkly crimson gown. Her tiara glimmered in the sunlight, and the white sash across her chest proclaimed her Cotton Queen.

"Janie Hightower," Ben said under his breath. "Her mama owns the little ritzy boutique in town."

"Ah. She's cute."

He leaned down from behind her, circled his arms around her collarbone, tickled her ear with his warm whisper. "Who needs cute when I've got gorgeous?"

She elbowed him again and he grunted. "Don't forget feisty," she said sweetly. He rolled his eyes and turned his attention back to Mayor Stiles, who was tapping the microphone.

"I'd like to welcome ever'body to our great Republic's fiftieth anniversary celebration!" The mayor's amplified voice echoed off the school buildings and across the pond. The crowd cheered and waved flags. Wolf whistles speared the air. "Alright, alright. Ever'body settle down. Now, y'all ready for some lumberjackin'?" Once again, the crowd erupted.

One by one, the mayor announced the contestants. As he called off the names, Ben leaned down again to Cora's ear. "Don't worry about me, Doc. This time, I won't cut myself."

She looked at him, puzzled. He pointed to the pair of chainsaws lying on the ground a dozen paces away from the makeshift stage, then to the pinkish scar on his forearm. She felt the color drain from her face even as he laughed.

"Lord, have mercy," she prayed aloud. How could she have forgotten?

The next hour was full of chopping and buzzing, sawing and thunking, as man after burly man proved his brawn wielding axes and chainsaws. True to his word, Ben handled the power tool like a hot knife through butter, rather than a grizzly chain-toothed death monster biting through a log nearly two feet across. She watched between the gaps of the fingers covering her face. After the three different chop events, the single buck and the hot saw, Ben was in second place. He stood gulping water handed to him by the simpering Cotton Queen, her pearly teeth shining as she batted her lashes at Ben. Cora had to give the girl credit, flirting with a man fifteen years her senior. She was more amused than annoyed. She caught Ben's eye, and wiggled her own brow in question. He grinned and shrugged, sweat rolling down his face and dampening his sandy brown hair. Bits of wood and sawdust clung to him head to toe. He looked like he was having the time of his life. Her fingers tingled, ached to touch him, to scrunch her hands in his hair and command a kiss. She shuddered and blinked, very thankful that no one could hear her thoughts.

The contestants moved over to the speed climb, a set of vertical cedar spars sunk into the ground standing sixty feet high. Steel-core ropes hung from the tops of the poles to aid the men in climbing. Some looking up at the height had turned a slight shade of green, and two bowed out of the competition at that point, leaving eight men standing. Cora watched Ben and the other competitors strap on their spurred climbers. Soon, a judge yelled go, and two burly men scampered up the soaring poles, their sights set on the bell at the top of their spars. One bell rang right after another, and down they came. The crowd cheered and friends clapped the winner on the back. The next two scaled the heights nearly as quickly as the first two, though the faster of the set finished three seconds ahead of the other. Cora's heart beat rapidly as she watched the following pair, closed her eyes as she realized Ben was next. She was so engrossed in her thoughts, eyes squeezed shut, that she didn't hear the bells ring or the crowd cheer for the third pair when they landed on the packed ground.

Someone grabbed her arm tightly. "He's next!" Cora's eyes flew open.

Beth gripped Cora's bicep, and a curly-haired man stood right behind her.

"Beth! You're here!"

"Sorry we're late. We had a mare give birth unexpectedly this morning." Beth pointed to the man at her side. "This is Ronnie, my husband. Ooooh! Here he goes. Go, Ben!"

Cora didn't want to watch, but she couldn't pull her eyes away. She uttered a prayer for his safety as he prepared to climb. The judge yelled "Go!" and off they went, scuttling up the tall cedar spars. Halfway up, Ben's left leg slipped, losing contact with the pole. Cora's hand flew to her mouth, and her eyes grew wide just as the crowd gasped in unison. But he soon regained his footing and rang the bell a hair after the first man. Then it was a race to the bottom.

"He did it!" Beth yelled as Ben's feet pounded the dirt half a second ahead of his competition.

Cora couldn't speak. Her heart continued to thud painfully in her throat. Anxiously she watched the results board, and cheered with the crowd when she saw Ben's name move to the first place position. She hugged Beth in a jumping embrace, and turned back to find Ben.

As she edged closer to the contestants, pressing toward Ben, the crowd to the right of her parted. Where was he? There! He had bent over to remove the studded climbers. He glanced up and waved, a silly grin on his face. The crowd around her widened, and she saw a concerned look shadow Ben's face, worry evident even from a distance. He stepped toward her, arm outstretched.

Three microphones shoved into her face as she was swarmed, dozens of people reaching in, snapping photographs, a human noose tightening around her so that their lapelcams could capture live video. The seething mass was yelling, questioning, a barrage of language she couldn't interpret. Frantically, she looked for Ben, but she couldn't see him over the wall of reporters surrounding her. What was happening? Where was Ben? Shouts and yelled demands assaulted her ears.

"Cora! Cora Thomas!"

"What is your reply to these allegations?"

"Did you flee from America to get away from murder charges?"

"How long have you studied witchcraft?"

Left and right she searched, her head spinning as she backtracked away from the knot of people yelling foul accusations at her. "Ben!" she cried. "Ben!"

Through a gap in the crowd she caught a glimpse of Beth, Ronnie's tanned arms surrounding her as she tried to reach Cora. She looked like she was yelling, but Cora could hear nothing over the clamor and confusion surrounding her on all sides.

"Miss Thomas! Do you have anything to say?"

"Get away from me! Leave me alone. Ben!" she yelled.

And he was there, plowing through the throng as powerfully as he wielded the chainsaw earlier, cutting a path until he reached Cora, wrapping her in his sweat-drenched arms. He turned to the paparazzi, glared at the cameras and ignored the slender microphones now being shoved into his face.

He stood still, cradling Cora in his arms, her face buried in his musky chest. Tears leaked down her face. One by one, the reporters quieted, as if waiting for his statement.

Quietly, he commanded, "She has nothing to say to you. Get out of my way. Now."

Like the Red Sea, they parted. Once Cora and Ben were a dozen paces away, the buzz geared back up again, the reporters interviewing townsfolk, questioning her friends and neighbors, no doubt. Ben stalked away, holding her close to his chest. His heart pounded steadily, helped to calm her own. She stayed in his arms, tears tracking down her cheeks, until they were around the school and the crowd was blissfully left behind.

24

Ben carried her, around the high school, between the gymnasium and the middle school, until they reached the vehicle parking lot, his long legs chewing the distance easily. Cora glanced up, saw the knots behind his jaw and the focused look as he swung his head in either direction, watching for stray reporters lying in wait. The shocked crying subsided, but a hiccup or two still crept up. Her throat felt tight, constricted.

"Ben? Ben, you can put me down now."

Still he scanned the area, but he spared her a glance. "We're almost at the truck anyway, darlin'. Sit tight."

Cora gave half a laugh. "Like I could go anywhere if I wanted to."

She blew a curl out of her mouth, then another, brushed more stray locks from her face. Her face heated as she remembered where the hair elastic landed, in the dirt in the alley where Ben had kissed her silly. Well, maybe she could deal with the riot on her head a little longer. The day had been spectacular, up until the last five minutes when the ugliness of the world rammed her full-on. At least now she understood the cool reception at church.

He stopped at the driver's side of the pickup, smoothly stood her up. Her knees shook and her hands were cold, clammy. She was sure her face was a swollen, blotchy mess. If it mattered to him, Ben didn't show it. He cupped her face in his hands, and planted a chaste peck on the end of her nose.

Bluegrass echoed off the buildings, the plucky mandolin and banjo twang muted by distance. The crowd roared in unison, and applause briefly drowned out the live music from the bandstand.

"The competition! Ben, you have to get back over there!"

"It's not important," he replied. "You are." He cupped her face, tender and insistent, looked her square in the eyes. "When did you become so important to me?"

Cora shivered. She didn't know the answer, but she felt the same way. He mattered, more than any other person had in ages.

"Are you cold?" he asked, concern in his voice.

She laid her head on his chest, took comfort in the steady thump-thump of his heart.

"Let's get you home."

The school complex was about a mile east of Cotton Springs, so they backtracked through town and headed north to her little house on the edge of the forest. Patriotic banners adorned the gaslights, and The Square was decked out in red, white and blue buntings. Downtown businesses flew the Lone Star outside their shops, the flags drooping limply at an angle from the storefronts. The local business owners had pitched in and were sponsoring a town-wide barbecue as part of the evening festivities. In about an hour, all of the downtown streets were to be cordoned off for a giant block party, followed by a fireworks gala after dark.

As they passed the feed store, Cora sighed. "I'm sorry you didn't get to finish the competition."

"Did you feel the water? The pond is frigid. Can't say I'm all that disappointed I won't be doing the burling. Besides, you have nothing to be sorry for. You can't control the idiotic media."

"You're only saying it to make me feel better. But thanks."

"I'm sure the rest of those guys are glad I'm gone. It wasn't a fair fight, know what I mean?" She loved that schoolboy grin of his.

"Full of yourself, don't ya think?"

Eyes wide and innocent, he replied, "Nothing but the truth." He crossed his heart twice with his finger, making her chuckle.

"It feels good to laugh. But this makes me wonder. What's next? I have no doubt Gordon Wilkes is behind this."

He nodded as he turned down her driveway. "Gotta be. Probably leaked lies and half-truths to the right ears in the media. Any lawman has to have contacts within the news."

Cora saw no one near her home, no evidence anyone had been there. It was naïve to think her life would remain peaceful. Ben walked her to the door, taking the keys from her hand before she could unlock the house. Once again, Ben swept the house, looking for signs of an intruder. Satisfied with his precautions, he settled himself on the sofa near the fireplace.

"Does it work?" He pointed at the brick-faced fireplace.

"It's seventy-five degrees outside. You can't possibly want a fire today."

"I was thinking for later."

"Later?"

"Well, yeah. What's for supper?"

Stunned, Cora stared at him. "Supper?"

He looked at her with his head cocked, an eyebrow raised. "Yeah, you know. The meal in the evening?"

She plopped down on the couch next to him, shoulders slumped. "Crap. I guess we won't be going to the block party tonight." She pounded her fist on her thigh. "Is this ever going to end?! Will he ever leave me alone?"

"It is the way it is, Cora. We're going to do everything we can to fight back, but right now, we have to accept the present and move on."

"We?" She kept her voice low, smooth. Steady. Inside, her heart raced.

His eyes flared green fire. "Do I look like I'm going somewhere?"

Cora breathed deeply. This wasn't the time to have this talk. All she wanted was to curl up in his arms and shut out the world. Her breath came in short bursts, her chest tightening. In, out. But even as she told her mind to be quiet, her mouth blurted, "Ben, this thing we have. It's wonderful. But ..."

"But?"

Choosing her words carefully, Cora picked at imaginary lint on her pants. "He's attacking my faith, Ben. Not just me, but my belief in God. And you! You stormed off the one and only time I ever discussed it with you!" Why, oh why, did she bring this up?

He frowned, remained silent, as if the eye of a hurricane was passing overhead.

But now that she began, she couldn't stop the torrent from flowing. Weeks of emotion crushed the dam in her mind. Cora grabbed his hand, squeezed. "Ben, please look at me. I've been living in the moment with you, ignoring my head and listening to my heart. In here," she said, placing their joined hands just above her heart, "I want you. Need you." With the other hand, she tapped a finger to her temple. "Here? There's a voice telling me we can't keep this up. Jesus is a part of who I am, the most important one. You have to admit there's no real future if you can't take me as I am. Because it isn't going to change. And this is what Wilkes is after, my belief. The one you despise. I can't separate it anymore."

"So what are you saying, Cora?" He gazed out the front window. "You want me to leave?"

"No, Ben! I want a future with you. I'm saying I want you to give God a chance to heal your heart!"

He closed his eyes, angled his head toward the ceiling. He shuttered an exhale. With a gentle squeeze of their entwined hands, he let go. Her heart shattered into a million pieces.

"Cora," he whispered, clearing his throat. "Don't do this, not now. You know how I feel about it. Can't we go on like we have been? What we have is amazing. I've never felt this way about anyone. Let's leave your God out of it, and deal with this threat without it."

A knot crept up, wedged itself in her throat. What was she doing? Lord, why now, this moment, when her life was crumbling, in shambles? "I want to. My heart wants you. But I can't deny Him anymore. I can walk you through it, read the Bible with you. God loves you so much. And I--," she stuttered, "I need you, Ben. But I need you to want all of me, my faith included. This isn't only an assault against me, but against God. Can't you understand? I want you by my side!"

Ben rubbed his face, closed his eyes. "Why now, Cora? You've ignored this the whole time. We can keep things the way they are. There's no need to complicate us."

"But I haven't ignored it, Ben. It's always there, in the back of my mind, niggling at me. I *knew* this day would come. Lord," she pleaded aloud, "why are you making me choose?"

Ben, silent and grave, sat beside her, his warmth a false comfort she'd come to rely on far too much. The silence stretched, thin and taut. "I'll give Jimmy a call, get someone out here to keep the press away. I'll keep watch outside until the sheriff's department arrives."

He stood, positioned his back to her, faced the laced-curtained windows. His hands were tight-fisted knots at his side.

Tears welled in her already reddened eyes. "So that's it? You'll toss us away?"

"No, Cora. I'm not giving this up." He shook his head slowly side to side as he edged close to the door. "You are. I'll fight for us. But I can't battle this fantasy you insist on believing."

"Haven't you ever wondered if there's something more? Wanted to hope, to have faith in something larger than yourself? To know you were created, not an accident?"

He spun to face her, raging emotion fighting across his face. "The one thing I'm sure of is if there was a God, he wouldn't let all these horrid things happen to good people! You've been persecuted, hated, driven away from your family and home because of this, Cora. Wake up! You're a good person. Kind, caring, generous. Why would a loving God want all this to happen to you? You, who profess to love him so much?" He shook his head, ran a hand through his shaggy hair. "Why would a loving God let a man murder my parents, take them away from me and my sister for nothing more than a handful of gold and silver? What did they do to deserve that?" Ben was yelling now, "Answer me! Why would he let my parents die?"

She stood, walked to him as he stood by the door. He pushed her away as she reached out to him. "Please, Ben. The world is a broken and fallen place. I don't have all the answers. I wish I did. But I know God does, and I trust Him to bring me through whatever this world throws at me."

"I believe in these." He held out his calloused and worn hands, palms up. "I believe in hard work, and making my way in this world. Being a good person. I'm sorry it's not enough for you, Cora. These hands want so very badly to hold you."

Ben turned the knob, pushed open the door. "I'll sit on the porch until Jimmy can send someone out. I'm sorry. You brought this on yourself. Goodbye, Cora."

She sobbed as he closed the door firmly behind him without looking back, slid down the door frame into a huddled knot on the floor. "Please, Father, soften his heart. Ben needs your mercy." Her whispered hiccup echoed, resounded in her fractured heart.

Tears glided down her cheeks, plopped softly on the hardwood floor of her living room. Each one felt like a piece of her heart, falling out of her chest, and shattering into tiny pieces.

***

Ben sat on the top step of Cora's smooth-sanded porch, switched off his wrist communicator, cutting Jimmy off mid-question. He thought idly that Cora needed one of these.

Cora.

Even now, she was still there, nestled in the front of his mind. Both a sun to his soul and a supernova, warming and destructive. For the first time in his life, he let someone in, allowed a woman to hold his heart. Now she squeezed and he was suffocating, struggling to breathe.

Jimmy said he be out in ten minutes, and then he would leave. Ben scrubbed his whiskers, making a scritching sound. Maybe he'd go get a haircut, a shave. Groaning inwardly, he remembered that not only was it Independence Day, but it was Sunday, and not a single business in town was open. He would go by Nan's house. She was up and about, probably antsy and itching to have something to do. Anything except thinking about the fiery redhead inside the quaint cottage. Decision made, he stood, stretched.

The woods enveloping Cora's small home were quiet. The only sounds were the blue jays crying and the crows squawking, the occasional squirrel chittering as it scampered up a tree. Keeping the porch in view, he walked around the tree line out front, along the east and west sides. Here, too, all was peaceful.

If only his heart was as serene. The blasted woman tossed him to and fro, sent ripples along the fabric of his nature, rocking him to the core. After all she had been through, the hate and the disappointment, the strife and struggle, she still clung to her so-called faith. It irked him to no end. How did she put that kind of trust into something she couldn't see, couldn't touch? He recalled the way her hair tangled in his fist, the softness of her hand in his. He believed in what he touched, tasted, smelled. Faith in action, in making his own future, self-reliance. He believed in himself and the goodness of others. Not some unseen puppet master pulling the strings of the unwary. How could she be so naïve?

He punted a pine cone down the driveway, kicking up dust in the process. The gritty cloud hung in the air with no wind to dispel it. With so many gusty days lately, the still air was almost too tranquil, in direction opposition to his tumultuous feelings.

Jimmy's cruiser pulled into the drive, the solar-powered engine a hum above the crunch of loose rock under the tires. Ben waved in his direction, marched back toward the front deck. Billowy reddish-brown clouds trailed behind the police car, like a grainy fogbank on a sunny day.

The deputy still wore civilian clothing, jeans and a plaid button-down shirt. His badge was clipped to his belt. Pearl snaps and a gold star glittered in the afternoon sun.

"Ben."

"Jimmy. Thanks for coming out. Sorry to ruin your day off."

"Don't sweat it. How's our girl holding up after all this mess?"

"She's pigheaded stubborn," came the surly reply.

Jimmy raised an eyebrow. "No news there. You two have words?"

"Something like that." Ben ran his hand through his hair, pulled it down over his face. "I guess you could say we don't see eye to eye."

"She's had a lot to deal with, Ben."

He nodded. "I do. I get it. This is something else, though." Ben toed a rock loose from the driveway with his boot. "Listen, you mind if I ask you a personal question?"

"Shoot."

"Do you believe in God?"

Without hesitation, Jimmy answered, "Absolutely."

"Absolute certainty? Just like that?"

"Well, yeah. That what you two were arguing about?"

"Wasn't arguing," Ben said sullenly. "Just her dropping me on my butt and walking away from us."

Jimmy had the decency to look sympathetic. Heck, maybe he was. The deputy reached out, grabbed Ben by the shoulder. "Look, man. She's had a lot to deal with over the last year. But what matters most to her is not giving ground on the issue she holds dearest to her heart. If she does, then everything has been in vain."

He wondered why he couldn't be the thing she cherished above all. Then he felt like an idiot for being jealous of a fictional spirit. Ben cleared his throat. "So, you're okay watching her place for a little while? I need a little space, time to clear my head."

Jimmy nodded. "I got it. I'll keep our girl safe from those vultures with cameras. Bo will be here at 7 to relieve me. She'll get twenty-four hour protection. With the press stalking her and our unwelcome trespasser lurking, well, let's just say I'm being overly cautious."

"I appreciate it."

"Don't worry. I've got it covered. Go think things through. But Ben, you better come to your senses quick-like. I don't like seeing her hurt."

Ben glanced back at the house, saw a lace curtain fall across the window. Cora had been watching the two of them talk. His body instinctively turned toward her, ached to hold and comfort her. Why was she chasing him away, giving up on what they have? He growled and flung himself into the truck, threw it into gear.

He brooded as he drove towards Cotton Springs, the breeze from the lowered window assaulting his face. It seemed he lost everyone he cared for, every single person who mattered. Except for Nan, and he almost lost her to a stroke. He felt like he was at the bottom of a well, beaten, looking up at a blissful sky above him, and there was no way to climb out of the slick-sided shaft.

Where did he go from here?

25

He parked on the road behind Nan's home on Main Street, a modest slate blue two-story with white painted shutters. A clothesline ran between the house and the detached garage, the narrow strip of lawn around the T-posts mottled brown and green. Two cheerful potted mums flanked the back door, sunny yellow blooms popping against the dusky tone of the house. He rapped twice on the door, then walked in, yelling as he entered.

"Nan! I'm home!"

"In the living room, dear," came the softer reply.

Annie had her feet up on the worn beige ottoman, a ball of red yarn by her side. Knitting needles clacked in a steady rhythm. Another skein of yarn, this one a pearly white, sat abandoned on the cushion beside her, with a crochet hook stabbed through an intricate square in progress. Nan rested the fearsome looking needles in her lap when he sauntered in the room.

"Come give you grandmother a smooch."

Chuckling, he replied, "Yes, ma'am." He jutted his chin in the direction of the project in her lap. "Whatcha working on?"

"Knitting you a hat for the winter, dear." He winced at the red yarn, brighter than a newly washed fire engine.

"Well, thanks. You didn't have to knit me anything."

"Nonsense. I need something to keep my hands busy. You're always fretting over me. Sit, Benjamin. You're hurting my neck, making me look up at you. How your mother ever birthed such a giant, I'll never know."

Annie Hayes was a wee thing, barely five feet tall since age had compressed her spine. Her green eyes shimmered beneath hair as white as a snowdrift. She resumed her knitting, the knuckles on her paper-skinned hands flexing and bending as she wove the yarn together in knots. Her right hand was only slightly slower. The effects of the stroke were hardly noticeable.

"Mom wasn't short," he said defensively. Ben remembered hugging his mother's long legs, peering up at her, amazed at her height.

"Well, she wasn't an Amazon either. You get it from your great-granddad, Earl."

"So you've said a few hundred times," Ben murmured.

"Nothing wrong with m' hearing, now is there?" She winked at him from a lined face.

"Nan?" a female voice called. "Who're you talking to?"

Nina—Beth—ambled into the room from the back hallway. "Ben? What are you doing here?"

"I could ask the same of you."

"Kids, knock it off." Nan reprimanded the two, looking from one to the other. "Don't make me get off this sofa."

"Sorry, Nan." Beth exhaled as she cocked her head and looked at her brother. "I thought you would be with Cora."

"It's a long story." Sullenness seeped past his defenses.

"Boy, sit down, and talk to your sister," Nan admonished. "Beth, park your butt and finish your granny square. It's not going to crochet itself."

"Yes, ma'am," the siblings said in unison. Beth looked up, gave him a smile.

"You need a haircut, young man," Nan said, peeking over her half-moon glasses.

"Shaggy." His sister grinned as the crochet wove in and out, knotting the pearly yarn.

Ben chose to ignore the jab. "Am I supposed to call you Beth now, after calling you Nina all my life?"

She rolled her eyes. "Yes, Ben. Please."

"All right. Just don't get feisty with me if I forget now and then. You can keep calling me Ben."

"Gotcha," she said with a snort. "Goober. What did you and Cora fight about?"

"Who said anything about arguing?"

"Why else would you be here at a time like this? She needs you, Ben."

"Agh! You females are all out to get me, I swear it!"

Nan piped up, not looking away from the looping yarn. "You better not hurt my girl. Cora's special."

Her girl, huh? Ben decided the only way to get them off his back was to tell the whole story, starting at the escape from the lumberjack games, and ending with his foot-dragging to Nan's back door.

Nan looked at Beth. "Poor Cora," his grandmother gushed. His sister gave him the stink-eye.

Irate, Ben stood. "Poor Cora?! What about me?"

"You can't fault a woman for standing on her beliefs, Benjamin," Nan said. "What would you say about a girl who dropped her faith, caved at the first sign of distress? No, she's the kind of woman you want. The kind who sticks to her guns, remains steadfast." Dropping the needles in her lap, his grandmother pinned him with the look that brooked no foolishness. She jabbed a finger in his direction. "She's the one you *need.*"

"What I *need* is a woman who doesn't swallow lies or allow herself to be brainwashed by half-baked myths and legends with no basis in reality!"

Nan pinned him with a narrowed stare. "And this is what your heart tells you?"

Beth leaned forward, the crochet forgotten. "Listen to me. Cora's a good woman. She helped me find my way, showed me the truth. Heck, she even gave me a Bible. Peace springs from belief, big brother. I know, because I've been where you are, and I know where I am now. There's no question God is real, and He loves me. Cora was my answer to prayer."

"You too?" he groaned. "I can't believe it. She's using you to get to me?"

The ball of white yarn hit him in the face before he could block it. "Are you kidding me? You pig-headed, selfish, self-centered...man!"

"Well, it's a little convenient," he shot back. "Don't you think?"

"This happened weeks ago, you big jerk! I didn't even know you two were seeing each other. She didn't know I was your sister!" Beth yelled.

"Kids, pipe down," Nan demanded. It was the tone which struck fear into the hearts of all her former students. "Ben, I love you. But you're an idiot."

"Nan!" he whined, even as Beth smothered a laugh. "Shut up, *Beth!*"

Setting her knitting aside, his grandmother rose, tottered over to the built-in bookcase. She plucked a leather-bound book off the shelf and returned to stand before him. Nearly eye to eye, Ben sitting and Nan standing, she passed him a worn leather-bound Bible.

"You've run away from this for long enough, young man. Be grateful I didn't whack you on the head with it. Your granddad read the Good Book daily. I expect you'll treat it properly. You call yourself a tracker?" When he nodded, she replied, "Good. There's truth in these pages, more important than anything on this forsaken earth. You seek out the truth. Read God's word, His love letter to us. Search your heart and listen close, because God speaks in a whisper. None of us are good enough, Benjamin. But God's mercy is never-ending."

He accepted the book, hefted it, eyed it askance. Such a little thing, but it weighed a ton. Ben wedged the book between his leg and the arm of the chair, anxious to get it out of his hands.

"So, *Beth*, why were you out at Cora's house?"

"Ben, you are absolutely insufferable. For your information, Mr. Noseypants, Ronnie and I want to start our family. We have tried for a year without success. Her experience as a midwife and physician is what brought me to her, but I think of Cora as a friend, now. She helped me through a pretty rough patch. It's my hope she'll deliver my baby, too."

For the next hour, they talked. Tensely, hesitant in the beginning, but loosening up as the minute hand wound around the clock. His shoulders transitioned from knotted to relaxed as the conversation steered away from Cora and her religion. Nan clicked her long needles together, and Beth had four squares stacked tidily beside her on the couch. His sister informed him the intricate squares were part of a baby afghan. The pearly white would go for either a boy or a girl, she pointed out. Ben found himself relaxing into his grandfather's plush chair. He listened more than talked.

Beth and Nan chatted incessantly, and he let himself slip away, his mind sliding to memories of his childhood.

As a boy, newly orphaned and taken in by his grandparents, he had terrorized the neighborhood. In no time flat, his name became synonymous with mischief, pranks and vandalism. The town paid the price for his anger, confusion and sadness. He uprooted dozens of planters on Main Street, stole gum and candy from the general store, and generally made a nuisance of himself.

Until the day he side-armed a smooth skipping stone through the plate glass window of the sheriff's office. Faster than a summer storm breaking, Sheriff Larrison laced his eight-year old hands behind his back, and locked him in a tight, barren cell. The sheriff wore his mean son-of-a-gun reputation as proudly as he did his crisp starched brown uniform and shined metal star. Ben had made the unfortunate decision to launch the rock about ten minutes after the barrel-chested sheriff decided to check in with the Cotton Springs deputies. The other lawmen in the area had tolerated Ben's outbursts for nearly two years, but the sheriff would have nothing to do with coddling a delinquent. One call to his grandfather and two hours in a jail cell straightened him out. Nan told him after his grandfather died that Pop had been willing to let him remain jailed overnight, or for however long it took for Ben to properly apologize for the offense.

Ben's grandfather and Sheriff Larrison shook on an agreement, and Ben spent the next three weeks cleaning the town, sweeping sidewalks, picking up litter, washing windows. Every day after school for an hour, and three hours each day of the weekend.

It was tough love, and he fumed with each piece of garbage he jammed into his sack. He held a grudge for months. But as an adult, Ben was grateful his grandfather had loved him enough to stop the self-destruction. Instead of dealing with the raw emotions of his parents' deaths, he had lashed out against those who loved and cared for him the most. It was easier to run than to face painful uncertainty.

Now, at thirty-five years old, he found himself lounging in his grandfather's recliner, and imagined he could smell his aftershave after all these years. The pressure in his chest built. He wanted to lash out, punch a wall, ignore the gentle camaraderie between his Nan and Beth. He couldn't help but feel like an elementary-school hooligan, out of control and bitter. Uncertain and frustrated.

Running away from love all over again.

***

Cora watched fireworks explode against an ebony sky. Brilliant sparkly reds, shimmering blues, strobing whites. Deep flickering purples, vivid flashing greens danced and drizzled over the tops of the yellow pines. The reverberating *boom-boom-BOOM-boom* echoed through the trees. The spectacular would have been clearer if she were sitting on a blanket in The Square, or lying in the open field by the school, but neither of those options held much appeal for her. More comfortable to sit in her front yard in a canvas lawn chair, than to face the gawkers and the press buzzards.

What a day. A morning spent with friends, celebrating the fiftieth birthday of her new country. Ben whisking her into his arms, making out like teens in the shadowy coolness, as breathless today as she was from the first kiss. And then out of nowhere, assault, confusion, paranoia. Ben abandoning her when she needed him the most.

Did she push him away? Yeah, maybe she did. Cora knew she was guilty of ignoring her conscience for the last few weeks. Every day spent with Ben was equal to another part of her heart she had laid at his feet. She was broken, shattered, in his absence.

As the replacement deputy, Bo Simmons, sat beside her, the brown of his uniform fading into the surrounding darkness, bitterness and depression hit like a tsunami. Bo was a nice man, but he wasn't the man she wanted with her tonight. She wondered what Ben was doing. Did he miss her, long to touch her face, caress her shoulders? Cora felt as though an organ had been ripped from her body, a physical hole that nothing but Ben could feel. Did he even miss her?

The *boom-BOOM!* pounded the air, resonating with her pulse. Each gorgeous light blossom in the sky was an explosion of her soul. Shimmering light flecks once a part of the whole, falling to the ground; the once dazzling fragments fading into coal black nothingness.

26

Monday, November 1, 2094
Bee Tree, Missouri District

Low, smoke-colored clouds scuttled across the afternoon sky. Bud Scallion slammed the cruiser door shut, activated the alarm and theft protection system. Beyond the two- and three-story brick and concrete buildings of downtown Bee Tree, the clouds were stacking themselves higher and thicker, looming overhead and bulging out across the horizon. From the parking lot behind the sheriff's station, Bud marched quickly across the pavement, turning up his collar against the harsh northern wind. Those clouds could mean snow, and doggone if the air didn't smell like snow was coming.

A gust of wind buffeted the building, thumping shut the rear door practically on his heels. Glad to be inside, he fixed his collar, walked down the hallway beneath bright halogen lighting.

Gene Holt looked up from his desk and flicked up his chin in greeting. How the man could find anything on the messy surface Bud would never know. Piles of paper were half-stacked, half-strewn across the desktop. Two dirty coffee mugs sat in one corner, while the one currently in use rested closer to Gene's hand.

"You know, Gene, all our cases and notes are in the system, right?" He grinned to take away the sting of his words.

"I like paper, Bud. You just don't appreciate my filing system," his messy officemate replied. He chewed the end of his pen. "Besides, the computer is always glitching. Not reliable in the least."

Under his breath, Bud retorted, "Operator error, huh?"

"I heard that."

Bud looked around the office. Nancy worked at the far side of the bull pen. Four other desks were equally spaced around the modest room, with barely enough space to walk between. The senior deputy was fortunate enough to get his own office, although it was nowhere near grand. Still, Bud coveted the privacy. He looked toward Wilkes' open office door.

"Gordon's out again, huh?"

Gene shrugged. Nancy spoke up from across the room. "He went up to St. Louis. Said he had to visit the district attorney's office to check on the progress of the extradition y'all got going on with the midwife."

"Why didn't he just conference call the D.A.?" Bud scratched his chin, a frown on his face.

Nancy rolled her eyes. "Who knows why the man does what he does nowadays. Ever since Missy passed, he's been a little..." Nancy twirled her finger in a circle near her temple. "Know what I mean?"

Bud agreed. Crazy, obsessed, just plain off. He understood mourning the loss of a loved one. He went through it a few years ago, when his girlfriend died from a brain tumor no one knew existed. Gordon's preoccupation was something else. Feral, bizarre, and alarming.

"Who's out on patrol?" Bud asked Nancy.

"Ryder. Daley is transporting an inmate to the county jail."

Bud ambled to the desk kitty-cornered from Gene, plopped down in the chair, leaned over and rested his forearms on his knees.

"Since Wilkes is out of the office, we need to have a talk." He brought Nancy into the conversation with a glance. "I've got a bad feeling about this alleged complaint against Miss Thomas. An itch between my shoulders I can't scratch."

Gene was nodding, and Nancy pounded the desk. She pointed at Bud. "I told Gene the same thing this morning, didn't I?"

"Yep. And I agree. Something weird about it."

Bud leaned back, kicked a heel up on the corner of his organized desk. "All right, so let's dig a little, find out more concerning this Natasha Smith. Either of you know any of Gordon's informants?" Nancy shook her head, and Gene shrugged. "Doesn't matter. Let's take a look at mug shots for the last few months. I know her printscan came up clean. She's a little too squeaky. Let's go back, say, six months. Narrowing the search field by age should help, but be sure to look past hair color and style. We need to match facial points, search aliases."

"I'll get in touch with my friend Shirley in St. Louis. She's in the dispatch office there, bless her heart. She'll keep an eye out for Gordon," Nancy offered. She was already click-clacking away at an email. "There, on the way. I'm telling you boys, Gordon's just not himself. I hope he's not planning something stupid. Especially with his son in the middle."

Gene snorted. He had four kids of his own. "The man has nothing to do with his son. I can count on one hand the number of times Gordon said the baby's name." He shook his head, disgust painting his features.

"I'll activate the tracking system on his cruiser, as a precaution. Remember, not a word of this to anyone else. Not even Ryder and Daley. They're too new to even understand the concern, and they'd tip him off. Man, I hate having to do this."

Surveillance on a fellow officer didn't sit well with Bud, made him feel like an internal affairs sneak, a State-funded mole. But Wilkes left them no option, and he was still one of them. They'd monitor it in-house as long as they could. He settled into his chair, watched the mug shot database scrolling one mugshot after another, front and side-views tumbling across the screen.

This was going to take a while.

***

The circus had come to town, and it was camped at the end of Cora's driveway. Dozens of reporters parked their satellite news vans and personal vehicles on the edge of her property. She slid the lace curtain to the window frame, but instantly regretted the peek. Several photographers began clicking away, and reporters waved insistently, demanding a statement. They wouldn't get one.

In the middle of the night, near 2:00 a.m., she had been awakened by the *bang-bang-bang* of pounding on her front door. Thinking it had to be the deputy guarding her place, she went to the door to let Bo inside, wiping crusty sleep from bleary eyes. Only, Bo wasn't the one knocking. Bo had drifted to sleep in his cruiser, and a too-perky-for-the-middle-of-the-night blonde reporter shoved a microphone in Cora's face while the cameraman filmed away.

The only thing Cora had to say to her was, "You're trespassing on private property. Leave, or I'll have you arrested." She slammed the door, knocking the microphone out of Perky's hand to land with a thud on the wooden front porch. She heard the unmistakable sound of the cruiser door closing, and Bo's deep voice as he escorted them away. Fully awake, shaking, she lurched back to bed, where she laid staring at the ceiling for an hour. She arose with the sun at 7:30,

213

stumbled to the kitchen to slurp on a piping hot mug of coffee. As her butt hit the dining chair, a knock sounded at the front. Growling, she stood and stalked to door, ready to dump the hot contents of her cup on whatever nosy reporter was standing there.

Instead, Jimmy's smiling face greeted her, and she chanced a glance past him to the media encampment near the road.

"Ugh," she mumbled, stepping aside and motioning for him to come in.

"Good morning to you, too, sunshine," he laughed. He carried his hat in one hand, and a rolled newspaper in the other.

"Let's just say I didn't sleep well. But your deputy did."

Jimmy winced. "About that. Bo feels awful terrible about falling asleep. He's a good man. Try not to take it out on him. He had the night shift the day before, but skipped sleep to go to the festivities in town."

Great, now she felt like a heel. She ran a hand through her riotous red curls, remembered she hadn't pulled it back yet. Oh well. What did he expect this early in the morning?

She nodded to the rolled newspaper. "Mine?"

"Yeah, it is, and Cora," he said gently, "you'll need to sit down."

"O-kay?" It came out more of a question than a statement.

They sat at the round dining table. He unrolled the periodical, and on the front page, near the bottom, was a photo of her and Ben, snuggled together watching *The Wizard of Oz* the Friday before. The photographer skillfully captured both them and the movie scene in the shot. The green face of the wicked witch snarled, frozen with the snap of the camera. The headline below it read: The Wicked Witch of Cotton Springs?

Cora's mouth gaped open, closed, open again. "Are you freaking kidding me, Jimmy?"

"I wish I were. I want to laugh because it's so outrageous, but I'm furious at the same time."

"This is a nightmare."

She read the sorry excuse for an article. The reporter had obtained detailed information about Missy, the delivery, and Gordon's accusations of witchcraft. Allegations and suppositions filled the small, three column report, the majority gossip and hearsay. There were claims she had enchanted a local man, Benjamin Tucker, with either spells or potions. More troubling was the vague quote from an anonymous local citizen.

"Listen to this," she said, grabbing Jimmy's arm. "'I've always had a strange feeling about the woman, like she was hiding something'. Unnamed source, huh? Coward!"

"None of your true friends would say such things."

She stood up, went to the kitchen to refill her mug. "You want some coffee?"

"Naw, thanks. I need to get back outside before one of those idiots decides to come onto your property again."

"I appreciate you bringing this to me. You're a good friend."

He put his hands on her shoulders, looked her square in the eye. "It'll pass. I know it's hard, but you've got a whole passel of friends looking out for you."

"He's behind all this, isn't he? Gordon, I mean."

"Probably."

She sighed. "It's so hard. I feel sorry for him, deep down. But right now, I'm so angry! I keep hoping something bad will happen to him for a change. And then I feel awful, because I know it's the wrong attitude. Gah!"

"Well, we'll do our best to keep you safe."

"Hey, I forgot to ask," she said, trying to lighten the mood. "How ever did you meet Sandy?"

He blushed, looked down at the floor. "Aw, well, it was kind of a blind date. You know Betty at the office?" Cora nodded. "Sandy is her cousin by marriage. Betty's always trying to set me up with someone, and every time she claims *this* time it's a perfect match." He chuckled. "Sandy's a bit … peppier than I'm accustomed to."

"Seemed like it," Cora laughed. "I wish you all the best. I'll get you some earplugs for a wedding gift." She winked at the deputy. He rolled his eyes.

"Speaking of dating. You hear from Ben today?"

"No, but it's a little early, still. Honestly, I don't think he'll call."

"Give him some space. I think God's working him hard. He's stressed."

"Mae warned me about him, and I just didn't listen."

"You listened with your heart, Coraline."

And look where it got me, she thought.

27

Five patients occupied time slots in her appointment book for the day. By three in the afternoon, four had canceled. A local woman, Georgia Pickens, seven months pregnant with her third child, showed up with a bouquet of daisies and a big hug of encouragement. She felt awful that Georgia had to plow through the knot of reporters at the road to get to her house, but the genial woman waved it off when Cora apologized.

"Don't worry about a thing, Doc. You're a wonderful person who's just going through a rough patch. You hang in there. Besides," she confided with a wink, "if they mess with me I have no problem plowing right through them."

Listening to the rapid *thump-thump* of the baby's heart was the highlight of Cora's day. The cheerful yellow daisies in a vase on her desk helped to spread a bit of sunshine, too.

Another deputy, one she hadn't met, replaced Jimmy around four o'clock, but the press vultures had begun to thin, losing interest when they realized Cora planned to remain inside. At least, she hoped it was the reason. The woods surrounding her home provided enough cover should any of the leeches want to violate her privacy from another angle. The last thing she wanted was more trespassing on her land.

She paced the house a hundred times, back and forth between the rooms, tidying and reorganizing, preparing meals and freezing them, doing loads of laundry. She tried to read, but couldn't focus on the story. She tossed the book on the coffee table with a frustrated grunt. A nap sounded wonderful, but sleep evaded her, despite the exhaustion from the interruptions the previous night. The one reprieve had been Georgia's monthly checkup, a brief flash of happiness in an otherwise groan-worthy day.

Cora was bored. Not only bored, but antsy, crabby. She craved air, sunshine. Determined to taste the fall air, she laced up her boots, walked out the rear kitchen door. Rusty needed some attention. Feeding and grooming the horse would do wonders for her mood.

With a curry brush in one hand, and a bucket of feed dangling from the other, Cora entered the little paddock attached to the side of the faded red barn. She whistled for Rusty. The mare wasted no time galloping to the enclosure. Cora hummed as she brushed the horse. Rusty bobbed her long face up and down, as if she appreciated the rock-a-billy tune. Handfuls of russet colored hair littered the ground. First day of November, and Rusty was already thickening her winter coat.

Cora put away the feed bucket, hung the curry brush back on its nail, and was ankle deep in mucking out the barn when she heard someone calling her name urgently. She poked her head out of the white-trimmed red door, leaned against the shovel with her hip cocked.

She cupped her other hand around her mouth and hollered. "Over here, Jimmy!"

Red-faced and flustered, the deputy stomped back to the barn. "Cora, you scared the mess out of me! You weren't in the house."

Shrugging, she apologized. "Sorry. I was getting cabin fever, had to get outside on this gorgeous day. And I am sick of being controlled by someone else."

"Well, next time leave a note or let the deputy guarding you know. I just tore into Scott for not paying attention on his watch."

Abashed, her cheeks colored. "I didn't even think of it. I'll do something nice for him to make up getting reamed on my behalf. So," she joked, "miss me already?"

"Ha ha, funny lady. I wanted to bring this out to you in person, rather than showing you on screen."

He held out an 8 x 10 photo of a man, scraggly hair stringy with oil, faced lined by age and sun.

"Recognize him?"

"Yes! From Mae's front yard, the day Dabney got hurt! Where did you get the picture?"

"DNA and prints came back. Rupert Gallow, age 33, resident of Imperial, Missouri."

Floored, Cora shifted her gaze between the photo and Jimmy's face. "I've don't recognize him. And from my home town?"

He nodded, sliding the photo back into its protective envelope. "No warrants out for him, just a misdemeanor about a decade ago. You sure you don't know the guy?"

"Positive. It has to be someone spying on me for Gordon, don't you think?"

"All I know for sure is he's over here illegally. Which means, when we find him, we can arrest him for illegal entry."

"Have you shown this to Ben? Checked to see if he's the guy from the diner, just to be sure?"

Jimmy took off his hat, scratched his head, replaced the hat. "Couldn't find him to ask him. Dixie said it's our guy, though. You haven't talked to Ben?"

She shook her head. "He doesn't want to talk to me. I'm crazy and delusional, remember?"

"Aw, come on now, Coraline. He's a man with a thick skull and a hard heart. He'll come around."

"So you keep saying."

"Well, at the least we have a name to a face, and all local business owners will get a copy of this photo. He'll be in handcuffs soon, mark my words. It's progress."

Cora walked with Jimmy around the front of the house. Two die-hard members of the press staked out her driveway, but the rest had bailed and went in search of another story. Or, at least, she hoped. She lifted a hand in farewell as Jimmy drove away, narrowly avoiding the toes of the two nosy reporters. Cora stifled a laugh.

Scott Marcus leaned against the hood of his cruiser, reading a something on a paper-thin viewscreen. She course-corrected and veered toward the officer, instead of the porch.

"Hey Scott, sorry about Jimmy's scolding. I was out at the barn. I should have let you know, though. Won't happen again."

"Don't worry about it all, Mrs. Thomas," he drawled. His thick country accent drew the Mrs. out like Mizz. "This here's the easiest gig I've had in a while."

"Mind if I take a peek at your reader, there?" She tipped up her chin to indicate the gizmo in his hand.

"Not at all. It's sweet, ain't it?" His voice was like cold honey sliding down a Mason jar. Liquid sweet, and slow. "My wife gave it to me for my birthday. Check this out!"

He rolled it into a thin tube. It kind of resembled an old fashioned scroll, but it stayed closed without any visible restraints.

"How come it doesn't flop open?"

"There's a tiny magnetic strip built inside. It holds the edge in place once it's rolled. So small you can't even see it with the naked eye. And see?" He flicked the edge, and the screen opened up smoothly, laid perfectly flat. He tapped the lower left corner lightly, and the home screen flashed to life.

"Incredible! I have to get one of these!"

She brought Scott a glass of sweet tea, then busied herself inside making supper. She threw two juicy steaks on the grill outside, tossed a green lettuce and spinach salad, and baked a couple of monstrous potatoes. They enjoyed a quiet meal inside, away from the unwanted attention of the media. As thanks for feeding him, Scott let Cora play around with his new reader. Not only was it a reader, but it was a complete computer system with wireless capabilities. Cora cringed at how behind the times she was. She had a viewscreen system on her desk. But at half an inch thick, it seemed a clunky dinosaur compared to the deputy's toy. Even the flexible keyboard she used seemed ancient. Scott's projected an infrared keyboard on whatever surface the sheet was placed, whether on a desk or the hood of a police cruiser. She rolled the thin sheet into a tube again, noticing the name on the outside. *Papyrus*. Interesting. It definitely made her think of a scroll.

As Cora rounded up the dishes, Scott smacked his head. "Dang, hang on. I forgot something in the car. Be right back."

She rinsed off the plates and glasses, loaded them into the dishwasher. The screen door slammed shut and the front door clicked closed.

"Good news from the circus front. Looks like the media has given up. Your mailbox is safe again." He held out a small wrapped package.

She exhaled, relieved. "That *is* good news. What's in the box?"

"Jimmy asked me to give this to you earlier, before he found you in the barn. We scanned it, came back clean. No name on the return, though."

Cora shucked off the thick brown exterior wrapping, and opened up the simple white box. Inside was a wrist communicator, its silvery shine gleaming. Folded into a small square was a note.

Cora,
You need a new communicator, so don't argue. I'll be in touch soon. Just need to figure some things out.
Love,
Ben

A sad smile crossed her face as she fingered the note. Inside the box nestled what appeared to be a simple, yet elegant, silver watch, with Roman numerals around the larger watch face. The round dial slid aside to reveal a sophisticated operating system, and two small diamond stud earrings.

"Hey, now who's got the fancy toys? Impressive. Someone must like you."

"I don't even know how this doohickey works!"

"There's instructions at the bottom of the box. Man, my wife will be so jealous!"

For the rest of the evening, Cora fiddled with her new gadget. The deputy made himself comfortable outside in his cruiser, no doubt fiddling with the *Papyrus* reader. She discovered Ben had already preprogrammed a few contacts. His number, as well as his grandmother's, the Crocketts, and the sheriff's office. After half an hour of lip chewing and growling under her breath, a few more numbers were stored. The earrings, it turned out, were wireless receivers and transmitters. She test-called Scott and Jimmy. Both agreed the reception and transmission was flawless.

Ben claimed she was a puzzle to him, but she thought the feeling was mutual. Maybe there was still hope for them. Hesitantly, she spoke into to the communicator.

"Call Ben." Her cheeks flushed at the silliness of talking to a watch.

Rather than the call tone, his voicemail immediately answered. She ended the call rather than leaving a message. She would end up sounding as desperate as felt.

Before snuggling into bed, she padded down the hallway in her pajamas and fuzzy slippers. A singer from the early twentieth century, Billie Holiday, crooned softly from the sound system. Though many modern artists were trying their hands at the sweet, soulful sound, none came close to the original. She intended to shut down her viewscreen for the night, but noticed the little blip which indicated a new email.

John, her brother, sent his greetings, with a short message. Their mother was healing well, but still in a sling for the broken collarbone. Two investigators had interviewed him and their parents about a complaint filed against her. She detected the concern in the tone of his writing, and made a note to reassure him everything was fine. Cora hated to lie to him, but she didn't want him to worry. Besides, what could he do from Missouri? No, it wouldn't serve any purpose to have him know Gordon had once again set out on his witch hunt.

Cora typed out a brief reply, hit send, shut down the slim computer. She flicked off the lights in each room as she walked through her home, snatched the book off the low table in the center of the living room. Through her bedroom speakers, Lady Day crooned of how she loved her man. Still humming along, she muted the track.

The occasional cricket chirped low outside her window in the cool November night. In the narrow space between the curtain panels she glimpsed stars winking alongside gray clouds as they mingled in the pewter dark sky. She snuggled into bed, book in hand, the bedside lamp spilling mellow gold light in a puddle on the floor.

Before she finished a page, Cora was asleep, dreaming of Ben's arms around her.

28

Ten days slogged by, each day more difficult for Cora than the one before. Though not all of her patients were no-shows, she had more cancellations than kept appointments. Too many days like this, and she would need to consider other employment options. The clinic addition had sapped her savings.

A morose November rain fell in sheets outside her window. Little beads of water snaked down the clear glass panes. As children, she and her brother would pick two drops and guess which would slide down first, winning the race. No lightning flickered, no thunder boomed. Just a good old fashioned downpour. If it hadn't rained for the last four days, Cora would have enjoyed it more. However, mucking through the soggy, slippery mud to do her outside chores was getting old, and she was growing irritable with all the time spent in the house.

Rusty was fed and dry, housed in the stable. Every glass pane in the house sparkled, not a speck of dust remained on the furniture. Floors gleamed and smelled of orange oil. Vegetable soup simmered on the stove for supper in a few hours, and fresh bread dough was rising in a bowl on the counter. Hand on her hips, Cora wondered what else needed to be done.

In the exam room, she noted her supply of antibiotic ointment was diminishing. Relieved she could do something productive, she gathered a few neatly labeled jars and a block of beeswax in her arms, and strolled back to the kitchen.

She flicked on the radio for background noise. The hum of the falling rain on the roof made her want to take a nap, but she had slept enough the last few days. Austin had become the Nashville of Texas, and all new music had its roots in the country's capital. She recognized the song. The Hillbillies were one of her favorite bands. Their songs had the twang of country, mixed with some indie drums, and a killer bass guitar. Tapping her foot along with the beat, she grated a couple ounces of the beeswax. She combined it with the coconut oil simmering on low heat in her double boiler.

Cora joined in with the chorus, belting out the lyrics as she shook her hips and added vitamin E oil, a little bit of tea tree oil, and a few drops of lavender and lemon essential oils. No sooner had she added the last droplets than the call screen at the end of the counter flashed and the little alarm sounded, automatically muting the radio to a barely noticeable chatter in the background. She slung a hand towel over her shoulder and spoke to the screen. "Answer, video on."

Beth's face appeared on the screen. She dabbed at her nose with a tissue, and her eyes were red-rimmed and puffy.

"Oh, good, you're home." Beth sniffled and wiped again, plastered a smile on her blotchy face.

"What's wrong, Beth? Are you hurt?"

Ben's sister blew her nose, rolled her eyes. "I should have left the video off. Oh well. I just needed to talk to someone."

"Hang on a sec." Cora grabbed a barstool. "Okay, I'm set. Lay it on me. What's got you down? Baby stuff?"

She waved her petite hand in dismissal. "No, not that. I will say, however, Ronnie did not like the *not* practicing until prime time. But let me tell you what … those three days were pretty amazing. Fingers crossed! I'll know in a week or two."

"Well, since it's not baby-making blues, what's going on?"

"Ben. My brother makes me so angry!"

Cora chuckled sadly. "I know what you mean. He hasn't called, written, come by the house. The only contact, if you could call it such, was him leaving me a new communicator at the sheriff's station and them delivering it." She held her wrist up to the screen, and Beth let out a low whistle.

"Nice! Proof he's not a complete imbecile, I guess."

"He's still a man. Hardheaded and stubborn."

"Preaching to the choir. We fought, Ben and I. We've been doing so well, trying to get along and make peace with one another. And I won't lie and say it's been easy. I've tried putting myself in his shoes, attempted to see things through his eyes."

"Let me guess," Cora replied, eyes narrowed. "You mentioned God and he flared up?"

"Yes! Agh! Why is he so obstinate?"

"Honestly, I think God's doing a number on Ben's conscience. It's hard to sit back and do nothing, but Beth, I think the only thing we can do for him is pray."

"I know. I guess I pushed too hard."

"Been there and done that a couple of times."

"Yeah, well, he's gone."

Cora blinked. "Gone?"

Beth nodded. "Gone. Left. Accepted a contract and is on his way now."

"You have got to be kidding me!"

"It's his way of dealing with things. At least this time, he checked with Nan first and made sure she was okay with him ducking out for a few days. Told her he needed space, wanted to clear his head and think about things."

Cora chewed the edge of her bottom lip, then realized her old habit had crept up on her. She ceased nibbling, began tapping her foot instead.

"Anyway," Beth said, "I wanted to let you know he was out of town, in case you were looking for him."

"I'm sorry the two of you fought. Sorry he felt like he had to run. I still feel like it's my fault he's not here."

"Nonsense. He knew your feelings from the beginning, right? Well, he should realize how difficult it was for you to stand up for your faith despite how much you love him."

Eyes wide, Cora spluttered, nearly fell off the stool. "L-Love him?" She shook her head. "No, I like him a lot. I care for him deeply. But I'm not in love with Ben."

Beth rolled her eyes. "Oh, come on. I know love when I see it. And he loves you. He's being a big old baby about it. You're perfect for each other. Both hardheaded stubborn." She laughed.

"Whatever. I *can't* love him. But … would you call me if you hear from him again? I worry too much when he's not here."

"You got it." Beth stared at her a moment too long with a smirk on her face. "Pah! You don't love him. Don't worry, girl. Your secret is safe with me. Talk to you later."

Cora found herself dazed, mechanically standing in front of the stove chewing on Beth's statement. Mentally shaking herself, she focused on her work. She stirred the melted oils with a wooden skewer and turned off the flame, gathered a few of her sterilized stubby amber jars and laid them out, tops off. Cora listened with half an ear to the music on the radio. As she poured the liquid ointment into the jars, the melodic jingle announcing the news sounded.

President Nicolas Titus, along with six other heads of state, was scheduled to attend a summit meeting in Washington, D.C. concerning the adoption of a universal currency.

Could she be in love? The thought was scary, terrifying.

A Texas Ranger was found beaten in a ravine off the highway, clothed only in his underwear near Beaumont, and was being treated for extensive wounds and exposure.

When Cora was away from Ben, like these last couple of weeks, her heart felt empty, incomplete. Is this what love felt like? She'd had boyfriends in the past, but none in the last decade because it interfered with her studies. Never had she felt for another man what she felt for Ben.

Mudslides in the hill country near New Braunfels had claimed the lives of two teenagers who had been camping. Names were being withheld until positive identifications were made and the parents were notified.

With the last cap screwed onto its container, Cora placed her hands on the counter, looked out the window at the curtain of rain obscuring her view.

Aloud, she said to the rain, "I love Ben Tucker." Great. Now what?

***

Nancy wedged the pen behind her ear, flicked off the call screen, tapped her fingers on the desk. Bud Scallion sat behind his own meticulously organized aluminum desk, pecking out the final report on a recent B&E. Gene Holt was out on patrol, as was one of the newbies. The other rookie was home sick with the flu. The dispatch office was quiet, a squawk here and there punctuating the stillness.

"Still no hits on the woman?" Nancy inquired.

Bud shook his head, leaned back in his chair. "I went back ten months, but I'll dig deeper. I don't know, Nancy. I could be chasing a phantom, but this hunch won't let up."

For the last week Gordon had ghosted in and out of the office. Nancy noted each unauthorized patrol, every hour without a check-in.

"Sheriff called. Wilkes is officially on vacation."

Bud snorted. "No kidding. The boys are tired of picking up his slack."

"Well, at least now we don't have to worry about him traipsing in while we're digging behind his back."

Nancy jumped, put a hand to her ear. "Go ahead, Gene." She paused listening, her eyes widening.

"Can I put you on speaker?" She paused. "Okay, you're on. Just me and Bud in the office, so repeat what you told me."

His voice was clear, crisp. "Drove by the corner where the unlicensed escorts linger, and lo and behold, who do I see but our girl Natasha. They scattered like a grenade had landed in the middle of them when they saw my cruiser, but it was her. I reviewed the film. Let's narrow the search to unlicensed prostitution, see what we get."

"You remember how tall she was? Might help."

"Five two, five three. I'm almost back at the station. Holt, out."

Nancy scooted the rolling chair, click-clacked on her heels over to Bud's desk. She leaned over his shoulder as the mug shots scrolled across the screen.

"Wait! Go back. There!" She jabbed a red-painted nail at the screen.

Bud nodded. "There's our girl. Let's pull her up. Hmmm. Natalie Ann Munson, a.k.a. Leelee Anson, a.k.a. Natasha Manson. Looks like we can add another alias, huh? Prior convictions. Who-wee. Natasha, you're a busy girl. Unlicensed prostitution, document forgery, unauthorized possession of a stun gun."

Gene walked through the door. "What've we got? You two look like cats in the cream."

Nancy pointed to Bud's screen. "Our girl's got a record. Someone has fiddled with her file, too, because none of this popped when we scanned her for the statement."

"Scooch over, Bud. Let me work my magic."

Gene's fingers flew over the keyboard, seemingly typing in nonsense which ended with a dramatic final key.

Eyebrows near his hairline, Bud stared dumbfounded at his colleague. "What in the world?"

Gene pointed at the screen. "Ha! Look. See anything different?"

"Well, I'll be."

There, below the prior convictions section, was a full warrants section.

"How did we not see this before?" Nancy asked.

"It was fixed, altered." A few more keystrokes, and a photo appeared on the screen. "And this is who did it."

Bud sighed. "I hate it when I'm right."

"I'll call the district attorney, let him know to stop the extradition application." Nancy stalked over to her desk, her heels clacking against the hard tile floor.

Gene looked at Ben. "Question is, who's bringing in Wilkes?"

29

Ben anguished over the decision to accept the contract, but he needed some space to think, to breathe. To be alone and figure out what the heck was happening. Life was a tornado and he was a leaf, caught up in the whirlwind.

Buying the truck was one of his better decisions. He sped down the highway, the windshield wipers whisking away the deluge bucketing from a steel gray sky. The bounty contract was for a parolee, Devon Watts, a no-show with his parole officer for an entire month. Though not a violent criminal, the felon was convicted for cybercrimes, including identity theft, robbery, and forgery. The bounty was set at a hefty amount for his recovery. The man had stolen millions, but they could only prove a small portion of it in court. Luckily for Ben, cyber-cons rarely covered their physical trails as well as their hack tracks.

Early yesterday he had stopped into the sheriff's office to check in with Jimmy, go over new developments in Cora's case. The affable deputy was more than happy to update Ben. And berate him for not being with her.

The stalker had vanished, like warm breath in the cold night air. Ben remained certain, however, the stranger—no, he had a name now, Rupert Gallow—lurked, watching for an opportunity. No business owners reported him patronizing their establishments.

Jimmy believed Gallow got spooked and bolted, his tail between his legs. Ben disagreed.

Wilkes, likewise, had ceased contact with Cora, and the precinct in Missouri reported the deputy taking vacation. The threatening note Cora received weeks ago appeared to be the words of an unstable man letting off steam. Media attention trickled to nothing, once the initial explosion on Independence Day settled. For days, the newspaper ran speculative articles featuring rumors and suppositions, but interest wavered, then faded. Jimmy suggested pulling Cora's protection detail, and she agreed, giving the authorization for the continued surveillance to come to a halt. Ben read each notation in her file, the lines of his forehead coming together in a frowning V. Based on evidence, the menace surrounding Cora had fizzled. Off the record, Jimmy confirmed Cora's patient load dwindled to a few faithful patients, and Beth told him that while Cora appeared strong, the slight from the community stung her pride.

Ben questioned the wisdom of getting information about Cora from secondhand sources like law enforcement, but he refused to get into another philosophical debate with the woman, no matter how tight she held his heart. He would continue to look in on her from afar, talking to Jimmy and Beth for updates. It was the best he could do until he figured out what to do with her.

And his sister. Beth. To him, her name was Nina and had been for over thirty years. Calling his sister by another name was both foreign and frustrating, but he would do it if it meant mending the fences he destroyed in the past. And yet, last night he and Beth had argued yet again. Nan had thrown her hands in the air and huffed to her room when the quarrel burned hot and mediation proved impossible. The slamming door down the hall let the siblings know just how irritated his elderly grandmother was.

His thoughts drifted to their argument as he skimmed the asphalt toward Austin, the last known location of his fugitive. Rain sheeted off the tempered windshield, reminding him of Beth's tearful pleas the night before.

"Beth, just leave it alone! I don't want anything to do with a mythical higher being who did absolutely nothing to prevent our parents from being killed. Do you hear me?"

She had ignored him, of course. "If you would just open your heart, read the Bible that Nan gave you. I promise, God is so much bigger than any of these problems we have in life."

"What would you know of problems?"

Tears filled her eyes. "You have no idea the things I've been through. Alone, because you deserted us. I needed you and you weren't there!"

"Needed me for what? You had it so easy growing up. Friends who supported you, homecoming queen, college scholarships, a good marriage and a successful business. What has been so hard about that? Huh?!"

"I killed my baby!" Her hand flew to cover her mouth as the tears poured over her high cheekbones. In a barely audible whisper, she repeated herself. "I killed my child."

Struck dumb, Ben slumped, stared over her shoulder at the painted landscape hung on the wall. Seconds ticked by, a minute. Beth asked, "Ben?"

"What are you talking about?"

She asked him to recall the time he came home on leave after the end of his first enlistment, to the conversation overheard at the bar.

He remembered it well. It was the reason he deserted the family, abandoned Cotton Springs and everyone in it.

Tears streamed from his sister's eyes, but she kept her voice low and soft. "Three weeks after you left, I found out I was pregnant. I was terrified, but I loved him. Thought we would get married. Instead, he threw money at me, told me to get rid of it. Our baby." She hiccupped through the tears. "I did. I had an abortion. You're the only one I've told, Ben. Even Ronnie doesn't know. Neither does Nan." She peered down the hallway to their grandmother's closed bedroom door.

"Why are you telling me this?"

She swiped her hand across her face. "Because you need to know God has forgiven me for it. It haunted me every day. Still does," she admitted. "I'm working on letting go of the guilt, the shame. But God has shown me mercy. What did I do to deserve his love? Absolutely nothing! And yet, He loves me still. I deserve to die, judged guilty of murder and all the other bad things I've done throughout my life. But Jesus paid the price for all my incredible screw-ups." She reached out a hand, gripped his tight. "Ben, He loves you so much. No matter what, mercy and grace await you. All God asks is that you repent and ask His forgiveness."

"No. No! This just proves my point. A loving God would never allow babies to be killed, allow women to face that decision. I'm done. I have to leave, breathe. Get out of here and figure out what to do next. Will you be here for Nan if she needs help?"

Beth nodded, still crying, but thrust a pleading hand at him. "Please. Talk to Cora! She's a good woman. Without her help, I don't know where I'd be. Still hopeless."

And he ran, like always. Stopped by the station to pick up the contract, then home to pack a few days' worth of clothes and toiletries. Beth was gone, and his grandmother scolded him as he zipped the ditty bag. His sister had ridden home in the rain, and his grandmother laid the blame at his feet. Nan wanted to know why the two of them couldn't get along, act as adults rather than children. An inner voice acknowledged the veracity of his grandmother's criticism. He told his conscience to shut up.

Nan's stroke had rushed him home, the dread of losing his grandmother driving him back to Cotton Springs. Then, the chainsaw accident tossed Cora smack-dab into his life. Even as his wound healed, he felt his heart doing the same. Healing. And then, the whole issue of deity, constantly swirling around him, threatening to uproot everything he thought to be truth. His heart desired to grasp Cora tight and never let go, to protect her from harm. He yearned to discover what she looks like in the morning, just as the sun climbs past the horizon and floods the bedroom with light. She pulled at him, a force stronger than the tides, more powerful than gravity. And yet, he fled, desperate to avoid answering the questions plaguing him even now, as the asphalt glided beneath wet tires, the wipers thumping out a rhythm against the steady smack of the rain.

Could Cora be right? Is there a God? And if God exists, what does it mean for him? For the first time in his life, Ben doubted. He doubted himself. No matter how he wished for it, the barely audible voice in his head wouldn't go away.

He needed this trip, to distract himself with the contract, track this cyber-con, apprehend and convey him to the authorities. Use the time to think, to clear his head.

Jimmy assured him Cora was safe. The deputy continued to send patrols out to her house, despite the termination of official surveillance. Even the forest rangers had been alerted to monitor the back side of her land, where the National Forest boundary kissed the property line. Plus, she had the new communicator he had given her. No, Cora was fine. Safe.

He shoved away the memory of his promise to her, that no one would harm her or touch her, nudged the guilt aside and drove towards Austin, with the smatter of raindrops and a bluegrass station to keep him company.

She wouldn't even miss him.

***

Dixie kneeled behind the high counter, filling her arms with napkin-wrapped stainless steel utensils. She peeked over at the tinkling of the bell, tipped her chin at the newcomer. "Find a seat wherever you like, hon'. I'll be right over."

She dumped the awkward load on the countertop, grabbed a menu and sashayed over to the newcomer. He sat in the booth, facing the door. Outside the window a curtain of rain obscured the view of the street. On the table, the man's steel coffee thermos sat beside the salt and pepper shakers. His hat occupied the space beside him, his shorn head sprouting a silvery gray sprinkle of new growth. His full goatee was mostly silver, with a few brown and black clumps mixed in. Despite the gray, he looked younger, maybe in his forties. Definitely built, she appraised.

"Want me to freshen up your coffee there?" She smiled brightly to counteract the gloom outside.

He wrapped his hand around the base of the silver cylinder, shook his head. "No, thank you. I'm kind of particular about my drink. You understand, right?"

"Sure thing, sugar. Here's a menu, and I'll be back in a few to get your order."

"What's the special?" he asked before she could turn, his voice a little gravelly.

"Chicken fried steak, green beans and mashed potatoes. Or you can have a salad instead of the taters."

"Sounds perfect."

Dixie returned to the counter, slipped the order ticket in the pass-thru for the cook to grab. She filled a glass of ice, added water, picked up a paper-wrapped straw.

Besides the newcomer, only two other tables were occupied. The rain the last few days kept most of the locals in their own kitchens. The other patrons swam in the door, drenched head to toe despite the umbrellas they carried. This one, though. He was damp, but not soggy. And since she'd never seen him before, she was fairly certain he had a vehicle outside in the parking lot.

He removed his leather jacket just as she brought the glass of water to the table. "Now I know you didn't ask for it, but I brought you some water, just in case."

The man nodded his thanks. "Appreciate it."

"What kind of badge is that?" She pointed to the silver emblem on his belt. "If you don't mind me asking."

The star within a circle gleamed beneath the overhead lights. "Texas Rangers."

"I knew it! See? All my screen time paid off for something. Hey, what brings you to town?"

"Work. Just passing through."

Eyes wide, Dixie asked, "Does this have anything to do with the Ranger found beaten near Beaumont?"

Taking a sip of water, the officer nodded. "Yes, ma'am. Sure does."

"I bet you're investigating it, huh? Oh, oh!" She wiggled a little jig. "This is just like the shows on-screen."

"Yep, I'm a part of the enquiry."

"Wait 'til I tell Stella I met a real Texas Ranger!"

"Well, now, I know it's exciting. But to be honest, we need to keep this as quiet as we can. Think of it as helping out federal law enforcement, aiding the investigation. If the assailant is in the area, we wouldn't want him to know anything, would we?"

Her eyes climbed her forehead. "Your secret is safe with me, mister." She sealed the deal with a slow, deliberate wink.

"Order up!" belted from the kitchen, and she retrieved his loaded plate.

"Enjoy. Best chicken fried steak in the county."

The Ranger held her attention captive even as she serviced the other tables. He sipped on his coffee thermos, acting like he got a little too much down the pipes, wincing and whatnot. Had to have been some piping hot joe to make him cringe like he was swallowing fire.

She bussed tables, and cashed out the other patron, pocketed the tip. When she turned back around, the Ranger was standing at the register, his hat on his head and wearing his damp leather jacket. The thermos dangled from one hand.

"Much obliged. Food was good. Remember. Our little secret."

He ducked out the door, and into the flood.

***

Neither Dixie nor the Ranger noticed the man with oily, stringy hair standing across the street, dry beneath the red awning of the junktique store. As soon as the lawman was around the corner and headed to the vehicle lot, the man across the street dashed out into the rain, his faded and worn boots splashing as he ran down the sidewalk, headed north.

30

Scott Marcus pocketed the receipt, winked at the cashier. "Thanks, Margie."

"My pleasure, deputy. How's your mutt doing, anyhow?"

"Growing like the nettles in my pasture," he laughed, hefting the 50-pound sack of dog food, and throwing it over his damp shoulder. "Good thing he's part Labrador with all this rain the last few days."

Margie nodded through the open garage door to the loading dock. "At least it's finally letting up. Otherwise, we'll all need boats and waders."

Over his shoulder, Scott called, "See you next week, Marg. Tell your mama I said hello." His pickup—well, the county's pickup—was backed up to the loading dock of the feed store. He tossed the large sack into the bed of the truck, jumped down off the waist-high concrete ledge, landing with a splash. Margie was right. The incessant rain had slowed to a sprinkle. Maybe after four days the clouds had plum run out of water.

Scott steered the unmarked black truck out of the lot onto Highway 58, headed north toward home in the drizzle, tires whisking and hissing on the blacktop. Above him and on the horizon the clouds broke apart, the late evening sun making a watery appearance. A quarter of a mile down the road, Scott noticed a man running along the left lane, his checkered shirt and jeans plastered to his scrawny body, long hair dripping from the ends and plastered to his forehead. The deputy slowed to offer the pedestrian a ride.

The soggy man stared at the off-duty deputy with wide eyes, the whites shining in the dusky light, but faster than Scott could blink, the guy hung a hard left and trotted off into the thick tree line. He slowed the truck even more, pulled to the shoulder, and engaged his wrist communicator.

"Dispatch, Marcus. Over."

"This is dispatch. Go ahead, Scott," a familiar female voice responded.

"Betty, get Jimmy over here to Cora's place. Our stalker just veered off the highway into the woods near her property. I need back-up."

"10-4, Scott. Standby." He knew Betty loved it when she got to man the dispatch control station. "All right, Scott. Jimmy's three minutes out."

Cursing, Scott growled, "Tell him to make it two. Marcus, out."

Scott pulled onto the highway. Thickets and briars shadowed the ground beneath the trees on both sides of the road, hindering visibility. The consolation was it would be hard for their stalker, Gallow, to push through the undergrowth with any significant speed. In the rearview mirror, he noticed headlights drawing nearer, saw them flick on and off once, twice. Scott, and Jimmy in the cruiser behind him, slowed as they neared Cora's driveway, less than half a mile past the point where the suspect darted into the trees.

The shower had petered out to less than a drizzle, more like a misty fog. Scott slammed shut the truck door, strode back to Jimmy's cruiser as the other deputy was exiting his vehicle. Both men looked back towards town as the skimming hiss of wet tires approached. A blue all-terrain vehicle slowed. The driver, a middle-aged man with a silver goatee, stared, but continued north along the highway.

"Let's go in on foot," Jimmy suggested as the vehicle passed. "Her driveway isn't long, and if Gallow sees our vehicles he may be less likely to approach the house. We need to get him while he's clearly on her land."

Scott nodded. "Agreed. Should we call Cora, let her know?"

"I'll take care of it."

Jimmy reached Cora on his communicator as they crossed Highway 58. Their boots crunched on the wet gravel of the drive, rubber soles squelching in the saturated red clay.

"She agreed to stay in the house."

They took their positions, one where the open yard met the pines and oaks, the other hidden by the barn.

***

Cora watched as the two lawmen settled in to wait for this Rupert fellow who was so intent on destroying her solace. Finally, she would get some peace. Never before had she wished someone would trespass on her land and threaten her, but today she did. The deputies stood by, ready to haul him in for questioning. She craved answers as well.

She paced the living room, sneaking peeks out the front window even as the light dimmed outside. The sun displayed diluted rays through breaks in the clouds, letting the waterlogged people of Cotton Springs know he was still around, ready to shine again. Was it corny to hope her life could be the same? Storms turned to sunshine, new possibilities beaming from the dreary and woeful.

Minutes turned into half an hour, forty-five minutes, then an hour. Darkness descended, and with it came zero visibility of the men outside, lying in wait for Gallow. Cora settled into her sofa, kicked her feet up on the coffee table. She slumped in dejection, thinking it was too good to be true that the man would be caught red-handed.

Light flooded the side yard. She tensed, aware of movement close enough to engage the motion-activated security light. When he called earlier, Jimmy told her to act as normal as possible, so the man would get close enough to the house for them to circle behind him. Wondering which window the man would use to stare at her—she shivered in discomfort—she picked up the heavy photography book, thumbed through the pages. Just another quiet night at home, she pretended. Nothing to see here, nothing at all.

Yells broke through the night. She heard Jimmy barking at the trespasser. "Hands up, Gallow!"

She couldn't help it. Cora ran to the front porch. "I told you to stay inside!" Jimmy had his knee wedged between the man's shoulder-blades. Gallow squirmed and resisted, grunted, as Jimmy restrained his hands with the cinch strap. Scott stood to the side, stun pistol pointed and steady, alert in the event Gallow attempted escape.

Jimmy stood the man up as he informed him of his rights, told him he was under arrest for trespassing on private property. Red clay mud covered Rupert Gallow from stringy hair to worn leather boot.

"I didn't do nothing!" he spat, twisting his shoulders in an attempt to gain leverage on the officer. He shuffled and stumbled, his arms locked behind him. Jimmy gripped the stalker's upper arm to keep him steady. "Cora! You've got to believe me! I'm just trying to help!"

Jimmy hauled him down the driveway, the man cursing and growling excuses with every foot taken. Scott paused, turned to Cora. "Relax, Doc. This guy won't be bothering you anymore." The other deputy quick-stepped to come aside Jimmy and her would-be stalker.

The last thing she heard was Rupert yelling, "You don't know what you're doing! He's coming for her!"

Shivers snaked up her neck, made the fine hairs rise. The wiry man kicked, wiggled and bucked the entire length of the driveway until the three were out of sight, all the while viciously denying any wrongdoing and cursing in equal parts.

Cora tried to calm her racing heart. The night air was cool, crisp, fresh. She smelled wet clay and sodden leaves, saw stars twinkling serenely between the clouds. Crows called to one another, and the mockingbirds echoed their squawks. Her nerves jangled in the aftermath of the apprehension. She sat in the swing, kicked back and forth gently, even as she glanced out at the yard, between the stable and the paddock. She should feel relief, joy, since the mysterious man plaguing her the last few weeks was finally in custody, if only temporarily.

Answers. More than anything, Cora wanted answers.

***

"You have the right to remain silent, Mr. Gallow," Jimmy reiterated, "but you keep yelling that you're innocent. So you either need to shut-up and wait for a lawyer, or start talking. You're wasting my time."

Jimmy sat across from the trespasser at a metal table in the middle of a tight, neutral-colored room. The halogen lights cast a sickly glow to the beige walls. At one time, this served as a janitor's closet. On one side of the table sat Gallow, hands secured in front of him. His restraints connected to a bolted chain secured to the floor. Jimmy faced Gallow across the table, his chair leaned back on the two rear legs, the deputy's long legs crossed at the ankles. A small camera, about half an inch in diameter, was disguised and embedded in the concrete block wall, the lens camouflaged with a screen in the same shade of paint. The camera transmitted a feed wirelessly to any of the viewscreens in the office. Tonight, Scott witnessed the interrogation from his desk in the bullpen.

"I don't know any lawyers here, I keep telling you," Rupert complained. "And I wasn't doing anything wrong."

"Trespassing is against the law here in Texas, just like it is in Missouri." Seeing Gallow's eyebrows creep to his hairline, Jimmy nodded. "Yeah, we know you're here illegally. What we want to know is why. What did Wilkes hope to accomplish having you here?"

Rupert threw himself as far as the restraints would allow. "Wilkes? You mean Gordon Wilkes?"

"You heard me, Gallow. So why did he send you?"

"That psycho didn't send me!"

"Why else would you be here, watching Cora, camping out on her property, leaking information to the press?"

Rupert's mouth opened and closed, like a guppy. He tried to put his hands on the top of the table, but the chain kept them closer to his lap. "I wasn't doing anything except watching her, keeping an eye on her so I could protect her if that maniac ever showed up! And now you have me locked in here, and I can't keep him away from her. John's going to kill me!"

"Wait a minute," Jimmy said, glancing in the direction of the hidden camera, raising an eyebrow. "Who is this 'John' you're referring to?"

"Cora's brother, you moron!"

"Let me get this straight. You expect me to believe her own brother sent *you* to protect her against Wilkes?"

Nodding nearly hard enough to dislodge his head, Rupert tried once again to lean forward. "Look man, I'm telling the truth. Call John, ask him. He'll verify everything. But you have to do it quick, because I'm pretty sure I saw Wilkes tonight at the diner."

"What? You're saying Wilkes is here, in Cotton Springs?"

"I saw someone who looked sort of like the photo John showed me, but the guy's hair was gone and he had a goatee. Wasn't like that in the picture. It was raining buckets, too, when I saw him walking out. I just took off, ran towards Cora's house as fast as I could, hoping if it was him he wouldn't beat me to her."

Scott spoke in his ear, the little bud nearly impossible to see. "He's telling the truth, Jimmy. John Thomas just verified it."

Jimmy stood, throwing the chair back. He came around the table, released the restraint keeping Rupert tied to the floor. The deputy opted to leave the cinch strap wound around the man's wrists. "Come with me."

"Scott," he barked, dragging Rupert into the main squad room. "Pull up the picture of Gordon Wilkes. Image a goatee on the man and shave his head." Scott tweaked the image, getting information from Rupert along the way. When it was finished, Rupert lunged at the screen. "Yes! He's the guy who came out of Dixie's place. Oh, man! We've got to get to Cora *now*."

Scott stood, grabbing his jacket. "We've got another problem, Jimmy."

"What?"

"Remember the drive-by right before we pulled into Cora's place, the blue all terrain?"

Jimmy swore, grabbed his coat on the way out of the door, dragging Rupert Gallow behind him. "I hope we're not too late."

***

Cora glided out of the steamy bathroom moments ahead of a fog bank. A hot shower was what she needed to relax, calm her nerves. With a thirsty plush white towel she dried her curls, stepped around the doorjamb and into her bedroom. She pulled on comfy flannel pajama bottoms, sky blue with white snowflakes scattered about, and a white long sleeved t-shirt. In the quiet of the night, she heard tires crunch on the driveway, saw the flashing red and blue strobes of a law enforcement vehicle. Curious, she tossed the towel on the bathroom floor, and walked down the hallway towards the living room.

Headlights and flickering flashers flooded the front of her house. A swift knock on the door announced the visitor. Jimmy probably needed to get a statement from her about the arrest. Well, he'd just have to see her in her jammies.

She turned the knob, pulled it open. The cold gunmetal of a pistol pressed against her forehead, biting into her skin. Cora froze, stunned.

Gordon Wilkes stood before her. His hair was gone and he had a goatee, but it was most definitely Gordon.

He smiled, an insane light in his brown eyes.

"Did you miss me, witch?"

Gordon laughed, and the last thing Cora remembered was the butt of the handgun ramming the side of her head.

Then, darkness.

31

Ben pulled into an electrifill station and convenience store, just off the interstate on the eastern edge of Outer Houston. He needed to stretch his legs and get a shot of caffeine, before pushing through northwest to Austin. Erring on the side of caution, he hooked the truck up to charge, and stepped inside the glaringly-lit retailer in search of bottled liquid energy for his foggy mind. Days of rain had been detrimental to both his brain and the solar charging capacity of his vehicle. Yet another reason to rely on four-footed transportation. Except rain tended to dampen the riding experience, and his truck made the miles fly.

He paid the cashier, walked back to the vehicle and disconnected the charge plug. The bottom dropped out of the sky. Rain fell so heavily it was like a solid gray wall enclosing him within the confines of the filling station's awning. The roaring cacophony obliterated the sounds around him, drowning out voices and highway noise. He watched other customers trying to talk to one another, throw their hands up in the air in frustration. There was no way he could drive in this mess.

Great. Exactly what he needed. He slammed the door, pounded the steering wheel, slugged the iced coffee in three gulps. The downpour raged, effectively halting his pursuit contract. On and on, the rain fell. Five minutes, ten, fifteen. Fed up and frustrated, he punched on the radio. The auto-tuner rolled and scanned, finally picking up a single station. One station in Houston? He sneered at the hilarity of it. A soulful voice belted out her love for Jesus. Ben screamed in exasperation, banged his forehead on the top edge of the wheel. He tapped the power.

Nothing happened. The singer crooned her adoration, and Ben fumed. Punch, punch, punch. Nothing, zip, nada. He scanned through the stations once again, only to have it land on the annoying God station again. Irritated, Ben exited the truck, stood outside the cab watching millions of gallons of water descend from the heavens.

Livid, he shook his fist heavenward and bellowed at the heavy laden sky. "Is that all you've got?! You take my parents! My sister wrecks her life! And now I've lost the only woman who ever mattered to me!" Spent, broken and torn, Ben heaved deep breaths in, gasping for air. Belatedly he realized the people in the sedan two bays over were staring and whispering. He opened the truck door, shaking his head, dejected. There was nothing left. Nothing except a raging storm and a broken heart.

The roar of the rain on the steel awning filled his ears, but in the midst of the white noise Ben clearly heard, "Listen."

He jumped, looked around the confines of the interior, startled. The only sound was the falling rain, and the song on the radio. The lyrics made the short hairs on his arms rise.

How many times must you fall?
How many miles must you crawl?
How many times must you hit the wall
Before you learn God is your all?

No. No, no, no, no. He ignored the growing tension in his gut, like someone had tied a rope around his spine and was dragging him over a cliff. He dug his mental heels in. Growling, he placed his

251

forefinger on the starter pad, anxious to move, drive, do something. The truck remained silent. Ben pulled his finger off, replaced it. Still no ignition. His wrist communicator chirped. The dial flashed *Angelina County Sheriff's Office.*

"Answer call," he instructed the voice operating system. "Ben Tucker."

"Ben, it's Jimmy. Where are you, man?"

The tone of Jimmy's voice made the alarm bells ring in his head. "Just outside of Houston, near Old Cleveland. Why? What's going on?"

"It's Cora. Ben, he took her."

"Who took Cora? What is going on?"

"Gordon Wilkes. Get home. I'll give you the details in person."

"End call," Ben barked with a press of his finger to the starter pad once again. The truck remained silent, no ignition. He thought of getting out of the truck, checking the starter, but as he reached to open the hood, the locks engaged, trapping him inside. Stunned, he stared at the dash, then yanked on the door handle. He banged and smashed and pushed every button he could find in the truck, all to no avail.

Anger boiled, his face flushed. Fury clawed its way from his throat in a savage cry. At the top of his lungs he shouted, cursed, flung his wrath into the universe and at the God who created it. When the rage subsided, he was left a gasping shell, empty and hopeless at the bottom of his soul's well. Tears streamed down his face in a torrent, a perfect reflection of the storm wailing outside. Numb, alone, trapped, with nowhere to turn.

Defeated, he cried out to God. "I'm done. I can't do this alone. God, oh dear Lord," he pleaded as tears continued to fall, "please, help me. I have to get to Cora. I'll do anything, whatever you ask.

Lord, I've messed up so many times, walked away and abandoned those I love. Don't abandon me now. I don't know what to do. Just please, don't take Cora from me too."

Sobbing, wracked by emotions penned up for decades, doubled over in pain, Ben was barely conscious of the locks disengaging. The radio station previously blaring praises to God spewed white noise, the sound of an unoccupied frequency. Wiping his eyes, he looked up, saw the rain diminish to a drizzle. His forefinger engaged the ignition, and the truck rumbled to life. Ben stared, amazed and humbled.

"Lord, take me. I don't know what it means yet, but I know I cannot do this without you," he whispered in the wake of the miracle. Blinding joy burst in his chest, burning away the sorrow, and empowering him to move, to find his way home. In the still small place of his soul, he heard the words, "Go, son," caressing his heart. This. This is what Cora was talking about. An explosion of all-encompassing love surrounding his very soul, a radiant light that penetrated each and every dark crevice. He laughed, threw his head back and laughed, cried, jubilant.

Loved. He was loved beyond measure.

Alive with purpose, burning with an overflowing love, Ben threw the truck in gear and sped eastward. Back to Cotton Springs.

Back to Cora.

32

Ben stormed into the sheriff's office less than an hour later. The door banged and rebounded as he pushed through. Betty took one look at his face, and pointed to the bull pen. "They're waiting for you."

Scott and Bo, two of the deputies, hovered near the wall map of Angelina and the surrounding counties. The junior lawmen pointed and spoke in hushed tones about various dotted locations. Probably projecting escape routes Wilkes could have taken. A tap of the screen enlarged a portion. Scott used his finger to drag and refocus the terrain. Jimmy sat behind the desk in a video conference. He looked up when Ben entered the room and motioned him over to the screen.

"Gentlemen," Jimmy said to the officers on-screen, "this is Ben Tucker. He's the best tracker in this area and he has a vested interest in getting Miss Thomas safely home."

Two men filled the screen, one wearing a sheriff's badge, the other a deputy. Ben nodded in their direction. "I'll do whatever it takes to get Cora home, you can count on it."

The older, portly sheriff wrinkled his nose, scrubbed a hand across his chin. "Like I was saying to Deputy Wilson, if Wilkes is in his issued transport, we're in luck. Your deputies described what sounds like his ride, but a different color. We all know it's not hard to change the color of a vehicle, so I'm betting it's one and the same. Wilkes is smart, so he's probably disconnected the transponder already. There's a confidential secondary backup, put in place by the federal government. Bud, here," he said pointedly to his colleague, "is going to pretend he doesn't know about that particular tracking feature for the rest of his life, since it's above his pay grade."

The other deputy cocked half a smile and nodded. "I've worked with Gordon nearly five years. This last year has been rough, with his wife passing away and all. But lately, he's worse, and I'm afraid for the little lady. He blames her for Missy's death." Bud pointed to three bottles of various size and shape, all holding small amounts of clear liquid. "We thought these were water. He always had one with him. Here in the office, on patrol, wherever. It's vodka, not water. I have no idea how long he's been drinking or to what extent."

Jimmy spoke up. "Sheriff Moynahan, let's go ahead and try the first transponder, the standard issue one, and see what happens. Our maps have interfaced with your tracking system and are ready."

The sheriff flicked something out of view. No lights, no blips showed on the interactive wall map.

"All right, now the backup, please, Sheriff."

Again, a flick of the switch, and a tiny red dot blinked on the map. A sigh swept across the room.

"We've got him," Ben smiled.

"Where is he headed going *that* way?" Jimmy nibbled his lower lip in thought. The red light moved slowly, but steadily along a small state highway south and east, toward the border of Texas and Louisiana District.

A thought occurred to Ben. "Sheriff! Tell me his vehicle has a kill switch."

A malignant smile spread across the rotund lawman's face. "That it does, son."

Moynahan tapped a code on a switchboard behind him. In the Cotton Springs bullpen, the red dot halted. The room erupted in cheer. The lawmen ended the call, and the screen went black.

Jimmy stood. "All right, everyone. Listen up. We have an unauthorized American citizen on our soil, and that person has abducted one of our own. Ben," he nodded to the long table along one wall, "we haven't been sitting on our thumbs."

Polymer casts of boot soles, bare feet, and tire tracks sat on the surface, as well as Cora's new wrist communicator, and bloody swabs sealed in vacuum containers. Various other bits and pieces, tiny debris, had been gathered and logged into evidence. Ben formed a picture in his mind.

He nodded at the bloody swabs. "Cora's?"

Jimmy nodded, wincing. "It's our theory he knocked her unconscious somehow, based on the droplet pattern. Most likely when she opened the door."

"Why would she open the door?"

"Crap. I forgot to fill you in on the stalker."

Quickly, concisely, the deputy ran through the arrest and questioning. In conclusion, he explained his theory. "She probably thought it was one of us, especially if he used his flashers."

"Let me get this straight," Ben rehashed slowly. "The guy we thought was hounding her on Wilkes' orders was actually here because her brother sent him as a sort of guard? It makes no sense."

Jimmy explained his conversation with Cora's brother. John thought Cora would balk at having someone there to guard her, think he was overreacting. Weird things had happened around the Thomas farm, and he didn't want to alarm Cora if it wasn't necessary. He sent Rupert Gallow, a hired hand from the ranch, to watch and guard her from the shadows should Wilkes show up. Since Cora had never met Gallow, she wouldn't suspect her brother sent him.

"It's too bad she wasn't wearing the communicator you bought her," Jimmy groaned.

"You're a genius! Did you find the earrings?" Ben paced the floor in front of the evidence table.

"Earrings? No."

"Both earrings can function as the receiver and speaker for the communicator. But they also have a GPS tracker beneath the diamonds, mounted between the stone and the setting."

Ben withdrew a folded thin tablet from his back pocket. "I can track her from here, as long as she is wearing the earrings." A few swipes and keystrokes later, he held a miniature version of the wall map. A blue triangle blipped on the screen.

"There you are, baby," Ben whispered. "I'm coming to get you."

***

Cora's eyes fluttered open, but reflex squeezed them closed. The light hurt, daggers knifing her skull. Where was she? Thinking was nearly impossible, like her head was clogged with cotton. Her jaw throbbed in time with her pulse. She attempted to swallow. A gag was stuffed in her mouth.

The monotonous tone of tread-grooved rubber on asphalt told her she was in a vehicle. In a flash she remembered opening her front door, to find Gordon standing on her porch beneath the warm yellow light, darkening her welcome mat. The feel of a cold, steel barrel pressing into her forehead, his evil smile. A jolt of pain, then nothingness.

Until now. Wilkes had knocked her unconscious, kidnapped her. Where were they? Did anyone know she had been abducted?

A hair's width at a time, Cora cracked her eyelids, slivers of light glaring green and blue from the vehicle's console. She was gagged and hogtied in the rear cargo area of what appeared to be an all-terrain type vehicle, but the computer array in the front reminded her of Jimmy's cruiser.

Gordon sat rigidly in his seat, the ropy muscles of his neck taut against a stiff collar. Good, she thought. Let him be nervous. Occasionally he would turn his head left and right, checking his mirrors. She kept her eyes lidded, fearing his reaction if he knew she was awake.

No raindrops slapped the windshield, but the highway was wet, the tires hissing and humming. Trees lined either side of the road, the thick, dense undergrowth illuminated by the headlights. Lights within and outside glowed brightly one second, and the next snuffed, all power from the vehicle extinguished. He cursed, banged the steering wheel, and manhandled them to the shoulder as the last of the momentum coasted the vehicle to a stop.

"This cannot be happening," her captor growled. He flicked a look in the rearview mirror just as Cora eased her eyes completely closed. Foul language poured from his mouth as he exited, slamming the door behind him. She heard rather than saw him as he beat the side of the transport, frustration turned to fury. He grew quiet, but the silence was short-lived.

He yanked the rear hatch open. Gordon grabbed the rope section between her hands and feet and pulled, hauling her to the edge of the cargo area. Despite her best efforts to appear unconscious, she groaned in pain.

"Awake, witch? Ah, good. I'm not carrying your filthy body anywhere."

Cora heard the *whisk-click* of a pocketknife opening, felt the rope give way as her hands and feet sprung apart. Her shoulders and back screamed in agony, but she denied him the pleasure of crying out again. Gordon hauled her out of the vehicle, into the stinging November night air. He secured her hands in front of her, rather than behind as they were before. Her bare feet scraped against the rough asphalt of the highway. She cringed and gasped as he dragged her into the ditch, sharp rocks and splintery sticks biting into the soft pads of her bare feet as he led her deeper into the undergrowth. Briars and thorns clawed her face, arms and clothing. Where was he taking her?

"Don't you dare try to remove that gag, witch," he warned. "Now come on. We ain't got all night."

Lord, she prayed silently, *I don't want to die. Please help Ben find me.*

33

The sliver of moon hanging in the inky, cloud-blotted sky did little to illuminate the cluttered undergrowth of the forest. Thicket seemed an inadequate word for the foliage she stumbled through, her bare feet bleeding from hundreds of tiny cuts. Her unbound hair snagged every branch and briar. Gordon trudged, heedless of the darkness, pulling and yanking her forward when she fell behind. Time played a ruthless game. Minutes slugged by, each second agonizing torture, but it seemed days since Gordon seized her. Cora thought it was close to midnight, but she wasn't certain. If only her watch adorned her arm instead of resting on the bathroom vanity.

For the hundredth time she longed for the wrist communicator. What good were the earrings if she didn't have their counterpart? Still, they were a gift from Ben, a connection to him, and she clung to that hope, a lifeline. She focused on the memory of his face, the lines around the eyes she loved, shocks of sandy hair in need of trimming.

She stumbled, flailing as she tripped over a fallen oak tree, the rough pitted bark scraping a hole in her flannel pajama pants and cutting through to skin. Her knee seared with a flash of pain as she fell. Cora braced herself with cuffed arms outstretched at the last second. Pain exploded in her right elbow with a blinding *snap!* She cried out, falling to the forest floor, crumpling in on herself as she attempted to cradle her broken elbow. Too late she remembered her wrists were lashed together. Weeping, she groaned, huddled on the leaf-littered ground. Pine needles stabbed through her thin t-shirt, but she barely gave them a thought.

Gordon returned, stomping through the undergrowth.

She tried to speak, but the gag prevented it. With her elbow broken, she couldn't remove the taped wad if even she did dare to provoke his wrath. He reached down, grabbed her bound wrists in his hands and hurled Cora to her feet. A scream erupted from behind the wadded gag, tears streamed down her face, as her broken arm protested. Lights flickered around her vision, sight tunneling towards a black hole.

"Get up and shut up!"

She planted her feet, swaying, broken twigs and sharp sticks making the stance excruciating on her already battered feet, vision wavering under a mountain of agony. Her right elbow swelled and throbbed, blood trickled from tiny briar cuts all over her face and neck. Blackish-red blood ran in crusty drips from temple to cheek, from the grisly wound left by the pistol whip. Leaves and twigs cluttered her hair. Cora stood as tall as she could, feet spread in a firm stance, and stared at Gordon. As degrading as it was, she grunted, making noises hoping he would remove the gag, tears cutting paths through the dirt on her face.

He shot her a venomous look. "What? You're going to be brave, now, are you, witch?"

His open hand struck her left cheek, and she rocked back, once again saw flecks of light dancing. Though more tears fell across her stunned and blazing face, she stood firm once again, rolling her shoulders square in defiance. She would not back down. Behind the gag she growled at him again, shaking her head left to right, willing him to understand her request.

It must have worked, because he leaned forward and said, "If you scream, I will cut out your tongue. Do we understand one another?"

She nodded once, bracing herself for the rip. Cora winced as he yanked the tape from her face. She refused to give him the satisfaction of hearing her cry as long as she could help it. The cloth wad shoved into her mouth stuck to the tape, a blood and saliva coated ball of fabric, and she coughed and spluttered at its removal.

"You have to stop," she panted. "Turn around. Let's walk out of here."

He threw back his head and laughed. Even in the darkness she saw the insanity behind his eyes. "I've waited too long for this to stop now. You're gonna pay for killing my Missy. Now, get moving!"

"My arm is broken." She had to keep him talking, distract him, buy some time. Surely someone was trying to find her. "Can you at least untie my wrists?"

He snorted his reply and spat at her feet. "Walk."

Every second, every minute agonized. Her elbow blazed with throbbing fire; minced and grated feet bled with each step. Time blurred into a tortuous haze. Finally, she collapsed, unable to lift her legs. Gordon was five paces away before she saw him spin around, searching for her. He glowered as he backtracked, raised his hand to hit her again.

Cora braced herself for the blow. "Gordon, it's late. My feet are shredded, I'm thirsty, and I can*not* walk another step."

Amazingly, he lowered his hand, withdrew the strike with a frown. He spun in a lazy circle, taking in the surroundings. "Over here," he uttered, walking to a tall pine, about a foot in diameter.

From his pocket he withdrew a coiled length of wire, narrow and silvery in what little moonlight filtered the canopy overhead.

"I said get over here, witch!" He reared back to kick her, and Cora haltingly scuttled to the trunk. He shoved her down roughly, her back bit into the bark. He wound the filament around her and the tree several times, securing it tightly below her shoulders with a clamp of sorts. He pulled on it to gauge the slack. Nodding in satisfaction he gloated, "Don't think you'll get loose, just because it's thin. It's military-grade wire. Not what I was planning to use it for," he chuckled, "but it's handy right now."

He gathered fallen limbs, dead pine needles, and crunchy oak leaves, mumbling barely audible nonsense as he worked. Soon, a teepee of deadfall blazed, the damp wood casting clouds of smoke that danced in a swirling pillar overhead. Gordon leaned over the fire, rubbed his hands together. "Ah, now that's better."

A thousand agonizing daggers assaulted her body. From her position a few feet away from the fire, Cora barely felt the warmth of the flames. Her eyes watered from the smoke and the glare. Yet somehow the red, orange and yellow of the fire gave her hope, bolstered her resolve.

"I bet you're thinking someone will see the fire, be able to find you out here in the sticks." Maniacal laughter filled the night, as if his blackened soul leeched from within to join the surrounding darkness. "No. Your friends in town can't find us. I disabled the transponder on the vehicle before I left Missouri. More horses than cars in these parts anyway. Just you and me, witch."

"I'm not a witch. I serve God, not his enemy."

"If your God existed, he would not have taken my Missy from me. She was a good woman!" The veins in his neck bulged in the light of the bonfire. He dropped his voice to a crackling whisper. "I loved her so much." He jabbed a finger at her. "Until *you* took her from me, witch. I saw you chanting over her, casting your evil spells."

Sadly, Cora shook her head. "Missy asked me to pray for her. I did. That's all you saw, honestly." Her voice was a weakened croak. Unconsciousness flirted at the edge of her vision.

His fists knotted at his sides. "You expect me to believe your word?!"

"It's the truth. There's nothing in this world I would want more than to have Missy alive. She was my best friend."

"She was never able to conceive a child after she met you! Explain that, you evil filth. And you brainwashed her! Filled her head with lies and fairy tales, when you knew full well that religion was illegal. Making a deputy's wife break the law. She didn't get pregnant until I ripped her away from you and all your wretched lies. What kind of friend are you? Tell me!"

"The kind of friend who was worried about more than this life." If only she could make him see, help him understand. It was her only hope. "She needed the saving grace of Jesus everyone needs. You need it, too, Gordon. If you'd like, I can …"

"Never! I'll have none of your craziness, now just shut up and let me think! Shut up or I'll gag you again, so help me!"

Cora stared at the fire, mesmerized by its simple beauty. Flames leapt and danced, swirling sparks into the night sky. She stared unblinking, envious of the fire's freedom. Tears leaked from her swollen and bruised eyes.

She must have dozed off, or passed out. She awoke with a jerk, stifling a cry of anguish. A low mewling escaped her lips. Cora fully expected another blow to land on her face. Left and right she looked, searching for Gordon, but he was nowhere in sight.

***

Ben and the search team sped down the back roads, taking the shortest route to Cora's location. Her earrings continued to transmit a signal, the little blue triangle gently flashing on his screen. Neighbors and friends had gotten word of Cora's abduction, and flooded the precinct office with volunteers. Much to Mae Crockett's obvious chagrin, Dabney insisted on hobbling over to help out. The citizen workers stayed behind to monitor communications.

Ben rode with Jimmy in the police cruiser. Bo Simmons and Scott Marcus trailed them. Jimmy had made contact with the Texas Rangers to brief them on the situation. They were to meet Ben and the others at the last known location of Wilkes' vehicle when it was shut down. While Jimmy drove, Ben scrutinized the screen and the flashing blue triangle. Until now, it had meandered in a northeasterly pattern toward Toledo Bend Reservoir, snaking through the Sabine National Forest.

"She isn't moving. Jimmy, how far out?"

He consulted the console display. "Two minutes or less."

"Looks like he's taken her nearly a mile into those woods."

Jimmy hissed. "Nasty thicket out there, briars and prickly bushes wedged tight underneath the trees. I'm surprised they made it that far."

"They had a few hours head start. I know, I know. I'm not blaming you." To the glowing screen he whispered, "Why aren't you moving, Cora?"

"It's nearly one in the morning. Maybe they're resting." Jimmy shrugged. "There, look," he said, pointing. In the light of the headlights he spotted a blue all-terrain transport, half pulled off the two-lane back road, the tail-end jutting out onto the road.

Ben gazed into the thick shrouded forest, the fringe illuminated by the beams of their headlights.

"I'm coming to get you, baby. Hang on."

34

Cora thrashed against the restraint, but the thin cable was every bit as durable as Gordon had touted and her strength waned steadily. Panting, she jerked her head left and right, searching for any sign of her tormentor. He was nowhere to be seen.

Pulling against the wire dug the filament into her upper body, with only the thin t-shirt buffering. If she couldn't break the wire, maybe she could slide out. She inhaled deeply, forced every ounce of breath she could muster out of her lungs, and pushed herself tight against the tree, back and downward.

Each agonizing millimeter was a victory, fueling the fire of perseverance. She prayed Gordon stayed away from the makeshift camp. The longer he was away, the more time she had to escape. One inch, two, she shimmied behind the tightly-wound wire, until it slid over her shoulders to lay limply against her collarbone. With hands tied in front of her, she attempted to grab the wire and guide the coils over her head, but the broken elbow made it impossible. Cora groaned as a wave of nausea rolled over her. The pain of trying to bend her fractured elbow was more than she could bear. Frustrated for losing precious time, weakened by pain and exhaustion, she continued her downward wiggling motion, strategically tucking her chin and turning her head. The three loops of wire slid upward over her chin, scraped past her nose, and finally over her head.

Her battered, bruised and blood-smeared feet throbbed in time with her pulse, but she forced away the anguish. She had to run, escape this madman! Cora furtively looked in every direction, but the dying firelight wreaked havoc with her night vision. The forest circling the small blaze was as black as pitch. She took one step, two, praying the path she chose was the one they cut earlier. Once past the outer reach of the fading light, she threw herself into the woods.

Days of rain did little to dampen the sounds underfoot as she crashed through the thicket. She was lost, with a sliver of moon to light her way and a psycho prowling nearby. Her brain screamed *RUN* and she obeyed, tripping and stumbling. Every yard away from his clutches was one closer to freedom.

Dark, so dark, but she ran. She collided with what she thought was a tree, but this tree had arms. Rough arms wrestled her to the ground, jarred her broken elbow. She screamed, no longer gagged.

Gordon loomed over her, his features fuzzy and gray in the wan light. "Yell like that again, and you'll pay."

She didn't care. "HELP ME!"

Cora never saw the fist connect with her jaw, knocking her unconscious.

***

Ben and Jimmy both strapped high-powered headlamps around their foreheads. Jimmy had an emergency kit bound to his back. They stood at the edge of the narrow two-lane road, where the glow from the headlights faded into inky blackness. Bo and Scott remained with the vehicles, manning communications and as backup in the event Wilkes returned to his deserted transport.

The night held its breath, with barely a whisper of wind to stir the emaciated branches of the oaks and sweet gums. Scattered clouds hid the cold slice of moon. The early morning chill had teeth. The damp earth would yield prints, and if Cora was barefoot, as they suspected, her feet would soon leave blood tracks as well. Anger boiled inside him, thinking of Cora hurt. He had vowed Gordon would never touch her, and he broke his promise. Selfishness and pride lured him away, but he was a changed man. He would to never make the same mistake again.

Jimmy took off into the woods, but before he could penetrate the tree line too deeply, Ben grabbed him by the bicep, squeezed tightly.

"We need to do something first." Ben hesitated, wary, but unable to deny the force living inside him now. "Will you pray with me?"

The deputy's startled eyebrows climbed his forehead. "Well, yeah, of course." Aloud, he prayed, "Lord, help us find Cora. Show us the way, and keep her from harm. Protect all of us out here tonight, and help us see justice done. In your Son's name we pray, amen."

Ben clapped him on the shoulder. "Thanks, man. I'm still learning the ropes."

They stomped into the brush. "I want to hear your story, after this is all said and done, brother."

"After she's in my arms. But trust me, it's a good one."

In the quiet of the woods, footfalls were magnified. Each crunch, every snap was amplified. Critters scooted under bushes, up trees. With the piney canopy and cloud cover overhead, Ben was thankful for headlamps.

He consulted the handheld map screen, the blue triangle steady, close to a mile away. Then, movement, heading in their direction, albeit slowly. As quickly as the movement began, it ended. Ben halted, studying the map. The tiny triangle which represented Cora backtracked in the same direction from which it came. Strange. It was almost as if ...

"I think she just tried to escape," Ben pondered aloud.

"Let's get moving. Here, I'll hold the map, and you check for signs they've been this way, in case we lose her signal."

"We entered on their tracks, I'm sure of it. Trust me, Jimmy. This is what I do."

The men stalked as swiftly as they dared. Ben focused on the trail, and signs his prey preceded them. Twigs snapped in odd places, grass and weeds flattened, and there, a few hundred yards into the trees, blood. Her feet must be shredded, scraped and bruised. Sweet gum trees dropped gumballs, round ball-like flowers which were as hard as stone and surrounded with spiky protrusions. Stepping on one hurts; stepping on thousands was akin to torture.

Ben quickened the pace, determined to find his girl. Make no mistake about it, she was his, if she'd have him. He had messed up royally, and he couldn't wait to beg for forgiveness. Cora was alive. He refused to believe otherwise. If there was one thing Cora had taught him, it was that faith was necessary to life. He knew the truth, now, and had faith she would be in his arms soon.

A loud crack shattered the night, like a peal of thunder compacted into a single clap echoing through the trees. Birds launched into the night sky.

"What was that? A firearm?" Jimmy nearly dropped the illuminated map.

"I'd say it was, though I've only heard them a few times." Ben's mouth was set in a grim line.

Neither had to encourage the other to step up the pace. Ben snatched the glowing map from Jimmy's hand. Less than half a mile to go.

"Try to keep up," he advised the lawman.

Ben ran.

***

She came to, groggy and confused. Her left eye was swollen shut, her cheek and jaw aching and swollen. Cora tried to assess her situation, but her vision was gray around the edges, fuzzy. The effort to raise her head was excruciating, and she moaned when she saw her surroundings.

What she mistook for hazy vision was dense smoke from the nearby fire. Gordon stood over it, stoking the blaze with pine straw and dead limbs.

"Please, Gordon. Don't do this."

She was tied standing to a dying weathered oak, little more than a giant stick of kindling with roots. The same thin cabling which restrained her before held her upright again. This time the wire bit into her chest, under her arms. Withered and desiccated sticks, limbs and branches littered the ground around her feet, an unlit bonfire piled to knee height.

As he fed the other fire nearby, he spoke. He seemed pensive, thoughtful. Calm.

It chilled her to the bone.

"I didn't know what to do, how best to punish you. But I knew after you were cleared of all the charges that justice still needed to be served. You needed to pay the price for causing Missy's death. For months, I planned and schemed, tried to figure out the perfect execution. That wire holding you up? I thought about hanging you. Stringing you up, watching you dangle and thrash. But see, it didn't feel right. Enough.

"So, I bought an illegal handgun. Broke the law so that I could see justice done! Want to see it?" The flickering firelight added to the crazed look on his face.

Gordon brandished the pistol in front of her. "Oh yeah, you've already met Mr. Colt here. I forgot! Gave you a nice kiss on the temple, huh?" He chuckled at his joke, withdrew a flask from his back pocket, swigged a long gulp with a wince.

"But I don't think shooting is the right punishment either. Over too quickly. You need to feel the pain. It needs to linger." He could have been discussing the weather by the tone of his voice.

The man was insane. How could she reason with a madman? Instead, she prayed. *Lord, you are the God of miracles. I know you can deliver me from the hands of this madman. I'm so scared.*

A deafening boom sounded. Her ears rang with the concussion. Gordon was in her face, yelling, his spittle flying in her face. "You're not listening to me, witch!"

"I don't know what you want me to do," Cora pleaded. Her voice was tinny in her head, not even seeming a part of her. Her head throbbed to the rhythm of her beating heart. The pistol whip, backhands and punches were taking their toll. Cora knew from her distorted vision she suffered from a concussion. Her voice slurred despite her concentration. "Missy had a blood clot travel to her lungs,

Gordon. There was nothing I could do. Please, think of your son. Think of William."

"You leave my son out of this! You have no right!"

His breaths came in heaves, sharp inhales and exhales, his eyes rolling, insane. Gordon snatched a limb from the fire, its end ablaze with yellow-orange tongues tasting the cool air.

"I couldn't quite figure out how to punish you for taking my wife from me," he repeated. "But as we were taking our little moonlit walk out here, it came to me. In the old days, do you know how they punished witches?" His smile was evil.

"They burned," he cackled. The man danced around in a loopy circle, waving the firebrand above his head, laughing at the sky. "And so, you'll meet the same fate as your ancestors, witch. You'll feel the heat roast your skin, feel it burn every layer. Just a little preview of the Hell I'm sending you to."

Tears fell down Cora's cheeks, salty drops she couldn't wipe away if she wanted to. If this was the way she would leave this earth, she was prepared to meet her Father. Her only regret was she didn't get to say goodbye to her family, to her friends. To Ben.

As Gordon maniacally danced around the tree, Cora closed her eyes.

***

Ben watched from the perimeter of the tiny clearing, while Jimmy circled around for a second vantage point. Cora stood lashed to the oak, head down, shoulders slumped, with a heap of timber and tinder piled at her feet. The way Gordon danced around with a blazing branch left no question about his intentions. Ben had to keep the fire safely away from Cora.

As Jimmy edged around behind her, Ben stepped out into the light of the fire.

"Wilkes!"

Cora's head snapped up, eyes wide. His gut knotted in a hard fist at the sight of her face. She was battered, bloody gashes oozing down her beautiful face. The left side of her head had taken the brunt of Wilkes' abuse. The man would pay for what he had done to Cora.

Gordon's arm glided into a firing stance, the antique pistol straight and steady, even as the firebrand dangled from his other hand.

To Cora, Ben said over Wilkes' shoulder, "Hey darlin'."

She began to cry in earnest and Gordon yelled. "I told you to shut up, witch!"

"Wilkes, listen to me." Ben inched forward one baby step at a time. He had his hands up, showing he was unarmed. "Let's talk this through, try to see reason."

"Look," the madman growled, "I don't know who you are, but this is between me and the witch. Leave or die."

He had to keep him talking, distract him so Jimmy could reach Cora. "Ammo for your weapon is difficult to obtain. You already fired one shot. I'm betting you had some target practice before coming too. Want to bet how many rounds you've got left?"

"Shut up!"

Ben took another step forward, drawing his attention away from Cora. Over Gordon's shoulder, he caught a glimpse of Jimmy behind the tree, working on the wire release that secured Cora to the trunk.

A dozen paces stood between Ben and Gordon, with the tiny campfire between.

"She's mine, Wilkes. I won't let you hurt her anymore." Cora shifted. Jimmy had released the catch.

"I'd like to see you try and stop me." The madman waved the firebrand over his head, but kept the gun aimed at Ben. Behind Wilkes, Cora moved slowly in the direction of safety. But despite her obvious caution, a limb snapped beneath her foot. Gordon spun at the noise, arm still poised to fire. "NO!" he yelled, firing the pistol. The shot went wide, and Cora stumbled into the trees.

Ben barreled into the psychotic kidnapper with two-hundred and eighty pounds of force, knocking the smaller man to the ground. The gun slammed out of his hand, tumbled a few feet away. Gordon shimmied out from under Ben, turned and landed a glancing kick to Ben's kidney. He grunted, shifted, and lashed out with a punch to his opponent's stomach. Gordon doubled over, and Jimmy came up behind him, aimed his weapon and stunned the man before he could regain his feet. Gordon lay on the ground, motionless.

Jimmy quickly scuffed dirt over the flaming branch that had fallen from Gordon's grasp. Cora burst from the darkness, her hands still tied in front of her. She hobble-ran to Ben, sobbing. She was covered in cuts, gashes, scrapes and bruises. She was beautiful. He had no idea how she was still standing. He rushed to her, enveloped her in his arms even as she collapsed.

Ben sat on the cool autumn ground, in the middle of an inky black forest, cradling the woman he loved. The light from the fire danced on her bruised face, highlighting tears falling like rain. He rocked her back and forth, whispered reassurances. He ran his hand through her tattered leaf-strewn curls, her hair like the fire blazing a few feet away. Jimmy gently sliced the restraints around her wrists, and she whimpered in pain. Ben thanked God for His perfect timing, even as a tear from his own eye joined the puddle of hers on the damp ground.

He would never let her go again.

35

Cora remembered scenes from the previous night in flashes, like looking at snapshots in a photo album, an observer glimpsing flickers and bursts, rather than living every moment in real time.

Flash. Gordon Wilkes standing on her porch, then darkness as the pistol collided with her temple.

Flash. Waking hog-tied in a moving vehicle, praying she would survive.

Flash. The agony of a thousand cuts burning, her feet mangled, face scratched, bruised, swollen, throbbing.

Flash. Blazing fire, running for her life, his fist connecting with her face, and darkness once again.

Flash. Bound to a tree, the rough bark digging into her back. Gordon, deranged, flailing about in a macabre dance waving a makeshift torch, ranting and screaming. Terrified of dying in a conflagration, executed for a death she couldn't prevent.

Flash. Ben's voice, hope exploding in her chest, a fire of her own banishing the darkness, clinging to faith. Her lifeline.

Flash. Praising God as she felt another set of hands working to release the ratchet fastener.

Flash. Freedom! Escape into the safe murky darkness of the forest, hiding in the thicket, watching her rescuers battle her tormentor.

Flash. The safe cocoon of Ben's arms around her, his scent filling her nostrils. Snug and shielded, protected. Home.

Flicker. Red and blue strobes shattering the still night. Gordon slumped in the cage of Jimmy's cruiser, defeated. Ambulance doors open wide, paramedics rushing in her direction. *Flicker.* Her hand in Ben's as paramedics tended her wounds. *Flicker.* Harsh overhead lights, doctors swarming. A sharp pricking as the intravenous line was inserted into her left arm, and then oblivion, clinging to Ben's smile, his emerald eyes her anchor as she slid into the soft satin black.

Cora awoke in a hospital room. A garden of bouquets surrounded her, their heady scent penetrating the sterile antiseptic air. Ben slept in the reclining chair, his head thrown back, mouth open to the ceiling, snoring. She couldn't help but smile. The first time she had heard his snore, he was passed out in her spare bedroom, recovering from a chainsaw wound to the arm, sedated. She may have even loved him then. He spilled out of the convertible chair, his long powerful legs splayed out in front of him, larger than life. His eyes snapped open, as if somehow aware she was conscious.

He leaned forward abruptly, smacking his lips together, swallowing. "Thank God you're okay."

"You were snoring."

"I told you," he smiled, "I don't snore."

"Do too."

"Do not."

"Did I hear you say 'Thank God' just now, Benjamin Tucker?" Was her imagination running wild?

A grin split his face, light shining brightly from within. "You heard correctly. And I've prayed it at least a million times since last night."

It hurt to smile, but she did anyway. Tears threatened to fall, but she swept them away as best she could. "When?"

"I'm not sure you'll believe me if I told you."

"Try me."

He recounted his experience at the filling station. The radio phenomenon, truck locks engaging on their own, the ignition failing despite a full charge. The audible voice telling him to "Listen" and the chorus on the airwaves. It was all so incredible, miraculous.

"God had my attention, and He made sure I had nowhere to go. I finally surrendered. Let it all go. The hate, the anger, the guilt. I asked God to help me, and he filled me with wonder, with hope. Joy. Without God on my side last night, I don't know what I would have done to Gordon," he admitted. "It was tough enough, restraining myself, not killing him on the spot."

Ben scooted closer to the hospital bed, clasped her hand with both of his. "Cora, you were right all along. I never realized how much hate I had living inside me. God took it all away, and for once in my life, I don't feel the weight, the burden. Last night, while you were sleeping, I was so wired. Couldn't sleep, couldn't relax. I read the Bible instead. It was in the drawer of the nightstand." She nodded, happy. "I read about his grace, and his mercy. It's still hard to imagine He loves me despite the years I spent hating Him. But I'm grateful. So, um, thanks," he concluded, a little flushed from embarrassment, joy, she couldn't tell, "for praying for me."

No longer able to hold them back, tears streamed from her eyes. Her face was a mass of bruises, abrasions, larger lacerations, and tiny cuts. Her arm was broken and casted, her mangled feet wrapped in gauze. She had survived a nightmare abduction at the hands of a killer.

She had never been happier in her entire life.

Ben stood, kissed Cora on her forehead. His green eyes gazed into her blue. "I screwed up so badly. I left you when you needed me the most, broke my promise to protect you. I know I don't deserve it, but ...will you give me another chance?"

Unable to speak around the lump in her throat, she nodded fiercely, winced at her pounding head. Ben sighed in relief, happiness softening the worry lines around his face.

He gently cupped his hands around her face, careful of her battered and bruised left cheek. "I don't know when it happened, Cora Thomas. I think it was when I first opened my eyes, and you were standing over me, the sky behind you, and me flat on the ground in front of your house. But whenever it first happened doesn't matter. I love you, Doc."

Swallowing the lump in throat, joy filling her heart, she reached up with her good hand, placed it on his. "I love you, too, Ben Tucker. So very, very much."

36

Cora's ordeal captured national attention. Once again, the media flocked to Cotton Springs. Rather than the wicked witch persona, the fickle press painted Cora as the misunderstood hero subjected to the whims of a psychotic killer. One local news anchor went so far as to issue a public apology. A nationally-broadcast morning show, *Rise and Shine Texas!*, interviewed Cora in her own home, just days after she was discharged from the hospital. She sat on her plush sofa, feet up, casted arm resting in her lap. Her bruised face was untouched by stage makeup. The perky and perfectly coiffed reporter perched opposite Cora, asking probing questions and sounding genuinely appalled in all the right places.

It was likely she would not have to cook another meal for three months. Casseroles, side dishes, and desserts were jam-packed into every nook and cranny of her refrigerator and freezer. Stella had organized a chart, and people in the community signed up to help with chores around the house until she got back on her feet, literally. She had a total of thirty-seven lacerations across the soles of both feet, numerous bruises, nicks and slices by the hundreds. Doc McMullen had ordered her to remain wheelchair-bound for ten days, to help keep the suture gel intact. The old man even threatened her with old-fashioned stitches if she didn't comply. Her right elbow was another matter. A cast covered her arm from armpit to wrist, bent at a ninety degree angle, immobilized for the next six weeks.

Her cheek went from red and purple, to greenish yellow brown in a few days. Gordon had given her a hairline fracture in the cheek bone, but her jaw remained intact. The swelling in both the jaw area and in her gums made chewing a challenge for a few days. The cuts and scratches marring her face healed rapidly, thanks to the antibiotic ointment she had prepared the day of her attack. The concussion headache abated after three days.

In connection to her abduction and recovery, the media focused on Gordon Wilkes. While in custody, he confessed to luring the Texas Ranger from Beaumont to a secluded area on the outskirts of town in order to steal the badge. Forensics confirmed Gordon's story that he beat the officer, loaded him in his transport, and dumped his battered body just off the highway. The man's blood was found in Gordon's Missouri-issued vehicle. Wilkes told the investigating officer his original plan had been to serve falsified extradition papers under the guise of a Texas Ranger, but the arrest of Rupert Gallow had provided the perfect window of opportunity for Gordon to sneak in under the radar and snatch Cora. There was no need for the papers after all. Among the evidence were the forged extradition orders, found in the glove compartment.

The Republic of Texas petitioned the American government to try Wilkes in the Texas court system, and the State granted the request. Wilkes was transferred to the prison in Huntsville, awaiting his trial date.

Cora no longer felt sympathy for Gordon, but neither did she feel hatred, fear, or any other emotion. She told the reporter who interviewed her for the morning show, when asked the question, she felt absolutely nothing for the Missouri man. She truthfully stated she had given those emotions to God, and she trusted Him to get her through the future rough patches.

Beth came to Cora's house every day. Cora was humiliated the first few times she had to have help going to the bathroom and bathing, but Beth was a natural nurse. She joked that maybe she had missed her true calling. The two spent their days together, often times with other women of the community dropping by. Ben's grandmother insisted on accompanying Beth one day, and brought her basket of yarn and crochet hooks. After hours of attempting to make it past the chain stitch, Cora and Annie came to the conclusion crochet was not her forte.

She also learned being a good patient was harder than it seemed. A week into her recovery, Doc McMullen stopped by to check on her progress. He examined her feet, and eyed her beneath droopy white eyebrows.

"Two of the cuts are infected. I want you to stay off your left foot for a couple more days."

"I'm sick of wheeling around this place!" She threw her left arm up in the air. "Fed up!"

"You'll either do as I say, or you'll make it worse. And then," he growled, pointing at her, "you'll be in the wheelchair for a lot longer. So what's it gonna be, Red?"

She muttered and snarled, but eventually agreed. The healing cuts itched as the skin knitted itself together. The tender skin beneath the cast itched. She wanted to comb and put up her own hair, not have to rely on Beth to do it for her. She grew tired of depending on others to do things she knew she was capable of doing herself, dagnabbit. But the fuming, and the raging, and the flying off the handle felt good for mere moments. Afterwards, she was always ashamed and frustrated.

Through it all was her constant, Ben. He reassured her he had enough in savings to take another couple weeks off, despite the weeks spent nursing his grandmother after her stroke. He took odd jobs around town, living off his army retirement pension. He patiently taught her to play chess and gin rummy, gritted his teeth when she won every checkers match. Ben's horse, Goliath, and Rusty became fast friends, galloping across the pasture or hanging out in the paddock. Cora learned to listen for Rusty's knickering when Goliath turned up the lane.

Ben encouraged her when she was low, and listened when she needed to vent. He told her to suck it up when she was whiny, and massaged her shoulders to help her relax.

Simply put, he had become her best friend. They held hands on the porch swing, on the days when the autumn sun warmed the nippy air. Each night he stole a kiss that she willingly gave, the kisses deeper and sweeter, somehow, than before, as if he knew what would cause her to sigh in contentment, or moan and demand more. Most nights, though, Ben would escort his sister, Beth, home to her husband, and the kisses would be a peck on the forehead or a swift nip on the lip.

Cora found herself dreading the day when she could stand on her own feet once more, because she was afraid Ben wouldn't be around the house as often. Beth had become the sister she had longed for as a child, and she cherished the time spent with her. She would miss her company, too.

On the Monday of the fourth week in November, Doc McMullen pronounced her feet healed. The wheelchair nearly slammed into the wall, Cora was out of it so fast. And just as quickly she regretted it, overestimating her leg strength. The older physician silently held out an arm as her cheeks flared in embarrassment. Ben, on the other hand, laughed hysterically, and Beth joined him. Doc maintained his bearing, but a grin split his face.

"Laugh it up, all of you! You try sitting in a wheelchair for ten days and see how you like it!"

"You and Dabney would sure get along with each other, right about now," Mae said from the kitchen, the screen door banging shut behind her.

"Mae! What are you doing here?"

The older woman caught Cora up in a tight squeeze, brushed her loose red curls over her shoulder. "You should wear your hair down more, dear. It's extremely becoming. Anyway," she waved, "I figured I'd come over here and see what y'all's plans for Thanksgiving were."

Eyes wide, Cora's hand flew to her mouth. "I completely forgot about it! It's this Thursday!"

"Yes, dear, I know. I was hoping you and Ben, Beth and Ronnie, and you," she said, nodding to the doctor, "would join us at our house to celebrate. We have a lot to be thankful for."

"I'm in! And I will bring *all* the food. Have you seen how many casseroles are in the fridge? What about Annie? She doesn't need to be alone on Thanksgiving."

"I've already spoken with her, and she's joining us. So how about it, you two? Think you can get along long enough to eat Thanksgiving dinner with us?"

Beth said slyly, "I think I can handle it. Not sure if Hardhead, here, can though."

Ben laughed. "It'll be tough, but I think I can manage. Mae, can I talk to you for a moment?" He nodded to a corner and led her away.

They chatted, heads together, low enough so they couldn't be heard. Cora asked Beth, "Do you know what that's about?"

Beth shook her head, grinned. "Not a clue. If he's cooking up something, it'll be interesting."

37

For the first time in nearly two weeks, Cora bathed alone. No aid, no one standing by in case she fell. Her house was blissfully quiet, with the exception of the passionate croon lilting from the surround speakers. She sang, not quite off-key, to a soulful mix of indie blues and classic jazz, as she sat in a bubble bath, the scent of lilac filling the steamy bathroom. In a few hours she'd be gorging herself on gifted casseroles, pigging out on donated desserts. And she would walk up to the Crockett's door on her own feet.

With her casted arm resting on the side of the porcelain tub, Cora enjoyed the feel of muscles unknotting and bubbles tickling her chin. Such small things she took for granted before, now brought her great joy. The nightmares were fading, but there were still mornings she awoke in a cold sweat, the insane light of Gordon's eyes sliding from memory in the late morning light. No. She squeezed shut her eyes, willing the image away. Today was about family, gratefulness, and the Lord knew she had much for which to be thankful.

Later, with the bathroom sufficiently fogged, and tendrils of steam swirling from the open door, Cora made her way to the bedroom in her fuzzy white robe. Dressing remained a battle, but one she intended to win single-handedly. She laughed aloud at the unintended pun.

Her hair...ah, her hair. The best she could manage was to comb the damp mess and apply a styling lotion that allowed the curls to air dry without frizzing into a lion's mane. Satisfied with what she saw in the mirror, she walked slowly to the kitchen. The soles were healed, but her feet remained tender. Before she left the hallway behind, a knock sounded on the front door. Ben was early.

Smiling, her cheeks flushed with the anticipation of the kiss he would greet her with, she opened wide the door. And nearly fainted when she saw her mother, father, brother and his family standing on her front porch. Towering behind them, Ben grinned broadly, his own face rosy amid his freckles.

"Mom! Dad! John! Oh my goodness, how--? When? Ben, did you do this?!"

She was swept up in a maelstrom of hugs, her nephews doing their best tornado imitations. Her mother cried, and her father stood shoulders back, ramrod straight, but with a smile spread across his face. John grabbed her in such a hug her feet left the ground, and Sally, John's wife, kissed her on the cheek, a tear streaming down her face. Cora was overwhelmed.

"Come in! Hunter! Heath!" she addressed the boys. "I've got cookies in the kitchen. Why don't you ...?" They streaked past her with a squeal, ran directly to the kitchen. Boys were just little men, she thought. Always led by their stomachs.

Her father sat stoically on the sofa, his arm around her mother, who was still crying. "When Benjamin called us and told us what that horrible man had done, I just couldn't stay away," her mother cried.

"Now, now, Faye. Our girl's okay. She's as tough as we raised her. Ben, we owe you so much. We owe you our daughter." Her father, Charles, wasn't a man of many words, but he always made the ones he spoke matter.

"Mom, how's your collarbone?"

"Oh, that," Faye dismissed. "It still pains me some, but I'll be fine. I guess we'll never know what happened, but I'm just glad I wasn't hurt worse."

"Me too," Charles agreed, squeezing her mother's knee.

Cora noticed Ben and John eyeing one another. She caught Sally's raised eyebrow in question and rolled her own eyes in response. It was like watching the peacocks at the zoo, comparing tail feathers.

"Ben, would you mind feeding Rusty? I haven't had a chance to get out there yet today." Would it be too much to bat her eyelashes at him? Probably.

"You don't need to be around the horse yet. Of course, I'll go out there. Um, John, would you want to come outside, meet Cora's horse?"

John grumbled a response and followed Ben out the back door. Those two were like alpha wolves, circling one another.

Over the next hour Cora reunited with her family, laughing and crying, hugging and telling stories. Her father spoke of the last few months, losing the mare John had written about, but also about delivering twin calves and bringing in a surplus tobacco crop. Surprisingly, her mother had taken on a herd of sheep, adopting them from a neighbor who was no longer able to care for them. The wool had brought in a tidy sum, and promised to be a lucrative hobby in the future.

Cora told of her experience as a small-town midwife, physician, and herbalist, how most of the townsfolk were hesitant concerning apothecary theory, but how a select few had embraced her tinctures and creams. She recounted the babies she delivered, of becoming a part of a community. Which led to the question Cora knew was coming since she saw her family standing on her porch.

"Coraline," her father began, "now that Wilkes is out of the picture, will you come home? We've missed you."

"Dad, I've missed you all more than you could know. But Texas is home now. I couldn't bear to leave. Can you understand?"

A tear rolled down her mother's face. "Of course, we understand, honey. You do what you feel is best. Your brother has promised to keep in touch better than he has," she said with a twist of her lips.

Her sister-in-law, Sally, piped up. "Looks like you have one enormously *tall* reason to stay in Cotton Springs." Cora's face flushed, but she didn't disagree. Sally cackled at her lack of response.

Thinking of her new home town reminded Cora of the time, and looking at the clock on the mantle, she gasped. "Oh! We're supposed to be at Mae's house in a few minutes!"

As if on cue, she heard her brother and Ben coming in the back door, followed by the twins darting in the house like fish in a pond.

"Ready to go?" Ben asked the group. "The Crocketts are waiting on us."

Cora walked up to Ben, looked up into his face. "You did this," she said, waving to the clan gathering their belongings behind her. "Didn't you?"

He smiled, nodded. "I got tired of you whining about how much you missed your family. Not a big deal." But his grin gave away his pleasure.

She shook her head. "It *is* a big deal, and I love you for it," she whispered. "I don't whine."

He planted a chaste kiss on the top of her head, wrapped her in a hug.

They descended on Mae and Dabney's home like locusts on a garden. Thanksgiving took on new meaning this year, and every one of them had an attitude of gratefulness. Cora's smile threatened to overtake her face as they gathered around the elongated wooden table, hand in hand, and Ben said the prayer. As hard as she tried, Cora couldn't keep the tears from flowing.

She had her family from Missouri and her family from Cotton Springs, the love of a man committed to his newfound faith. Bounty from generous townsfolk filled the table, laughter filled the air. It was the best Thanksgiving she could remember.

Later in the evening, Cora's house was nearly bursting at the seams. Her parents took the guest room, and she insisted on John and Sally taking her bedroom. Cora could easily sleep on the couch, and the boys would make a pallet on the floor nearby to keep her company. It was well past midnight before the snoring began, and Cora slept soundly, dreamless. She awoke with the dawn, and made coffee before everyone began to stir.

The day blew by like the autumn wind, in gusts and spurts, swirling with activity. The twins were excited to go to Movies in the Park, and Cora admitted she was too. It was to be her first outing since the kidnapping. Instead of his truck, Ben arrived with Goliath hitched to a wagon. They caravanned into Cotton Springs, a constant chatter accompanying the clip-clop of the horses' hooves on the packed ground. The weather smiled on them. A warm front was predicted to stall-out over the weekend.

As always, blankets dotted The Square, and families squawked and children squealed in the moments before the movie began. Tonight's feature was *Mary Poppins*, one of Cora's favorites. She was already humming "A Spoonful of Sugar" under her breath as she snuggled up next to Ben. Her parents sat on a blanket next to them, her brother and his family on the other side with the boys wiggling and giggling incessantly. The lights around the park dimmed and brightened, and a hush settled over the crowd.

Nash Wainwright stepped in front of the crowd. Curious, Cora leaned forward, wondering what was going on. He tapped a head-set microphone, cleared his throat.

"I'd like to thank everyone for coming out to Movies in the Park," he began, pausing for the polite applause. "I wanted to give a special welcome to Cora Thomas, who's finally back with us." This time the crowd roared, and her cheeks flamed. "Also, please welcome her family from Missouri." Again, applause and whistles. "All right, everyone. Let's get quiet and enjoy the show."

The gaslights dimmed, and the audience quieted. The white brick of the building flickered with the opening credits of the film, but it seemed they were having a bit of a problem with the movie. Someone turned the lamps up a hair, not fully lit, but giving The Square a romantic ambience. Nash's voice floated disembodied over the gathering.

"Just a moment, people. A little technical difficulty. Hang on…one…sec. There, here we go. Ok, everyone, enjoy the show."

A white frame lit the side of Wainwright's Pharmacy. But instead of the peppy credits and music playing, a message appeared on the wall.

Hey Doc,
Will you marry me?
Love, Big Ben

It took a second to sink in, but when it did, she gasped. All heads swiveled in their direction, and she turned, staring at Ben.

When had he moved? He was kneeling on one knee, with a small black velvet box in his enormous hands.

"Without you, Cora, my life is nothing. You are my everything. Will you be my wife?"

Happy tears leaked from her eyes, and for once, she didn't care how puffy her face got.

"YES!" she cried, as he opened the box.

A roar erupted around her, enveloping them in a rumbling cocoon. He leaned in and she heard him say, "This ring belonged to my mother. I would be honored if you would wear it."

"Oh, Ben. Yes, a thousand times yes!"

EPILOGUE

Seven months later

Outside the second story window, the sun glared in shimmering waves rising from the asphalt parking lot. A smattering of vehicles soaked up the generous solar rays. Trickles of sweat still ran in rivulets down her back, but Cora hardly noticed them in the coolness of the air conditioned waiting room.

"Dr. Tucker?" a familiar nurse called. Cora stood, and the nurse nodded. "The room is ready for you now."

"Perfect, Chelsea. Thank you. You ready for this?" Cora asked as she turned to give Beth a hand up from her chair.

Beth laughed, a hand on her swollen belly. "I'm not an invalid. Just of whale-like proportions." Ronnie got to his feet, affectionately rubbed his wife's shoulders.

"I can carry you in there," Ben offered, "if you'd rather not waddle on your own." A smirk played across his face.

Beth swatted her brother and shooed her husband. "I'm fine, you ninnies. And I don't waddle. Let's go, Cora. I can't stand waiting another minute!"

They gathered in a comfortable room, with couches and chairs in a U-shape around three walls. Positioned on the fourth wall was the ultrasound machine and reclining table. Beth hitched herself on top of the table. "I'm ready!" She flipped her shirt up over the baby bump with a laugh.

Cora keyed in Beth's information, inserted the clear holographic slide for recording the imaging. She draped the belly-wrap over Beth's rounded abdomen, had Beth sit forward so she could fasten the wrap around her back.

"This has over a hundred mini transducers woven into the fabric. Don't worry about baby. The sound waves are precise and directional once it calibrates to your body, which should be right about … now."

The opposite wall of the viewing room was a giant screen. All eyes were glued to the wall as baby's form took shape.

"Oh, look!" Beth snagged Ronnie's hand, held it tightly. "The baby's sucking its thumb! Oh, Ronnie, just look!" Tears flowed, and Beth rolled her eyes as she swiped at them. "Stupid hormones."

They watched, entranced, as the little one squirmed and kicked, grew tired of the thumb, and threw out some mad kung fu moves. Beth crooned, "Easy, little one. Don't kick Mama too hard."

"Do you want to know the gender?" Please say yes, please say yes.

Beth exclaimed "Yes!" at the same time Ronnie answered, "Nope."

Her sister-in-law threw her hands up in the air. "We talked about this, Ronnie. Puh-lease?" she whined. "I can't stand calling the baby 'it' anymore."

Ronnie lost the staring contest of wills to Beth's puppy-dog eyes. "Oh, fine!" he ceded. "Lay it on us, Cora."

Using her fingers on the belly-wrap, she zoomed in on the baby. "Uncross those feet, little one. Come on, come on. There!"

"Is that…?" Ronnie asked.

"It's a girl!" Beth boohooed happily while Ronnie grabbed her in an embrace.

Cora walked over to Ben, who was sitting on the sofa opposite Ronnie. "You're being quiet, Mr. Tucker."

He chuckled. "Don't worry, Dr. Tucker, I'm just taking it all in."

She glanced over at the screen, the 3-D image of their tiny niece twisting and turning filling the wall. She squeezed his hand, and whispered in Ben's ear. "Isn't it wonderful?" Ronnie and Beth had their heads together, talking lowly and occasionally laughing around tears.

"Just think, in four months you can hold your niece in your arms and tickle her feet." His eyes grew wide, and she could practically read his mind. "Don't worry, you won't break her."

He twisted his mouth to the side. "How do you do that? Know what I'm thinking."

"In this instance, it's because you're a man. Typical response," she sniffed.

"I don't think I could look at such a miracle and ever deny there is a God. What a fool I was all those years."

She plopped down in his lap, grabbed his head with both hands and looked deep into his beautiful green eyes. "The important thing is you are no longer a fool, Ben."

"Can you imagine seeing this for the first time, your own child growing?" he asked quietly, mesmerized by the screen.

Cora smiled. "Yes, I can. And in another couple of months," she whispered in his ear, "you can see our baby." She placed his hand on her still-flat stomach.

Eyes wide, Ben opened his mouth, closed it, opened it again. She placed a finger over his lips. "Shhh, this is our little secret for now. Today is their day," nodding at Beth and Ronnie.

A smile split his face from ear to ear.

They sat on the sofa, Ben cradling her on his lap, with his hand covering their child, and for the millionth time, Cora thanked God for his beautiful mercy.

About the Author

Jennifer Osufsen is a native east-Texan transplanted in the northwoods of Minnesota. She is a veteran of the United States Marine Corps, a homeschooling mother of five children, and the wife to her best friend of fifteen years, Jesse. When she is not wrangling kids, slinging grub, scaling mountains of laundry, or wading knee-deep in toys, she finds time to grab some sanity and write. Oh, who are we kidding? It's a miracle that *Mercy Springs*, her first novel, was completed in the first place.

www.ingramcontent.com/pod-product-compliance
Lightning Source LLC
Chambersburg PA
CBHW021207250626
47155CB00008B/2717